"Heartwarming . . . Rab and Susanna have a sweet relationship that slowly evolves into a sensual, loving romance. . . . This one's a keeper!"

—*Night Owl Reviews*
(5 stars, A Night Owl Top Pick)

"Sara Luck has skillfully interwoven a solid story line of greed and corruption with a just-right soupçon of romantic tension."

—*Publishers Weekly*

"It has everything a historical romance reader could want—love, danger, secrets, destiny, fate, seduction, passion, silver mining, and finding true love. An exciting story with strong characters and vivid descriptions of Americana history."

—*My Book Addiction Reviews*

"A promising debut."

—*Romance Views Today*

"Luck is an author to watch. Her well-developed characters, accurate historical settings, and hot naked men will have readers turning pages."

—*RT Book Reviews*

Marci's
Desire

Sara Luck

Pocket Books

New York   London   Toronto   Sydney   New Delhi

Pocket Books
A Division of Simon & Schuster, Inc.
1230 Avenue of the Americas
New York, NY 10020

This book is a work of fiction. Any references to historical events, real people, or real places are used fictitiously. Other names, characters, places, and events are products of the author's imagination, and any resemblance to actual events or places or persons, living or dead, is entirely coincidental.

First Pocket Books paperback edition June 2013

POCKET and colophon are registered trademarks of Simon & Schuster, Inc.

For information about special discounts for bulk purchases, please contact Simon & Schuster Special Sales at 1-866-506-1949 or business@simonandschuster.com.

The Simon & Schuster Speakers Bureau can bring authors to your live event. For more information or to book an event contact the Simon & Schuster Speakers Bureau at 1-866-248-3049 or visit our website at www.simonspeakers.com.

Manufactured in the United States of America

10 9 8 7 6 5 4 3 2 1

ISBN 978-1-4767-1315-1
ISBN 978-1-4767-1317-5 (ebook)

MARCI'S DESIRE

ONE

Marcia Diane Winters sat on a big rock on the shores of Lake Cayuga watching the sun dip behind the ridges that surrounded the lake. Her favorite subject for her paintings was this gloaming, and this evening she looked with a critical eye at her canvas. She thought she had captured the pinks and blues that were spreading throughout the low clouds.

Just then a low-flying vee of migrating geese flew into her view, and putting down her brush, she watched as the birds dutifully followed their leader, the honking sounds almost mournful as the birds wound their way toward the marshland at the end of the lake. When they were lost to her sight, she began packing up her paints and taking down her easel.

Marcia, who preferred to be called Marci, was in her third year at Wells College, and gathering up her belongings, she walked up the slope to the main building on the campus. The building was impressive without being ostentatious, in keeping with the desires of the late founder, Henry Wells. It had been his vision to provide an institution of higher learning for women that was fully equal to any men's college in both equipment and facilities, and in Marci's estimation the school had exceeded his stated goal.

When Marci entered the building, she heard the a cappella choir practicing in the music room. One of her roommates was Georgiana Hayden, and Marci recognized Georgiana's voice as she began the descant portion of the song. Marci smiled as she continued past the offices and the library on her way to the residence wing of the building. This wing housed the resident teachers and a little more than ninety girls.

Her room, which was intended to house four girls, now had only three—all New York girls, Georgiana from Syracuse, Marci, technically from Roxbury, although her parents were now in Washington, and Mazie Just, a New York City girl.

When Marci entered the room, she encountered Mazie, who was sitting in the middle of the floor, crying loudly.

"What has Lucien done now?" Marci asked as she put her easel in the corner of the room.

"I don't think he loves me. I haven't received a post from him in four days."

"For God's sake, he's a lawyer. Maybe he's too busy to write to you this week." Marci had a hard time keeping her patience with Mazie, who was quick to complain about everything.

"That's easy for you to say. You get flowers from

Stanton every week. Look, today he sent hyacinths. You'll think of your lover all night long because the smell will perfume the entire room."

"Stanton is not my lover." Marci shook her head.

"Well, maybe not in the literal sense of the word, but in his mind he's your lover. No one gets more notes and telegrams than you do, Marci Winters. And he's busier than Lucien Alexander will ever be. Stanton is all over Washington, or so you say."

"I do get a lot of attention from him," Marci said. "Why don't you come with me up to the gymnasium? If you work out on the Sargent apparatus, you'll feel a lot better."

"You go on. We've got a test tomorrow in zoology and botany, and unlike some people I know, I have to study."

Marci headed for the gymnasium on the second floor. Wells College was one of only twenty-six schools to receive the wonderful apparatus invented by Dr. Dudley Sargent, a professor of anatomy and physiology at Harvard University, and Marci made use of it daily. When one entered the cavernous room, it looked as if the iron frames and crossing bars were part of the ceiling, but they supported trapezes, horizontal and vertical ladders, and swinging hemp ropes.

She climbed one of the ladders and transferred to one of the bars of a trapeze. Pumping her legs, she got the swing going, then lowered her body so that she supported herself with the bend of her knees. With her arms hanging down, the feeling was exhilarating. She wished Mazie had come with her, so that she could have practiced some of the aerial somersaults she knew.

Just as she was dismounting, dropping down to the mat, which was more than a foot thick, she heard the door open and the distinct click of shoes on the gymnasium floor. Marci adjusted the split skirt of her exercise costume and stood ready to take her reprimand.

It is not becoming for a young woman to take such delight in the toning of her muscular structure.

When you take your place in society, others will look with disdain upon your prideful display of your body.

A Wells girl does not yearn to find her place among the acrobats who perform for Barnum and Bailey.

It is with much distress that I forbid you to use the apparatus for one week.

How many times had she heard Dean Smith tell her this over her three years at college?

"Miss Winters, I thought I might find you here."

Miss Helen Fairchild Smith was the dean of the school. A short woman, she always stood erect, exuding dignity and serenity. She took it upon herself to train the girls to accept their places in society. She embodied Mr. Wells's original philosophy in training every woman that passed through the college to realize that a woman's true and only sphere was her influence on the home and society. It was instilled in every student that the family was the real source of influence, and whether it be for weal or woe, the woman had the most influence over the future of civilization.

"Miss Winters, following the dinner hour, I would like for you to meet with me in the library. I will expect you there by eight o'clock."

"Yes, ma'am." Marci listened as Dean Smith walked the length of the gymnasium, her footfall once more sounding loudly on the hardwood floor.

Dean Smith had surely known what Marci was doing on the apparatus, yet the dean had not chastised Marci. And now she was asked to meet in the library. Was she being expelled?

She could vividly recall the last evaluation the dean had written to her parents: *Marci is one of my most challenging students. She is a natural leader—smart, talented, and personable. If only she weren't so headstrong and opinionated.*

Both her parents had reprimanded her for not conforming to the Wells philosophy, and DeWitt Winters had been particularly critical. He often reminded her of the privilege it was to attend the college where Frances Cleveland, the first lady of the United States, had matriculated. If Marci was being asked to leave school, how would she face her father? How would she face Stanton?

"Oh, I am sweating so," Marci said a few minutes later, speaking to Georgiana. Marci dabbed at her face with a towel.

"Nonsense, child, Wells women never sweat. They glow, elegantly," Georgiana said, perfectly mimicking Dean Smith.

Marci laughed out loud. "Yes, ma'am."

"I see you got your weekly delivery of flowers." Georgiana walked over to the table, then leaned forward to smell the fragrant pink and white hyacinths. "I didn't read the card, but I can guess what it says. 'With affection, Stanton Caldwell.'" Georgiana exaggerated the words as she said them.

"Well, this time you're wrong. It says, 'With *much* affection, Stanton Caldwell.'"

"Why does he always sign his first and last name? Does he think you'll forget who he is?"

"You just don't understand Stanton. He is a very formal person."

"Ha! You're about the most informal person I know."

"Ahch!" Marci clutched at her chest as she stood in her underwear before her roommate. "You would say that to a Wells girl?"

"Yes, a Wells girl who has no modesty. I still don't understand how you got stuck with a staid, old man like Stanton."

"He's not that old, and besides, I met him at President Cleveland's inaugural ball. No one finds fault with Mrs. Cleveland for marrying a man twenty-eight years older than she is, so who can say anything if Stanton is twelve years older than I am?"

"Oh, yes, how can I forget the budding socialite on the arm of her father, the secretary of the treasury, at the inaugural ball," Georgina said with an affected accent.

"He's not the secretary of the treasury. He's the second comptroller, so that means he's just a glorified accountant, and there are a lot of very boring

things he and his family are expected to attend."
Marci sucked in her cheeks, puckered her lips,
then tilted her head back. "'Oh, my dear,'" she said
in a stilted voice, "'how delightful that you could
come to the tea of the Washington Ladies' Society
for the preservation of our little feathered friend,
the needle-beaked twit.'"

Georgiana laughed out loud. "Well, after all,
doesn't the needle-beaked twit deserve to be pre-
served?"

Both Georgiana and Marci were laughing as
Marci continued to dress for dinner. She chose the
most conservative dress in her wardrobe as she
remembered the meeting she was to have with
Dean Smith. If she had to leave Wells, she would
miss the friendships she had formed while she was
here.

"I'm serious. What was there about Stanton that
made you attracted to him? He seems so different
from you."

"Actually, he chose me, but I don't really know
how he did it, because there were about ten thousand people in the Pension Hall for the inauguration. But what really impressed me was how much
he already knew about me. He knew my father's
position and that we'd moved from Roxbury and
that we were now living on V Street."

"Didn't that make you feel a little creepy?"

"Oh, no, not when I saw how handsome he was!
You know, Georgiana, he could be a model for
a Norse god—blond hair, deep blue eyes set in a
perfect oval face. There's only one thing I don't like

and that's his mustache." Marci smiled when she thought of the tickle his mustache caused when his lips brushed against her.

"All right. We accept that he's a good-looking man."

"He is, isn't he? And he's mature. Sometimes I have to pinch myself just to remind me how lucky I am to know someone like Stanton. Last summer we saw each other almost every week. And then when I was home for the holidays, we spent as much time together as we could, but he's always so busy."

"Whatever he did, in my book he's proven himself. What man sends his girlfriend flowers every week of the year?"

"Grover Cleveland," Marci said.

"Oh, yes. It must be something about a Wells girl. I wonder if Mrs. Cleveland's roommate knew she was going to be the wife of the president of the United States when she was getting all her bouquets. Tell me, will you invite me to your wedding?"

"Of course I will. I may even ask you to be a bridesmaid, but it may be a while, because he hasn't even asked me yet." Just then the clock in the hallway chimed seven. "We'd better hurry. I have a conference with Dean Smith right after dinner, and I don't want to be late."

"In the library?"

"Yes, how did you know that?" Marci asked.

"Because she asked me to meet her at eight o'clock."

Marci let out a deep sigh. "Thank goodness. It's not just me. I thought I'd done something really dreadful this time."

❦

Following dinner, Marci, Georgiana, and six other young ladies gathered in the library.

"What have we done?" Ellen Barker asked the group. "Does anyone know why we're here?"

"For her to ask us to meet at eight o'clock? That's really not characteristic of Dean Smith, especially when she knows we all have examinations tomorrow," Georgiana said.

"No one told about us sneaking out of the dormitory and meeting the boys from Cornell last weekend, did they?" Carrie Frey asked. "Maybe someone heard when they threw rocks on the windows."

"That was nothing," Marci said. "There were ten girls and two boys. If anything, the boys should get in trouble."

"Shh, I hear her coming," Georgiana said.

Everyone grew respectfully quiet waiting for the dean. When she stepped into the library, all eight women looked like soldiers standing at attention.

Dean Smith laughed when she saw them. "Ladies, how did you know what I'm going to ask of you? Please, sit down." She directed them toward a table, where she took the head chair.

"Every year at this time, certain women's institutions are invited to participate in a social engagement"—Dean paused for effect—"at the United States Military Academy."

There were several oohs and aahs as the girls tittered among themselves.

"This year, Wells College has been honored with an invitation to participate in this prestigious event, and it is my distinct pleasure to announce that you girls have been selected to represent us with your presence." Dean Smith lowered her head and clasped her hands before her. "I must say that not all of you met with my wholehearted support, but each of you had multiple advocates from the faculty singing your praises. Therefore, I have put my imprimatur upon each one of you to represent Wells. Do not disappoint me." The dean looked directly at Marci.

"Several of you are very close to Miss Nash in the art department, and I have selected her to act as your chaperone. Remember, ladies, it is an honor to be invited to West Point, for the United States Military Academy represents the pride of our nation."

All the girls reacted excitedly over the prospect of going to the academy, though it was Georgiana who found the courage to ask, "What is this social engagement?"

Dean Smith paused for a moment, then smiled, perhaps as if remembering something from her younger days, when she lived at Annapolis, where her father had taught mathematics at the Naval Academy. "You're going to a hop, my dear. A dance."

"Oh!" Carrie Frey squealed in delight. "Oh, yes, I saw a corps of cadets marching in the Fourth of July parade in Albany. They are all so handsome!"

"When do we get to go?" Ellen asked.

"The event will be this weekend. You will take the train into the city and then travel by boat up the Hudson River. I know that many of your homes are clustered not far from the river, and I might suggest that before boarding the train, you notify your parents should they want to visit with you. We will leave tomorrow as soon as all of you have written the zoology examination."

A general groan of dissent came from the girls.

"Why did you have to remind us of that?" Carrie asked.

"Because first and foremost, you are students. This junket is to be considered a pleasant interlude intended to enforce your academic experience. And now, ladies, I suggest you get a good night's sleep. I've been told by Professor Hart that you will be tested on primates tomorrow. I trust that your venture into the night air a few evenings past was for just such study. Good night."

"That woman knows everything," Ellen whispered as the girls made their way back to the dormitory.

When Marci and Georgiana returned to their rooms, Georgiana was bubbling over with excitement. "Oh, isn't this the most wonderful thing? Just think, a weekend at West Point. I wonder who I'll dance with. Well, it doesn't matter. It's like Carrie said, every cadet is handsome. I think they have to be handsome in order to get into the academy."

Marci laughed. "Don't be silly. Do you really think they'd look at somebody and say, 'You can't come here because you're too ugly'?"

"Well, it must be something like that. I've never seen a cadet who wasn't handsome. I just know this will be a wonderful weekend. Aren't you excited?"

"I don't know."

"What do you mean, you don't know?"

"I know what she means," Mazie said as she sat

up in her bed. "I wouldn't go because I'd be betraying Lucien. And if Marci goes, what about poor Stanton?"

"I don't think it's the same thing. Lucien has asked you to marry him," Georgiana said.

"And Stanton just sends flowers," Marci said with a laugh.

"What's the harm of a small social outing at West Point? When you look at it logically, it's practically a civic duty. Besides, you'll be here to take care of the flowers. You can pretend they're from Lucien."

"Oh, Georgiana, you're so logical. That makes perfect sense to me," Marci said, as she sat down at her desk and opened her zoology book.

The Wells girls waited on the platform of the Delaware, Lackawanna, and Western Railroad after having been brought by coach to Ithaca. They would change trains at Owego and reach Hoboken, New Jersey, in the early morning.

Many were doing as Dean Smith had suggested—notifying their parents that they would be at West Point for the weekend. Marci sent a telegram to her father and contemplated sending one to Stanton, but she decided against it. She knew he often shuttled back and forth between Washington and New York, and if he was in New York, he could cross the river and meet the train at Hoboken.

But something made her hesitate. She didn't want to see Stanton—not when she had to admit she was looking forward to this trip.

Often when she was a child, her family would travel up the Hudson, going as far north as Catskill to take a road to Roxbury that was at a lower elevation than was the most direct route through the mountains. When the boat passed West Point, she would look up at the gray granite buildings wondering who lived there. Now, for the first time, she would find out.

The boat drew away from the dock in Hoboken at nearly 10:00 a.m., plowing through the water toward West Point. A brisk breeze was blowing, but Marci stayed out on the deck, tying a veil over her hat and wrapping a shawl about her shoulders. One of the boat's crew found a comfortable spot for her to sit near the rail, and for a time she watched a passing steamboat. The wake from its screw formed a large, following vee, causing some floating ducks to rise and fall with the waves. Soon the familiar scenery between the Palisades and the Highlands, now just beginning to show signs of the spring foliage, began to slide by.

"Marci, you'd better step into the salon," Miss Nash said after at least three hours had passed. "All the other girls and I have been playing tiddledywinks and you've missed it. Anyway, aren't you cold sitting out here?"

"I've rather enjoyed the trip," Marci said, "but perhaps I should step in to freshen up a bit. My hair has gotten a bit unruly with the breeze turning every loose lock into a ringlet."

"You look presentable. The steward says we have less than an hour before we arrive, so I do need to give you information about our stay."

As Miss Nash was talking to the girls, the bell of

the steamer rang out to signal that it was about to land at the broad dock.

"All right, girls, let's make ourselves ready, and as Dean Smith always says, never forget you are a Wells girl."

West Point

After being dismissed from their morning formation, the cadets checked the chalkboard for orders of the day. One posting drew the most interest.

Those cadets who are not dragging to the hop tomorrow evening will please repair to Mr. Gurney's room, second floor, fourth division, at the close of duty hours today. Drawings for young ladies will begin promptly at 5:30.

That afternoon, John Gurney collected all the names of the arriving female visitors and put them into a box. The cadets who didn't have an invited guest coming to the dance, who weren't *dragging* as the men called it, gathered in Gurney's room to draw the name of the person they would entertain for the weekend.

"Understand that each of these young ladies will be able to accept or deny any invitations to dance. She will have a dance card, and you will be expected to honor her commitments," the superintendent told them. "If she does not have a commitment, it will be your responsibility to entertain her."

"Excuse me, sir, but what if we find the looks and personality of the young lady whose name we draw to be . . . incompatible with our preference?" one of the cadets asked in an Alabama drawl.

"Cadet Mitchell, not one young lady will be"—Colonel Ernst paused for a moment, then continued—"*incompatible* . . . with your preference. These women have made great personal sacrifices to make the trip to this institution. As gentlemen, I expect each of you to escort the young lady in your charge as if she were a princess."

"Yes, sir."

"Now, I leave Mr. Gurney in charge of the drawing."

Cade McDowell drew just before his best friend and roommate, Casper Conrad.

"Who'd you get, Cade?" Casper asked as he stepped up to draw a name.

Cade read the card. "'Marcia Diane Winters, Wells College, Aurora, New York.'"

"Ooh," Casper said, reading his card.

"What's the matter?"

"Hortense Atkinson. Hortense? And she's from Evelyn College."

"Remember," Cade said, teasing, "no matter what the rumors are about the girls at Evelyn, she's a princess."

After the young ladies were duly checked in to the West Point Hotel, they were summoned by Miss Nash to walk with her out onto a broad open area, which Marci had already learned was the Plain. Marci looked over at the turreted, gray pile buildings on the other side as they walked toward a group of women who were standing at the end of the Plain.

The air was brisk, and the sky was a clear blue,

with but a few downy puffs of white clouds floating overhead. Marci felt excited being here, and she wondered what the weekend would bring.

Ahead, they saw a formation of men in gray and white uniforms, standing as still as statues. Some of the girls waved and smiled, but not one of the men looked toward them.

"Well, that's sort of snobbish," one of the girls said.

"They're in formation and they must maintain their military bearing," Miss Nash told her.

"Then, how come one of them is coming toward us?"

"Because he's the one in charge," Miss Nash said. "You can tell because he has stripes on his sleeves."

"Ladies, I am Cadet Captain Edward Schulz, and on behalf of the United States Military Academy, I would like to welcome you. I would hope that while you are here, you have a pleasant stay.

"Each of the cadets that you see in formation has been assigned the pleasure of being your escort for the weekend. When I call the name of a cadet, he will come forward and identify the lady he has chosen from a random drawing, and it will be his responsibility to make certain your visit to West Point is a memorable one."

Marci furrowed her brow when she heard this method of choosing an escort. She wasn't sure how she felt about being handed off in such a way, but as she thought about it, she couldn't think of any method that would be more impartial.

"Cadets, at ease!" Captain Schulz ordered, and as

one, the cadets moved their left foot out and clasped their hands behind their back.

One by one the cadets were called from the formation to read off a name. As each girl's name was called, she stepped forward; then the cadet, offering his arm, led her away.

Several names had been called before one cadet stepped forward, looked at the card in his hand, then said loudly, "Miss Marcia Diane Winters!"

"I am Miss Winters," Marci said, responding as had the girls who were previously called.

The cadet smiled broadly.

Marci noticed the man who approached her was taller than most of the others, with wide shoulders and a broad chest. He was quite handsome—not in the classical, almost effete way of Stanton, but in a very masculine way, with dark hair, dark eyes, a square jaw, and a strong chin.

"Miss Winters"—he offered Marci his arm—"I am Cadet Myles Cade McDowell, and I'm pleased to be your escort."

"I am pleased to meet you, Cadet Myles Cade McDowell." Marci took his arm. "And it would please me very much if you would call me Marci."

The smile broadened. "It would be my pleasure, Marci. And, please, I would prefer that you call me Cade. I get to hear my Christian name used so seldom, it would be absolute music to my ears, especially when it comes from the lips of such a beautiful young woman as yourself."

Marci's eyebrows shot up, then she laughed. "If I have to listen to that kind of nonsense all weekend"—she paused for dramatic effect—"I fear . . . I fear the nausea will force me to my bed."

Now Cade laughed. "A woman who speaks her mind. I like you, Marci, and we're going to get along just fine."

Marci felt a sudden exhilaration as the man pulled her closer to him as they started walking away from the gathered group. He was dressed in a gray shell jacket over closely fitting, crisp, white trousers that left little to the imagination. She could see the sinewy muscles of his strong, compact form. He carried his head erect, his shoulders back, and walked with an elastic, measured stride.

"What are we supposed to do today?" Marci asked.

"We're just supposed to get to know one another, so you go first. What should I know about Marci Winters?"

"Well, I'm an only child who grew up in the Catskills, in Roxbury. My father works in the government, so now my parents and I live in Washington, but we go back home as often as we can. But now, I'm in my third year at Wells, where I'm hoping to get a bachelor of arts degree."

"What do you want to do when you finish?"

"I'm not sure. We're told over and over that a woman's role is supposed to be as the wife of a successful man, so I guess what I do will be determined by the person I marry."

Cade stopped abruptly and turned toward Marci. "Is this the same woman who just told me nausea would force her to her bed if she had to listen to my nonsense all weekend? You're going to tell me you'd do exactly what a husband told you to do?"

Marci wrinkled her nose. "That doesn't make much

sense, does it? So what about you? First, why did you choose to come to West Point?"

"I guess it's because of my mother. For my whole life, she told me the army, especially an officer in the army, was the most respected occupation anyone could have." Cade resumed walking. "My father was a captain in the army."

"You say *was*. What does he do now?"

"He's dead. He died with General Custer at the Little Bighorn."

"Oh, Cade, it must be a heartbreaking memory to have watched your father ride off to never see him again. Being at Fort Lincoln on that day would be a terrible thing for a child to remember for the rest of his life."

"My mother and I were living in Michigan, and to be honest, I have no real memory of my father. I don't know much about him, other than that he was supposed to be courageous and daring, and according to my aunt Libbie, I look like him."

"He must have been a very handsome man because you, sir, are quite handsome."

"Now who's talking nonsense? Come on, I'll take you to the Custer Monument. It used to be a lot bigger, but Aunt Libbie made them take the statue down, so now it's only a pedestal."

"Aunt Libbie? You don't mean Elizabeth Custer?"

"Yes, that is who I mean. She's not my real aunt, but now that my mother has passed, she's the closest thing I have to family."

"Then, both of your parents are gone?"

"Yes, my mother died last year. I wish she would have lived long enough to see me get commissioned."

"I'm so sorry."

"It rained," Cade said, seemingly out of nowhere.

"What?"

"During my mother's funeral, it rained. I know it sounds crazy, maybe even a bit maudlin, but I had the idea that God was crying."

"I don't think that's crazy or maudlin at all."

"Only a few came to mourn her passing. My mother was a very private person, but Aunt Libbie came, and I was glad she did."

"You must be very close to Mrs. Custer."

"I am. I don't have any living relatives—at least none that I know of, and Libbie Custer comes closest to filling that position. I'm pleased to have her as a friend."

Marci reached down to take his hand. "Well, now you have another friend."

Cade didn't answer right away, but he did squeeze her hand.

"It's because of Aunt Libbie's influence that I'm here at West Point."

"How's that?"

"Well, a person can't just choose to come to the academy on his own. He has to be appointed by a member of Congress, and Aunt Libbie convinced the Michigan senator to appoint me."

"Would that be Senator Stockbridge or Senator McMillen?"

"Senator McMillen, but how would you know the senators from Michigan?"

"There are only forty-four states. It's easy to keep track of eighty-eight men, especially when you've met most of them. And his daughter, Amy, is my friend."

"Hold up there, have I missed something about you? It's not every girl I've ever met who hobnobs with senators. Next you're going to tell me you know President Cleveland."

Marci laughed at Cade's comment. "Would you believe I did go to his inauguration and the inaugural ball, but who can forget the real connection I have to the president. His wife is a Wells girl, and that makes us practically sisters."

"Well, that's it, then. Mrs. Cleveland married well, and now all of you have to aspire to follow in her footsteps."

"In all seriousness, my father is a political appointee in the Treasury Department. During the president's first term, he was a clerk. Then during the Harrison administration we moved back to Roxbury, and when Cleveland was reelected, they remembered my father, and he was brought back to Washington as the second comptroller of the United States."

"Second comptroller? I guess that's sort of like second lieutenant," Cade said as they approached the bluff where the Custer Monument stood. "Here we are at the pedestal."

"That seems so strange to me. Why did Mrs. Custer want the statue removed?" Marci stepped up to the marker, which was taller than she was. "I would think she would want people to remember her husband."

"Oh, she does want that, but if I know my aunt Libbie, she wants people to remember him the way *she* wants him remembered. You could almost say her whole existence is a memorial to her husband—her articles, her speeches, her books—they're all about glorifying her Autie."

"Dean Smith assigned her book *Tenting on the Plains* for all of us to read. She said it was an example of how a woman could make a home anywhere, but Mrs. Custer doesn't make the life of a soldier's wife sound very attractive. It seems to me it's the man who chooses to be in the military, and the poor wife has no recourse but to tag along."

Cade was silent for a long moment after Marci's comment, then said quietly, "Perhaps she tagged along because she loved him."

"Oh, Cade, I didn't mean that the way it sounded. Please forgive me."

"Come on, let's leave here. It always makes me a little melancholy when I think about what happened to my father and the 267 others who were killed. Since we're so close to the river, would you like to go down to the lower rises of the cliffs? That's where my favorite place is."

"Of course. What's there?"

"The riding hall." Cade took her hand, and like two people who appeared to have known one another for more than just an afternoon, they carefully made their way down the stone steps that were cut into the steep cliff.

When they reached the bottom of the hill, Cade led her into a cavernous hall with a large, open floor covered with tanbark. The walls were high and had huge, arched windows all along each side, through which the sun poured to provide light. Between the windows were balconies from which one could look down onto the floor.

"My, this is huge," Marci said as she looked around.

"Some say it's the largest equestrian riding hall in the country. I wish you could see the men drill because I think what we get the horses to do is as artful as any ballet."

"You really enjoy it, don't you?"

"I do. Riding is the greatest pleasure I've had since I took my oath on the Plain. In fact, I've chosen the cavalry as my branch of service when I'm commissioned."

"Does that mean you'll be assigned some place far away?"

"I guess it does, but I've really never thought about it. I don't have anybody who cares where I go, so wherever the army sends me is where my home will be."

"The army is a strange life. I don't think I could ever get used to it."

Just then a signal cannon was fired.

"We need to get up the hill. You'll want to see the light battery drill." Cade was glad for the diversion because he didn't know how he would respond to Marci's comment.

As Cade and Marci were making their way up the hill, she couldn't help but think of the contrasts between their upbringings. She had been brought up with a father who doted on her, while by Cade's own admission he couldn't remember his father. With his mother no longer living, the closest person to him was a woman whose sole purpose was to make certain everyone remembered a man who lost his life fighting Indians.

Cade had said no one would care where he went when he graduated.

That was a telling statement. She wished she were in a position to get to know Cade better. She would care where he went.

TWO

With Cade holding Marci's arm, they walked along a flagstone path to the library, where they found other cadets and young ladies seated on the steps waiting to watch the drill. Out on the Plain, the battery stood hitched and ready while a line of saddled horses waited.

"Stand to horse!" the cadet commander shouted. "Prepare to mount—mount!"

The horsemen rose to their saddles and the cannoneers to the seats of the caissons. At the sound of the bugle, the cannons, with the black guns lying snuggly in their trunnion beds, and the caissons moved out onto the Plain with a low rumble of wheels.

"Trot, march!"

The dust rose beneath the speeding wheels as the caissons swept down toward the library, then, countermarching, returned up the Plain.

"Gallop, march!"

The well-trained horses leaped forward at the next note of the bugle and raced with precision.

At the order "Action front!" the cannoneers jumped down from their seats, lowered the trail to the ground, then spiked it into place. Had this been an actual battle, the guns would be ready.

"Battery fire!"

Together the lanyards were snapped back and the roar of six guns rolled out across the Plain as the recoiling pieces sprang back upon their trunnions to ground their trails into the sand.

Cade looked over at the beautiful young lady sitting beside him. He smiled as he thought again of Mitchell's comment "incompatible with our preference" and realized that none of all the girls who had arrived for the hop was more compatible with his preference than this one.

Many of the cadets had lady friends who corresponded with them and visited them when allowed. For just a moment, Cade allowed himself the fantasy of thinking that Marci had come here not as one of the officially invited young ladies, but to see him alone.

His thoughts were interrupted by the simultaneous roar from all six guns, and he felt Marci's reflexive reaction to it as she squeezed his arm more tightly. Protectively, he removed his arm and put it around her, drawing her closer to him.

She looked toward him with a wide-open smile, her cheeks rosy with the glow of the cool air, and her black hair dancing in the breeze.

Cade noticed that some of the other girls were well covered with hats and scarves, but Marci didn't seem to mind the breeze or what it was doing to her hair. One errant strand crossed her face, and Cade carefully placed it behind her ear. As he looked into her face, he had the almost uncontrollable desire to kiss her, as arousal stirred.

With an abrupt jerk, Cade returned his attention to the drill, dropping his arm from behind her.

For several minutes the wagons rumbled around the Plain as the gun smoke rolled up and away against the mountains, fading in a feathery mist. The thud of the horses' feet, the grinding of heavy wheels, the call of the bugle, the sharp explosions, and the precise and coordinated movements of the uniformed cadets all combined to create a theater of sight and sound against the marvelous background.

This was Cade McDowell's world. This was his family. He, who had grown up the son of a laundress, who had mucked the stalls of horses, was no equal to a woman who attended the inaugurations of presidents. He had to put this weekend in perspective. By the luck of the draw that he was with Marcia Diane Winters and not Hortense Atkinson.

When Cade left Marci at the hotel, he returned to the barracks, where several of the other cadets were assembled in his and Casper "Cass" Conrad's room.

"Cass and Cade, sounds like a couple of vaudevillians," Harry Stout had said once, and as a result their room was sometimes referred to as the Vaudeville Theater.

"Look here," Cass was saying, "you've got to help me out here. You've seen Miss Atkinson. Why can't you agree to sign her dance card? It wouldn't hurt a one of you to dance with her just one time."

"Not me," Harry Cavanaugh said. "I've already signed every line on Georgiana's card, and she'd be mighty upset if I left that pretty woman standing. What about you, Cade? He's your roommate."

"Yeah, Cade, you owe it to him," Mortimer Bigelow said.

"I don't know what the problem is, Cass. Miss Atkinson didn't seem that unattractive to me," Cade said.

"It's not that she's ugly," Bill Sills said. "She's a real chippie."

"A chippie?"

"She tried to make poor Cass take her out behind the barracks. I guess we know now why they say those Princeton men stand at the gates trying to get into Evelyn College," Sills said.

"If that's the case, we owe it to Cass to help him out. Everyone dances one dance with Miss Atkinson, but nobody dances with anybody else's girl, is that understood?" Cade asked.

"Thanks, buddy," Cass said, "and if anybody deserves the pig pot, it's me. I think we should double the money that we all put in."

"Oh, no, you don't. The pig pot's for an ugly girl, and believe you me, Miss Hortense isn't ugly. If she wasn't so damned horny, every one of us would be jumpin' at the bit wanting to dance with her," Bigelow said. "Which brings me to Miss Winters. We've not seen much of you, Cade. Where'd you take her?"

"We were down at the riding hall," Cade said.

"Uh-huh. With nobody there. Maybe ole Cade's

got a hot one, too. That's why he made it clear nobody dances with anybody else's girl. He's keepin' that little looker to himself," Bigelow said.

"You've got that right. She's mine, and I'm not letting any one of you pinheads even close to her."

"Oh, oh, Cadey's in love, Cadey's in love," Sills started singing.

"Just get out of here. All of you." Cade picked up a pillow and threw it at Sills.

When the others had left, and just Cass and Cade were alone in their room, Cade started to remove his jacket. "Is this woman really that bad?"

"Yes," Cass said. "Whoever selected her to come here this weekend really didn't know her. And where's the chaperone? If it weren't for our code of honor, I'd check myself into the infirmary and pretend to be sick."

"You'll get through it. I wish she was as nice as Marci," Cade said wistfully.

"You sound a little pensive, my friend. What's wrong?"

"For the first time in my life I've met a woman who's everything I've ever dreamed about. She's pretty, she's witty, she's smart."

"So . . . what's the problem? Every relationship starts with a meeting someplace. Why not consider this that meeting?"

"Because she has a disdain for the military."

"Cade McDowell, you're nuts. You can't make that kind of judgment when you just met her today."

Cade grabbed his towel and shaving kit and headed for the shower room.

"Yeah, I can," he tossed back over his shoulder.

∽∞⌇

The dance, which was held in the weapons room of the newly completed gymnasium, began at seven o'clock. The room, decorated with banners, flags, and pennants, as well as historical weapons, was already well filled with cadets and officers, all in full-dress uniform, and among the latter were the members of the academic board, the superintendent, and the secretary of war, in whose honor the battery drill had been performed.

The brass buttons of the uniforms sparkled in the electric lights no less than the gold and jewelry that glittered at the necks and on the ears of the young ladies.

The guest of honor at the dance was Secretary of War Daniel Lamont. He was standing in the reception line as the cadets and their ladies passed through. Cadet Captain Schulz was also in the reception line just next to the secretary. His task was to introduce each cadet and his special guest as they came through the line, referring to the notes he had in his hand.

"Mr. Secretary, this is Cadet Myles Cade McDowell, and . . ." Schulz looked down at the card to get the young lady's name.

"Miss Marci Winters," Secretary Lamont said, before Schulz could speak. "What a pleasant surprise to see you, Marci. I had the pleasure of lunching with your father just a few days ago, and when I told him I was coming to the academy, he didn't mention that you would be here." Lamont reached out to clasp Marci's hand in both of his.

Marci curtsied slightly. "The pleasant surprise is all mine, Mr. Secretary, and as for my father, my telegram was probably buried in his correspondence."

"DeWitt is a fine public servant, but he works too hard. Your family should take a cottage at Buzzards Bay this summer. When the president vacations there, it seems the whole government goes with him."

"I would like that very much." Marci withdrew her hand, aware that those in line behind her were straining to listen to this conversation.

"Mr. McDowell, you take special care of this young lady," Lamont said.

Cade, who had been genuinely surprised at the familiarity of the exchange between the two, nodded. "I shall, sir," he replied as he guided Marci away from the receiving line, cocking his head as if to pose a question.

Marci raised her eyebrows and shrugged her shoulders. "What can I say? Washington is like a small town, especially for those who work in government."

Cade just shook his head as he led her to the line forming for the Grand March.

Shortly thereafter, the bandleader raised his baton as a signal for both the music to begin and for the dancers to assume the promenade position. When Cade's hip brushed Marci's, it was as if he had touched her with a poker. Warm sensations began to radiate throughout her body, and she felt disappointed when they had to break contact to move out into the intricate patterns of the dance.

Marci had failed to get her hop card from Miss Nash, but it didn't seem to make any difference. Cade danced every dance with her.

The band tried to get the couples to try the polka or the german or a couple of other more athletic dances, but they soon found there was not much interest in reviving the old steps. So the dance continued throughout the evening with the band alternating between the two-step and the waltz.

At first, Cade maintained a respectable distance between them, but as the evening wore on, and several of the electric lights were extinguished, and the gaslights were lit around the dance floor, he pulled her to him. His hand slipped down to the small of her back as he exerted pressure to push her body against his. It was the most natural thing to place her cheek against his as he lowered his head to meet hers. She felt the movement of his head, and she knew he was going to kiss her, so she turned her head in anticipation.

At that moment came a loud explosion, much louder even than had been the fusillade of the cannons during the afternoon drill. The explosion was so loud that the chandeliers shook and jangled.

The music came to an abrupt halt, and confused couples scrambled to leave the building. Just then the gaslights flickered and went out.

"What's happening?" Marci asked, as she held on to Cade with trembling fingers as he led her through the darkness.

"I don't know," Cade admitted.

Thankfully, the electric lights were turned back on to push away the darkness.

"There's been an explosion in the coal house!" someone called.

As cadets and their ladies, officers and their guests, left the gymnasium, they saw a major conflagration at the coal house, which was two hundred feet long and fifty feet wide. Even from this far away they could feel the heat of the flames and smell the acrid smoke.

"This fire's going to be hard to handle," Cade said. "There's at least a hundred tons of coal in there."

"Officers, cadets, soldiers!" Colonel Ernst shouted. "Form fire brigades by companies!"

"What does that mean?" Marci asked.

"That means we're going to be busy for a while," Cade said. "Why don't you get your wrap and stand around the Thayer Monument. That way you'll be able to see what's going on but not be in the way. And if I can, I'll know where you are so I can come make sure you're all right."

"Where is this monument?"

"There, the southwest corner of the Plain. And, Marci"—a broad smile crossed Cade's face—"I'm sorry this had to happen. Especially right when it did. I have a feeling things were just about to get interesting."

"You're silly. Now go, and, Cade, be careful. I care what happens to you."

He squeezed her hand and ran off to join the other cadets who were now running toward the coal house.

From where Cade had positioned her on the Plain, Marci had an excellent view of all the action. She watched several men dressed in what looked like white canvas pajamas run by pulling a steam-powered pump engine toward the building, smoke pouring from the boiler. Next came a hose cart, and even before it was stopped, men were unreeling the hose and dropping it down to the river. By now the steam pressure was up and the pumper was ready to use.

Marci strained to see if she could find Cade, but she decided it was impossible when more than 250 men were all dressed alike. And then, as if he were an apparition, she saw him appear, and disappear, then appear again in the billowing smoke as he and several other cadets led horses out of the stable.

She tried to picture Stanton in this situation, and the thought almost made her laugh. Stanton's first thought would not have been the safety of the horses, but what the soot might do to his clothes. And for him to appear in public with a smoke-blackened face and mussed-up hair? Never. To say nothing of the physical courage it would require to run into the stable in the first place. No, Stanton would definitely not be risking his life to save a horse.

The horses were whinnying in terror as they trotted behind the cadets. They were being taken to the academic building, where a large open area doubled as another riding hall. She watched as the men and the horses ran back and forth across the Plain as more and more sparks landed on the roof of the stable.

"Please, God, don't let the stable catch on fire. Let him save the horses he loves," Marci said, not aware that anyone was standing near her.

"Better the horses die than humans," an older man who was nearby said. "If you ask me, those boys shouldn't be going in that building at all. If it catches fire, it's a tinderbox—all that straw and hay in there, and the dry wood. It's not granite like these other buildings. No, sir, I don't like the looks of that. We don't need to lose a young man just to save a horse."

A lump formed in Marci's throat as she prayed a silent prayer this time. *Please don't let anything happen to Cade.*

Several of the people who had been at the dance began to drift over to Marci's vantage point. Among them was Miss Nash.

"There you are, Miss Winters. All the other girls have returned to the hotel, but you—you always seem to be the outlier."

"I'm sorry if I caused you to worry, but my escort thought I'd be out of the way if I stood here."

"Did it not occur to you that the dance is over? As your chaperone, I think you should retire now."

"Miss Nash, please. Mr. McDowell thinks I'm standing by this monument, and whenever the fire is contained, I want to be here when he comes looking for me."

Joan Nash looked around at the little gathering. "I don't really like it that you're out here without an escort or a chaperone, but as long as you stay right here, I suppose it'll be all right." Miss Nash smiled, then held up her finger. "But mind you, don't go anyplace else."

"No, ma'am, I won't. And thank you."

Marci watched Miss Nash walk toward the hotel.

Marci didn't understand how people could have so little concern, or at the very least curiosity, that they could turn their back on the drama being played out here.

She saw Cade once again as he was bringing out still more animals. She knew it wasn't just a matter of getting them; bridles had to be put on the panicked horses as they reared and tossed in their stalls, and the flying hooves could injure anyone who got too close.

Even as Cade and the other cadets were rescuing the horses, others were playing water, not upon the fire itself, but upon the adjacent buildings—the stable, the armory, and the store.

"There goes the trestle!" someone called out, the shout followed by a loud crash. Marci looked over just in time to see the elevated railroad bridge, some 150 feet long, collapsing in a shower of sparks and clouds of smoke.

"These are the last of the horses!" one of the officers shouted, and Marci saw that Cade was the last cadet to leave the building, leading three horses across the Plain.

Finally the coal house was completely consumed, and while the large pile of coal continued to burn, there was no longer a danger of the flames, or sparks, involving any of the other buildings. That danger eliminated, the cadets were released.

Marci saw men silhouetted against the still-blazing flames as they came back through the darkness. Then she saw Cade, and she waved to him.

Smiling self-consciously, Cade approached her. "The supe says we can go back and finish the hop, but I can't very well ask you to dance with me when I smell like a chimney. I'm going back to the barracks and take a quick shower. Would you like to come with me?"

"If *supe* means 'superintendent,' I hardly think he would approve of that, and I'm sure Miss Nash would have something to say about it, too." Marci smiled broadly.

"Miss Winters! I am shocked that you would think such a thing." Cade crossed his hands across his chest in mock surprise. "Really, if you'd like to come with me, you can wait under the sally port while I change clothes."

"All right, I'll go."

"Good."

As they walked away, Marci thought of what she had told Miss Nash, that she would stay by the monument. Now she was deliberately disobeying that. Also, it was well on to eleven o'clock at night, and she was with a man. Prior to her coming to West Point, everyone's opinion, including her own, had been that she was practically engaged to Stanton Caldwell. This was not what a woman who supposedly cared for another man would do.

She stopped just before they reached the barracks.

Cade sensed her trepidation. "Is something wrong?"

"I feel guilty about leaving the monument. I told Miss Nash I would stay there. I probably should go back there and wait for you."

"Just stand under the sally port. It's not like you're going to be going into the barracks. And I promise, I'll only be gone a minute."

"All right, I'll wait here." Marci stepped into the covered archway and leaned against the stonework.

True to his word, Cade showered and changed quickly. Within fifteen minutes they were joining other couples on the flagstone pathway that led to the nearby gymnasium. The electric lights were blazing brightly, welcoming the participants back to the interrupted dance.

What neither of them saw standing on the balcony of the West Point Hotel was Miss Joan Nash.

"How could I ever have thought that girl was respectable?" Miss Nash said under her breath as she stepped back into her room.

The next morning Marci was awakened by someone's pulling the blanket off her shoulders, then shaking her forcefully.

"Is it morning yet?" Marci asked, not opening her eyes.

"It is, and everyone's up but you. All the other Wells girls got a decent night's sleep and they're dressed for chapel. I expect to see you ready to step out this door in ten minutes. Is that clear, Miss Winters?"

Marci sat up immediately when she realized it was Miss Nash who had awakened her. "Yes, ma'am, I'll be ready." Marci jumped out of bed, went to the washbasin, and began splashing water onto her face as Miss Nash left the room, slamming the door behind her.

"What did you do to get her dander up?" Carrie Frey asked.

"I don't know. I guess I slept in, but how did she know that?" Marci asked as she quickly brushed her hair and put it in a single plait that hung to her left side. She pulled out a blazer suit of gray serge with rows of tubular gold braid encircling the skirt and trimming the lapel and collar. This was not the costume she had planned to wear to the chapel service, but it was quick to put on and she was dressed with a minute to spare.

Just then there was a loud knock. Georgiana tiptoed over to the door and opened it.

"Is everyone ready?" Miss Nash asked in an authoritarian voice.

"Yes, ma'am," the four girls said in unison.

"Miss Winters, this is a church service, not a romp. Cover your head."

Marci spun around and withdrew a red tamo'-shanter from her valise. She cocked it on her head without looking in the mirror. When the four girls were leaving the room, Marci opened her eyes wide and shrugged her shoulders, trying to get one of the other girls to tell her what she had done.

Georgiana mouthed, *We don't know,* just as they joined the others and marched off to chapel.

The chapel was small, only seating about a hundred people. Other ladies were sitting in a roped-off area, and Marci and the others from Wells slipped into a pew near the back of the building. Several cadets were present and she looked for Cade, but she didn't find him. She decided he was probably still sleeping after the harrowing night before.

Instead of listening to the homily, Marci began to visualize Cade lying in his bed, or would he sleep on a cot? If he was on a cot, was it too small for his well-muscled body? She recalled the hardness of his chest as he held her against him during the dance, and she remembered the . . . *what am I doing?*

Marci was sitting in a church service, totally unaware of the homily that was being delivered, because her mind was on a man. Not Stanton Caldwell, but Cade McDowell.

To clear her mind of such thoughts, she began looking around the chapel. Even in this building, history was everywhere. Revolutionary War cannons were embedded in the walls, and black marble shields bore the names of renowned army officers: George E. Pickett, Thomas J. Jackson, A. P. Hill, and Robert E. Lee, among others. One plaque caught her particular attention: MAJOR GENERAL, BORN 1740. She thought it strange that there was no name or date of death. She would have to ask Cade about that.

The dismissal hymn brought her mind back from its wandering, and she breathed a quick and silent prayer, asking for forgiveness for her sins. She looked over at Miss Nash and quickly added the words *known and unknown* to her prayer.

When church was dismissed, Marci was disappointed to find that the women would not be reunited with their escorts until after lunch.

When Cade saw Marci in the reception hall of the hotel, he smiled. Marci Winters was unique. Her black hair was hanging in a braid that looked as if it had been done without much fanfare, while the other hairstyles looked as if every hair had individually been placed. Some were wearing dresses with flounces, lace, and ribbons with big, billowing sleeves. But Marci was dressed in a sensible outfit, just right for the tour of the post that the cadets had been charged to give.

"Miss Winters, did you choose what you're wearing on purpose?" Cade asked when he approached her.

"Oh . . . I . . . I'll go change," Marci said as she turned to leave the room.

"No, no. It's perfect for West Point. Look." Cade indicated his own gray tunic and pants. "Cadets have worn gray uniforms for almost a hundred years now, and that's why we call ourselves the long gray line. You couldn't have chosen a better costume."

"Well, good. I didn't exactly decide on this until the last minute, but I'm glad you like it."

"At least I don't smell like smoke today," Cade teased.

"I didn't smell the smoke last night. I smelled courage and compassion for those poor, frightened horses."

Cade smiled self-deprecatingly. "The horses weren't the only ones frightened."

"Ha! I don't believe that for a moment."

Cade offered his arm. "Are you ready for your tour?"

"I am."

"As you will see, West Point is more than a college; it's an actual army post. We'll start at the chapel."

"Oh, I went to chapel this morning," Marci said, and then her face flushed. This was the man who had occupied her thoughts during most of the church service. To cover her discombobulation, she remembered the plaque with no name. "The plaques. They're all generals who attended West Point?"

"Yes. They're from all the wars from the Revolutionary War up to the Civil War."

"There's one that just said 'Major General, born 1740.' That seemed strange to me."

Cade laughed. "You know who that's for? Benedict Arnold."

"But he was a traitor."

"He was, but he was still a brilliant tactician for some important Revolutionary War battles—that is, before he tried to turn West Point over to the British. Anyway, by not putting his name on the plaque or putting the date of his death there, the army thinks he'll never rest in peace."

"Cade, you really love this place, don't you?"

"Yes, I do. Let me show you some more of it."

THREE

Cade and Marci spent a leisurely afternoon walking the grounds of the academy, viewing what Cade called the military-Gothic architecture. They saw among other buildings the library, the Central Barracks, the superintendent's home, Professors' Row, the First Class Club, and the Boodler, where they stopped for a milk shake.

"This has been one of the most enjoyable weekends I've ever had," Marci said as she took a drink of her milk shake.

"I'm glad you came, and I'm sorry you have to leave so soon. I wish you could come back for the graduation hop."

"Perhaps I can," Marci said without thinking.

Cade smiled broadly. "Then, I have one more thing to show you. Trophy Point. That's where the graduation is held, and if you don't get to come, you can just imagine what it will look like."

Trophy Point was right beside the hotel, and it had without doubt the most beautiful view of the

Hudson River. It was called Trophy Point because this was where the captured cannons from past wars were displayed.

Cade was telling her all about the guns when, on a whim, Marci climbed up on one and sat on the barrel. "Where did this one come from?"

"It's an Armstrong gun, a hundred-and-fifty-pounder captured in North Carolina just three months before the end of the war," Cade said.

Just then a woman approached them. "Excuse me, sir, could I ask a favor of you?"

"Yes, ma'am, if I can help."

"I'm Emma Farnsworth from Albany, and I'm trying to make some pictures that are a little different. I want my pictures to have an artistic effect, and when your lady friend climbed up on the cannon, she looks so innocent next to the cannon, I'd like to take her picture."

"You'll have to ask Marci."

"All right. Young lady, will you pose for me?"

Marci attempted to jump down from the cannon. "Where's your studio?"

"No, no. I want it to be here. I want to shoot the picture with the sun in front of me. I've developed a technique where I put a stop between the lenses, so that I can control the amount of light that reaches the plate."

"What does that do?" Cade asked.

"It softens the picture a little bit. I like to say it gives my photographs soul and values."

"Then, I think Marci is the perfect subject for your photograph," Cade said.

"I'll do it, but only if Cade's in the picture, too."

Miss Farnsworth hesitated. "While I have to admit, your friend is a very handsome man, for what I'm trying to capture, I want the contrast—the softness of a woman pitted against the hardness of the cannon. May I take this one, and then take another one of the two of you?"

"Of course," Cade said, then looked toward Marci. "That is, if you want to do that?"

Marci climbed back onto the cannon, and Miss Farnsworth erected her camera on a tripod. She went about posing Marci in various positions, placing her arm first one place and then another, then moving her leg and draping her skirt. Finally, she even directed facial expressions until Marci struck just the right one. When the photographer was satisfied, she inserted a perforated metal disk between the lenses.

"Perfect," she said as she snapped the picture. "I'm trying to illustrate the Henry Norris 'Thirty-Fourth Ode of Anacreon,' and the last line is 'See! contrasted beauties shine.' This fits it beautifully."

"What about the picture of Cade and me?" Marci asked.

"Oh, I did say that, didn't I." Emma looked around Trophy Point. Seeing a big piece of chain that was affixed nearby, she began moving her camera. "Will you allow me to pose you near the chain?"

"Sure," Cade said as he helped Marci down.

Emma worked just as carefully to get just the right composition for this picture, arranging both Cade and Marci over and over. Finally she was satisfied.

When the photo session was over, she thanked them and requested their names.

"I plan to submit my illustrations for 'The Thirty-Fourth Ode' to the Postal Photographic Club competition. If these two pictures are as good as I think they are, I could win the whole contest."

"What line will this picture illustrate?" Marci asked.

"'As in love they fondly twine.' Thank you very much, Miss Winters, Mr. McDowell."

After Miss Farnsworth left, Cade and Marci lingered at Trophy Point.

"I admire someone like that," Marci said. "She seemed so confident, so sure that we would do what she wanted us to do. That's not the attitude most women have in our society."

"I suspect you're a lot like her."

"What do you mean?"

"I haven't known you for very long, Marci Winters, but you don't strike me as someone who is afraid not to conform."

Marci chuckled. "You sound like Dean Smith."

"We should have asked her to send us a picture when she develops them."

"Well, we know her name, and she said she was from Albany. I suppose we could contact her or we could watch for the Postal Club announcements. I know they publish the winners in the Washington newspapers."

"We'll have to do that," Cade said. "Say, how would you like to see how this chain was used?"

"I'd like that."

"It's a steep climb down the cliff, but I'll help you." Cade led her to a trail that led down to the shoreline of the Hudson River. They followed along the rocky trail until they reached some stoneworks.

"Here it is," Cade said. "This is where General Washington ordered a chain to be stretched across the river to deny passage to the British ships."

"I think it's amazing. How did they do that?"

"They made log floats and attached the links to them, then floated them out across the river to Constitution Island, over there."

"My real question is, how did they get those big chains up the hill? I dread climbing back up there myself."

"There's another way back."

"Then, let's go that way."

Cade had a mischievous grin on his face. "You may be sorry."

"Why do you say that?"

"The cadets call this Flirtation Walk and only a cadet and his escort can go there."

"That sounds . . . adventuresome," Marci said with a nervous laugh.

"We could go back and climb the cliff, if you'd rather."

"No, that's all right. I like adventure."

Cade reached for Marci's hand, and she hesitated for just a second, then she let him take it.

"It's all right," Cade said. "This is the only place on the entire military post where we can have a PDA."

"PDA?"

"Public display of affection," Cade said with a little chuckle.

Hand in hand, they started down the path. Marci was almost giddy. How could a simple thing such as holding hands cause so much anticipation? What had Cade said? Only a cadet and his escort could go on this path. That didn't mean anything, yet she knew something would happen before she returned to the hotel.

Did she want something to happen? And if so, what? Whatever it was, she wasn't worried. She knew, to her very core, that she was safe with Cade.

They wound their way among the trees that were just now beginning to leaf out. Neither said a word until they rounded a bend.

"There it is." Cade pointed.

Looking in the direction Cade was pointing, Marci saw that part of the cliff was jutting out over the path.

"There what is?"

"Kissing Rock." Cade led her under the overhang. He turned to Marci, and she had no difficulty in discerning his expression. "The legend is that if a cadet brings a girl here and fails to kiss her, the rock will fall on them."

"I wouldn't want that to happen to us," Marci said in a voice barely above a whisper, as her gaze fell to his lips.

Cade pulled her to him, timidly at first, then growing more daring, he pulled her closer, and she felt his body pressing against hers. His lips sought her lips as he began a tentative, hesitant kiss, testing her reaction. Then he pulled back and fixed his eyes upon Marci, as if searching for some signal of acceptance from her.

She gave it willingly. She wound her arms around his neck and boldly moved to accept another kiss. This time his mouth opened on hers, the action forcing her own mouth to open. At first she was shocked by it, but the shock was replaced by pleasure.

When she felt Cade's tongue invade her mouth, she felt an exhilaration that was both foreign and frightening, but she couldn't stop herself from following his tongue with her own, exploring his mouth as he had hers. Then, as she pressed her body even more tightly against his, answering some primeval urge to get as close to him as she could, she felt something hard and thrilling pressing against her.

Although this was a new experience, she knew instinctively what it was, and she was torn between the thrill of it and the idea that, somehow, this was not what a proper young woman should want.

She wanted him to stop, wanted to ask, to beg, him to stop, but the words couldn't come because she knew that, even more, she wanted him to continue. She put herself in his hands, subservient to his will, unable to muster any resistance.

Then, suddenly, abruptly it seemed, Cade stepped back. "I'm sorry. Please, forgive me."

Marci's pulse was elevated and her breathing was ragged. As they separated, she stole a glance toward the front of his pants. There was visual evidence of what, but a moment before, she had been feeling pressed against her, and she felt exhilarated knowing that she was the cause.

Cade turned and put some distance between them.

"I . . . don't think the rock will fall on us now, do you?" she asked in a quiet voice.

Cade laughed out loud. "No, Marci, my sweet, funny, wonderful Marci. I don't think the rock will fall on us now." Cade reached down and plucked a little white flower from the leafy mulch that lined the path. "Take this with you and press it in a book. When you see it, think of this moment."

Marci took the flower, and for just a second she thought of Stanton Caldwell. And in that moment, she decided Stanton Caldwell couldn't measure up to Myles Cade McDowell.

Georgiana and Carrie had gone on Flirtation Walk and also encountered Kissing Rock, and they talked about it with embarrassed tittering and giggles. Marci said nothing about her experience, though she certainly thought about it.

She would remember the kiss she'd shared with Cade for a long time. She'd wanted to talk to him again before they left, but that had been impossible.

The cadets may have had a brief respite for the weekend, but on Monday morning they would once again return to their regular routines of class and drill. As the girls were boarding the coach to take them to the boat dock, the men were on the Plain drilling. Every boot was polished, every pair of pants was creased, every posture was perfect, and every salute was snappy. Marci heard the commands barked and watched as the marching companies of men in gray moved with the precision of a Swiss watch.

As the boat slipped into the waters of the Hudson, Marci took one last look at West Point. She had an aching knot in the pit of her stomach. Something had happened to her this weekend, and she didn't know what it was, let alone how it would be resolved. Her relationship with Stanton had definitely come into question. If she cared for him as deeply as she had believed, could a man whom she had known for only two days make such an impact on her?

Tiny dust motes glistened as they floated in the still air, filling the bars of sunlight that spilled down through the windows of Hoboken's depot, to form glowing puddles of light on the floor. As the Wells girls waited for the train to take them back to Aurora, they gossiped back and forth about their experiences over the weekend.

Marci listened with interest, occasionally adding to the conversation, but not with anything substantive.

"Girls, our train is loading," Miss Nash said. "Collect your grips, now."

"It's too bad," Georgiana said as they started toward one of the many doors that read TO TRAINS.

"What's too bad?" Marci asked.

"It's too bad that we'll never see any of those men again."

"'Ships that pass in the night, and speak each other in passing, only a signal shown, and a distant voice in the darkness; so on the ocean of life, we pass and speak one another, only a look and a voice, then darkness again and a silence.'"

"Longfellow," Georgiana said with a little laugh. "'Ships that pass in the night.' It's so romantic."

Marci didn't reply. She had no intention of sharing her tumultuous thoughts with anyone else.

That night as Marci lay in her berth, feeling the gentle rock of the car, and listening to the click of the wheels passing over the rail joints, she tried hard to put Cade McDowell out of her mind. But she found it equally hard to think about *not* thinking about something.

She began to replay everything that had happened. The dance, the fire with Cade entering the building time and again to rescue the frightened horses, the conversations they'd shared about one another's background, and then there was Flirtation Walk and the kiss.

The kiss.

Stanton had never kissed her like that, and she had never reacted to any kiss the way she had this one. She had to confess she had never reacted to any man as she had reacted to Cade. She thought it odd that such a casual meeting could cause such a tumult of thought.

What was equally odd, though, was the way Miss Nash was acting. Maybe *acting* wasn't the word; maybe *looking* was the word. A couple of times she had caught Miss Nash staring at her with a most peculiar expression on her face, which could rightfully be called a glare. But Miss Nash hadn't actually said anything to Marci. And then she realized what was bothering her. Miss Nash hadn't said anything at all. For some reason, she was ignoring her.

∞

West Point

Cade smiled as he folded Libbie Custer's letter and put it aside. He thought of her as his surrogate mother, and he treasured the posts he received from her. Because she was the only person in the world who had known both of his parents, "Aunt Libbie" was his contact across time and space to the mother that he had known, and the father that he hadn't. He also realized that she was his only contact to the present, the only person who actually cared about his thoughts and experiences.

> *Dear Aunt Libbie,*
>
> *Yes, we did have a big fire here, but we, and the horses, are all safe. The newspaper account that you read may have been a bit exaggerated. It is now known that a barrel of oil exploded, setting fire to the coal house. The building was completely destroyed, but the coal pile, 110 tons, is still burning, and they tell us it could be weeks before the fire is out. Some enlisted soldiers have been assigned the duty of keeping watch on the burning pile, but it no longer seems a threat to any of the buildings.*
>
> *On the very night of the fire we had a hop, and several young ladies were invited from some women's colleges. We drew names from among those who were invited, and I was very fortunate to draw the name of a beautiful young woman with a most pleasing*

personality. Her father holds a position of some importance in Washington, and I was most surprised when Secretary Lamont greeted her by name and with the greatest familiarity.

At first I felt most remiss in not getting permission to correspond with her, but it is probably for the best. While she was a most delightful young woman in the conditions under which we met, I had cause to believe that she would not do well as the wife of an army officer. You, Aunt Libbie, are most unique in that you were the perfect officer's wife, and were I to compare any young woman with you, she would be found lacking.

I understand that your speaking engagements will take you abroad at the time of my graduation, and you will miss the ceremony. But, as I accept my diploma and commission, I will be thinking of you, and of your hand in providing me with this opportunity.

Your most obedient servant,
Myles Cade McDowell

Just as Cade was finishing his letter, Cass Conrad came into the room. "The mail clerk sent this for you." Cass tossed a package onto the bed.

"You'd better hope you didn't break those. The last cookies Aunt Libbie sent were just crumbs when they got here."

"That's not from Mrs. Custer."

"Oh, really?" Cade rose to inspect the package.

For an instant his mind flashed to Marci Winters. What if this was from her? But he dismissed the notion as quickly as he had thought it. She was back at college and had probably forgotten him.

Cade examined the package. "Emma Farnsworth?" he said aloud. "Who is Emma Farnsworth?"

"Ha! Do you have a secret lady friend you haven't told me about?" Cass teased.

When Cade opened the package, he saw that it was double-wrapped, so that whatever was inside was still unseen. There was, though, an envelope, and he opened it to find a note.

> *Dear Cadet McDowell:*
> *I want to thank you, and Miss Winters, for agreeing to pose for me. The pictures turned out very well, as you can see, primarily because of the lovely subjects. Please accept these photographs as a token of my appreciation.*
> *Sincerely,*
> *Emma Farnsworth*

Cade remembered the woman photographer then, and he opened the inner package eagerly. The first picture was of Marci, sitting on the Armstrong gun, her eyes shining, a slight smile on her lips, her dark, braided hair framing her face. She was beautiful, yes, but there was more than beauty here. There was also a hint of the whimsy that she had displayed that day, and he recalled not only the kiss, but her unexpected comment afterward: "I . . . don't think the rock will fall on us now, do you?"

The second picture was of the two of them together, and looking at it, he experienced a bittersweet moment. On the surface, it could be the image of any cadet and his lady, waiting only until graduation so they could marry in the chapel and emerge under an arch of crossed sabers.

Yet, he knew that wasn't the case. Marci Winters was but a casual acquaintance, a woman whose name he had drawn by lot. They were, as Longfellow's line said, *ships that pass in the night, and speak each other in passing.*

Miss Farnsworth had put the photographs in frames, and now he set both of them on his desk and smiled again, as he looked at them.

"Wow!" Cass said when he saw the pictures. "How did you get those?"

"There was a lady photographer taking pictures the weekend Marci was here. She sent them."

"Really? I hope she didn't get any pictures of Hortense and me."

Wells College

Marci had been summoned to Dean Smith's office over an hour ago, and now she sat in the antechamber watching the clock. She should be in her geology and mineralogy class right now, where Dr. Friske would be giving the last lecture before the final examination.

Marci tried to think of what she could possibly have done that would necessitate being taken out of a class, especially one as difficult as Dr. Friske's was. She had missed chapel a time or two, and her bed was not made on the last room inspection, but those were not serious infractions.

Then she began to worry. Maybe something tragic had happened at home, and the dean was charged with delivering the bad news to her. Maybe they were waiting for the doctor to arrive to revive her should she faint at the news. By the time she was called into the office, she had worked herself into an anxiety that was unusual for Marci.

"Have a seat, Miss Winters," Dean Smith said.

Miss Nash, who was standing at the window, turned and glared at Marci.

In an attempt to disarm the two women, Marci smiled broadly.

"I would think you'd wipe that grin off your face, you hussy."

"Now, Miss Nash, I thought we agreed we were going to handle this in a rational manner. It is my understanding that Miss Winters has not been allowed to explain her behavior. Is that correct, Marci?"

"I suppose not, because I don't know what you're talking about."

"Oh, yes, you do know," Miss Nash continued, approaching Marci with a menacing look. "You embarrassed me, but most of all you disgraced Wells College."

Marci looked toward Dean Smith with a penitent expression. "I'm sorry if I have done something, but if I've acted inappropriately, I have no awareness of it."

As soon as she said the words, she thought about West Point and her time spent with Cade McDowell on Flirtation Walk. But no one could possibly have seen her kiss him, and besides, both Carrie and Georgiana had done the same thing at approximately the same hour, and neither of them was here for Miss Nash's dressing-down.

"Do you deny that I asked you to go to your room the night of the fire at West Point?"

"You did."

"And did you not tell me you would stand by the statue until your escort returned?"

"Yes, ma'am."

"And did you do that?"

"I did."

"And when he returned, what did you do?"

"We went back to the hop."

"You have now added lying to your transgressions. Miss Winters, I watched you enter the sally port on your way to a gentleman's barracks, the entrance of which is strictly forbidden by a woman. I have no doubt that the man with whom I caught you cavorting has been expelled from the academy."

"Oh no, please tell me you didn't say anything to the officials at West Point! That can't be, the army is his whole life," Marci cried.

"There, Dean Smith. Is that proof enough? She did not have the fortitude to deny that she did enter the barracks, and I say she should be expelled from this institution, this very day. She cannot be gone soon enough."

Dean Smith folded her hands and dropped her head. It was several moments before she spoke.

"If you will excuse us, Miss Nash, I would like to have a word with Miss Winters."

When Miss Nash had left the room, Dean Smith spoke to Marci, who was now crying silently.

"Is what Miss Nash has reported the truth?"

"It is true that she did ask me to go to the room, and that she asked me to stay by the statue. When Cade returned, he smelled of smoke and he asked me to wait in the sally port while he went to change his clothes. And I did that. I did not enter any barracks."

"But you did disobey Miss Nash when she told you to stay by the statue?"

"I did."

"In view of your disobedience, and because Miss Nash feels so vehemently about this, I am going to have to ask you to leave Wells College."

Marci's lip began to quiver as she listened to the dean.

"Because we are so near the end of the term, I will allow you to write your examinations so that this year will not be totally wasted. However, I will not let you graduate with the class of '96. If you should be able to garner the recommendation from a prominent graduate . . . say, someone who may be on the board, I will readmit you to take your final classes and graduate with the class of '97."

"Would you be speaking of Mrs. Cleveland?" Marci asked.

"She is a board member."

Marci went out by the lake and sat on a big rock, looking out across the water. This was not fair. She had done nothing wrong. What would she tell her father? And then she thought of Cade.

"Please, God, please don't let me be the cause of Cade having to leave the academy. He loves it so, and he has nothing else. Please, and if it is so, let Mrs. Custer intervene on his behalf."

FOUR

West Point, June 12, 1895

For the last two days, every train arriving at the academy had had a full quota of people who would take part in the festivities that surrounded the commissioning of the class of '95. More than thirty-five hundred people were estimated to be in attendance, the majority of whom were young women who had come to be guests at the graduation hop. Cade had considered sending a personal invitation to Marci Winters, but had thought better of it. He had hoped that she would attempt to contact him since their meeting, but she had not.

This would be the last morning of Cade's life as a cadet on the Plain. For the past four years his life had been one of structure, but after today his life would forever be altered. He would be a second lieutenant in the United States Army, assigned to Fort Yellowstone, Wyoming. The closest he would come to acting as the officer for which he had trained to be would be in the telling of some tourist to stay away from a geyser. What would his father, who'd died in a historic battle, think about that?

It didn't matter. He stepped to the closet that he shared with Cass Conrad and withdrew his grays. Folding them carefully, he placed them in a packing crate, along with other mementos from his time spent at the academy. The last items to be packed were the two pictures that Miss Farnsworth had taken. He touched the photograph of Marci sitting on the Armstrong and relived that day, one of the happiest days he had ever spent. He could see her as she scampered down the cliff without fear or complaint, and he could feel her hand in his as they walked along Flirtation Walk. But what he wanted to relive most of all was the kiss—the kiss that caused a reaction that was both thrilling . . . and embarrassing. He smiled now and felt just a tinge of that same embarrassment today, remembering that he had turned away from her so that she couldn't see his obvious condition.

It wasn't fair to have someone make such an impact on another person, only to never see that person again. He put the pictures in the crate and nailed it shut.

A large tent had been erected in front of the library, and as the crowd swelled, more and more makeshift benches had to be set up. If not for the ameliorating breeze sweeping down the Hudson between Mount Taurus and Storm King, it would have been unbearable for the assembled crowd of people.

At precisely 10:30 a.m. the band began to play and the cadets marched to their seats under the leadership of Cadet Edward Schulz, who would graduate first man. For four years Cade had passed through the north sally port on whose keystone arch was spread the coat of arms of the academy and whose legend, DUTY, HONOR, COUNTRY, had inspired him, and now it was finished. They marched by class rank, and Cade, though his grades and military drill were among the highest, had significantly decreased his standing in the class due to an early penchant for acquiring demerits.

As a result of his activity, both good and bad, Cade graduated sixteenth in a class of fifty-two members.

Following the commencement speech, Adjutant General Ruggles stepped off the platform and exchanged salutes, then shook the hand of every cadet as he handed him his parchment.

"Lieutenant McDowell, congratulations on your achievement. I had hoped that our dear friend Mrs. Custer would be here to see her favorite cadet graduate."

"Thank you, sir. I, too, am disappointed that she was not able to attend."

"When next you see her, give her my regards."

"Yes, sir."

General Ruggles continued until he had distributed the last diploma, the fifty-second, to the new second lieutenant Daniel Duncan.

"Congratulations, Lieutenant Duncan."

"Sir, as the goat of the class, I am as proud of this diploma as any cadet who graduated at the head of the class."

Duncan's words were met with a hearty round of applause that was surpassed only by the final cheer when the superintendent rose from his place on the platform.

"Gentlemen of the class of 1895, you have completed your education and are no longer cadets. You are now commissioned officers of the United States Army!"

"Hurrah!" the graduating class shouted, as they threw their hats into the air.

Cade walked away while others were standing around with their friends and families. Unlike every other graduate, Second Lieutenant Myles Cade McDowell had no one to watch him receive his commission. While he felt a sense of profound satisfaction and accomplishment, he also deeply regretted that his mother had not lived to see this day.

When he got back to the barracks, he opened a can of black paint and carefully painted the address Mrs. G. A. Custer, 20 Park Avenue, Bronxville, New York, on one of the boards.

"Hey, Cade!" newly commissioned Lieutenant Casper Conrad called. "Hurry up! It's almost time for the day boat."

"You go on. I've got a few things to finish up."

Cass looked around the room. "It looks to me like you're done. If you're the only one not at the hotel for the class supper, that'll be bad. Most of the guys will leave for their furloughs tomorrow, so you won't get a chance to see anybody if you stay here."

"All right, you convinced me."

"Just leave your crate. Let the new plebes take care of it."

Cass and Cade hurried down to the boat landing

just as the Albany day boat rounded the S-curve in the river.

"Ah, so here you are, Son," Judge Conrad said. "You would think that four years of a structured school would break you of the habit of being last everywhere."

Cass laughed at his father's joke. "It wasn't me this time. I had to convince Cade to come with us. I didn't tell him you got us rooms at the Murray Hill."

"I'm glad you're with us," Mrs. Conrad said. "As Cass is the youngest of our three children, I confess that I miss having all of my children around. By the way, where are you going to go on your furlough?"

"I've not decided," Cade said. "Since my assignment is at Fort Yellowstone, I've thought about taking my time getting out there. Maybe just touring the country a little bit."

"That's ridiculous. You need to come back to Ohio with us. Cass is going to Fort Huachuca, and it's way out there, too. You could travel together," Mrs. Conrad said. "That is, if you're still speaking to one another after being roommates for so long."

"How could anyone not like me, Mom? You know she's right, Cade. We'll go fishing. Have you ever eaten catfish taken from the Ohio?" Cass held the tips of his fingers together and, after kissing them, scattered the kisses to the wind in his interpretation of a French chef. "Oooomwah!" he shouted.

"No, I can't say that I have," Cade said, laughing at his roommate's antics.

"Then, it's decided. You're coming to Ripley with us, and I'll take you out onto the river, and we'll catch so much fish the boat will be ready to tip over. What do you say about that?"

Cade took a deep breath. He had no plans at all for the next month, and it would be fun to be a part of a big family. He looked at Judge Conrad, who was smothering a smile as his son talked.

"Sir, I wouldn't want to impose," Cade said.

"Believe me, it's not an imposition. If you come, you'll keep Cass out of trouble."

"Well, all right, then. It's a deal."

Washington, DC, July 15, 1895

Stanton Caldwell spread a blanket on the South Lawn of the White House as the Marine Band were tuning their instruments preparing for a concert.

"I hope this doesn't last too long," Stanton said as he sat down.

"You know you like music," Marci said as she sat beside him.

"I do. In a symphony hall. Not out here on the grass."

"But there's nothing more rousing than the martial cadence of a spirited march—especially one of John Philip Sousa's compositions."

"That's the problem. Sousa's not here anymore, and it's all because Secretary Herbert wouldn't give him a commission."

Just then the director raised his baton and the band began to play a rousing rendition of "The Washington Post" march.

"Well, I don't care if it's John Philip Sousa or not. I like it, and I'm not the only one. Look at that little tyke over there. He's keeping perfect time," Marci said with a laugh as she pointed to a small boy who was "marching" to the music. "Isn't he cute?"

"That's disruptive," Stanton said. "His parents should rein him in."

"I certainly hope you wouldn't feel that way about our child."

"My child would know better than to make a pest of himself in a public setting."

It did not escape Marci's notice that Stanton had specifically said "my" child, rather than "our" child. "Of course he would know better." Marci reached over to take Stanton's hand in hers. "He would have the most handsome and the smartest daddy in all of Washington."

"Ah, Marci, I'm sorry. Mr. Hanna is moving to Georgia, and he's said I should go there, too." Stanton lifted her hand to his lips. "I've got to convince him that I need to stay in Washington, but that means . . ."

"We don't have to stay here if you don't want to."

"No, I know you like the music, and as I look around, I see several people I need to impress, so it's good to be seen on the White House lawn."

By her comment, Marci had not meant the concert. She would happily move to Georgia.

When she had returned from Wells, Marci had debated with herself whether she should tell her father of her dismissal. She hesitated because she knew that she had done nothing disgraceful. She had not remained by the monument as she had told Miss Nash she would do, but simply walking with

Cade to the sally port did not warrant an expulsion.

Marci knew that if her father found out, he would be profoundly disappointed, so she set about to find her own solution to the problem. And that solution involved Stanton Caldwell. If she could convince him to marry her, no one would question why she was not returning to Wells.

Once she reached that decision, the next step was to entice Stanton to marry her. Of course, she couldn't just ask him; the approach would have to come from Stanton. And at times during the summer she'd felt a comfortable relationship was developing, a relationship that she was sure was similar to that of a married couple.

Comfortable. Funny, but *comfortable* wasn't a word that she would use to apply to how she had felt when she was with Cade McDowell.

Cade McDowell? A ship that passed in the night.

She moved her hand to Stanton's arm, then leaned her head against his shoulder as the stirring music continued.

Here she was with Stanton, listening to music that had a definite martial air, music that meant little to Stanton, other than as a means for him to "be seen in the right places." Yet the military nature of the music had made her think of Cade. No doubt such music would stir his blood, as she felt it stirring her own.

For the rest of the summer, Stanton was in and out of Washington, shuttling between Thomasville, Georgia, where he met with his boss, Marcus Hanna, then Columbus, Ohio, where he visited Governor

McKinley, and then New York City, where he met with financiers. Anytime he had a few days in the capital, he was anxious to spend time with Marci. At times, in the shaded summer evenings, serenaded not by bands or orchestras, but the night-singing cicadas, crickets, and tree frogs, Marci and Stanton would share kisses. The kisses were pleasant and enjoyable, and Marci was beginning to think that the time was near when Stanton would ask her to marry him.

She told herself she could be happy with Stanton. The kisses they shared didn't make her feel exactly the way she had felt when she and Cade had kissed on Flirtation Walk, but she decided that was fine. Shouldn't a good wife be able to control her feelings?

It was near the end of August and Marci knew she would have to tell her father she was not returning to college. She felt terrible the way she had deceived her mother as they had prepared Marci's wardrobe for the winter, but she held on to the idea that any day now Stanton would ask her to marry him. But he did not.

Marci made an appointment to see her father at his office, and with much trepidation she made her way to the Treasury Building. When she arrived, she sat on a marble bench beside the statue of Alexander Hamilton, rehearsing what she would say to her father.

"I'm not going back to college because Stanton and I want to be married. I think it would be best if I spent the time here planning my wedding rather than putting that burden on Mother."

Yes, that was a plausible reason. She took a deep breath, then climbed the marble steps and entered the building.

"M. D. Winters. Now that's an original moniker," DeWitt Winters said when Marci was ushered into his office. "I've been expecting this meeting, although I did not expect it to be here."

"Daddy, I'm not going back to college," Marci blurted out.

Calmly, DeWitt opened his desk drawer and withdrew a letter. "Would this have anything to do with your reason?" He slid the envelope across the desk.

Marci recognized the distinctive penmanship of Dean Smith. She bowed her head, avoiding her father's steady gaze. "I don't know what she said I did, but whatever it is, I didn't do it."

"Oh? You didn't do it?"

"No, sir."

"Marci, what do you think this letter is about?"

"I think it's a letter that says I entered a cadet's dormitory while I was at West Point, but I swear, I didn't do that."

"What did you do?"

"Cade—Cade McDowell, who was my escort, asked me to wait for him under the sally port while he changed clothes after the fire, and I did. Miss Nash saw me and she told Dean Smith I went into his room, but I did not."

"It doesn't matter what you did."

"What do you mean, it doesn't matter?" Marci asked, jerking her head up for the first time.

"Marci, if you haven't learned before now, let this be a lesson to you. Perception can be as damning as truth. You won't be going back to Wells, and people will wonder about it."

"They won't have to. I'll be Mrs. Stanton Caldwell by the time school starts."

DeWitt made a sharp, quick intake of breath. "Mr. Caldwell has not spoken to me. Has he asked you to marry him?"

"No, but I'm sure he will before the summer is out."

DeWitt shook his head. "And I am equally sure that he will not. Nor do I want him to. Believe me, Marci, Stanton Caldwell is not the man for you."

"But I love him."

"Do you?"

"Yes, I do!" Marci said the words forcefully, almost as if she were trying to convince herself.

"And yet you were accused of entering another man's dormitory, not six months ago. Is this what you think one does if she loves someone?"

Marci had no answer.

"He earns his living convincing people to part with their money," DeWitt said. "And part of his job is the coercion, conniving, and, yes, even bribing members of Congress so that he may be privy to information to pass on to the Red Boss of Cleveland."

"If you mean Mr. Hanna, he doesn't live in Cleveland anymore."

"No, he doesn't. You've grown up in the shadow of politics. Why do you suppose a man who was a bank president, a partner in three rolling mills, a director of street railways, a shipbuilding executive, an oil and coal tycoon—why do you think he gave that all up to move to a quiet little town in Georgia?"

Marci shrugged her shoulders. "I don't know."

"He went there because he has plans to buy a presidential election for the governor of Ohio, that's why."

"But that has nothing to do with Stanton. He's not doing that."

"Stanton Caldwell works for Marcus Hanna, and Marcus Hanna is campaigning for William McKinley. McKinley is a Republican. Must I remind you that I hold my position because a Democrat is president?"

"I know that."

"At any rate, getting married has nothing to do with the business of government; this has to do with your life." DeWitt rose from his chair and walked around to sit on the settee beside Marci. "I don't think Stanton Caldwell is the one for you, honey. I just want to protect you. That's all."

"You know I'm going to be scandalized when it comes out I'm not going back to school. All my friends will speculate that I did something really bad, or even worse, they'll think I flunked. What am I going to do?"

"You're going to go to school."

"It's too late to enroll at another school. I'm so sorry I didn't tell you as soon as I came home. Then we could have done something else."

"My dear, arrangements have already been made to do something else. You didn't tell me, but Dean Smith did. And I think she believes in you. Perhaps you should have read the letter."

Marci picked up the envelope and, withdrawing the letter, began to read.

May 30, 1895

Dear Mr. and Mrs. Winters,
It is with great pleasure that I inform you that I have submitted the name of your daughter, Marcia Diane, to be a candidate for admission to the Académie Julian, the premier art school in all of Paris. She is a bright, talented woman, and I feel some time abroad will do wonders for her development.
Very respectfully,
Helen Fairchild Smith
Dean of Women, Wells College
Aurora, New York

"Why didn't you tell me?" Marci asked as she put the letter down.

"When you came home, you were so depressed. At first I thought you didn't want to go, and then I realized you didn't know what Dean Smith had done. I was just waiting for the right time to tell you."

"Does Mother know about this?"

"She does. Did you not realize that she steered you toward clothing that might better suit a bohemian?"

"I thought she was trying to make me the fashion plate of Wells College," Marci said as she began to laugh and cry at the same time. "I didn't have the heart to tell her I wasn't going back to school, and even if I did go back, all I would have wanted was leotards and bloomers."

DeWitt Winters enfolded his daughter in his arms. "Marci, I want you to know that no matter what you do, your mother and I will always love you."

Hearing her father's words caused Marci to cry openly.

"Now what's wrong? Do you want to go to Paris or not?"

"Yes, I want to go, but what am I going to do about Stanton?"

"Marci, if what you think you feel for Stanton—"

"No, Father, not what I think I feel. What I *do* feel."

"If what you feel for Stanton is real, and if he feels the same for you, then your relationship will certainly stand a temporary separation. You'll just be putting to a test the old saying, absence makes the heart grow fonder."

Marci left her father's office with conflicting emotions. She was relieved that she no longer had to keep up the pretext that she was returning to school, and she was equally relieved that she didn't have to pursue Stanton as aggressively. She had convinced herself that she did want to marry him. But her father had given her pause. Was she in love with him or was it just the idea of using a marriage to save face with her friends?

She mouthed a quiet prayer: *Thank you, Lord. And Dean Smith. Thank you for providing me with a solution.*

And what a solution it was. What young woman would not relish the idea of studying in Paris?

Her steps quickened as the horses pulling the cable car came into sight. The question now was, should she go directly to Stanton's office to tell him of her plans, or should she wait until he called on her? She would wait. He was probably out of town anyway.

FIVE

Fort Yellowstone, Wyoming, September 1895

The intruding notes of reveille played by the bugler rolled across the parade ground, then echoed back from Capitol Hill. Second Lieutenant Myles Cade McDowell turned on his bedside lamp, then rose from his cot and pulled on his light blue, wool trousers.

He stepped to the window of his room and, pulling the coarse drape aside, looked toward Sepulcher Mountain in the west. The snow on the mountaintop was becoming more and more visible, and it along with the jumble of travertine that made up the Mammoth Terraces was shining gold in the reflected light of the just-rising sun. He never tired of this view from the bachelor officers' quarters, and the setting had helped to ease his feeling of disappointment when he had read his assignment was at Fort Yellowstone.

As a cavalryman, his first choice for service had been at the new Cavalry and Light Artillery School at Fort Riley, Kansas. There, he would have honed his skills learned at West Point, but that was not to be. He was posted to a national park.

In the six weeks that he had been at Yellowstone, the most challenging duties he had been called upon to perform were to tell tourists to refrain from defacing the landscape, or to tell them to put out their campfires or to remember that the animals in the park were indeed dangerous.

This was not what he had envisioned for himself when he was training back on the Plain.

"Who's taking the formation this morning?" Lieutenant Scott called from the hallway.

"Our still-wet-behind-the-ears second lieutenant," Lieutenant Forsythe said.

"Would you be referring to me?" Cade called out from his room as he pulled on a blue blouse, tucking it into his pants.

"Is there any officer junior to you?" Forsythe asked.

"Are you talking about date of rank, or intelligence, charm, and good looks?"

"Were you absent from the class on humility?" Scott teased.

"Nevertheless, you're the only one who has to get up now," Forsythe said.

Cade lived in the bachelor officers' quarters with three other officers. Each had his own private bedchamber, but they shared a dayroom and a common mess in the basement.

Getting a cup of coffee, Cade stepped out onto the front porch, the wool uniform feeling good in the crisp mountain air. He watched as the bugler stepped up to the megaphone to play "First Call," which sent the soldiers rushing out of the barracks for morning assembly.

After the morning formation, Cade returned to the BOQ to join the other officers for breakfast.

"Any surprises at formation?" Nance asked.

"No, nobody showed up in long johns and poncho," Cade replied, and the others laughed. A few days earlier, one of the enlisted men had gotten out of bed too late and, so as not to miss formation, threw a poncho over his underwear and tried to hide in the rear rank.

"How's your chess game going with Lieutenant Moss?" Lieutenant Forsythe asked.

James Moss had graduated from West Point a year ahead of Cade. The two had become friends through a mutual love of chess. Moss, who was now posted at Fort Missoula, had engaged Cade in a long-distance game, exchanging moves by telegram and mail. The game had started soon after Cade had arrived at Yellowstone.

"He's down to a queen, one bishop, two rooks, and a knight," Cade said. "I've still got my queen, one rook, one bishop, but I have two knights."

The four were just about finished with breakfast when they heard "Officers' Call" sounded.

"Private, don't throw out my biscuits," Lieutenant Forsythe said as he pushed his chair away from the table.

When the officers reached the headquarters building, they hurried up the stone steps and into the orderly room.

The first sergeant and the company clerk stood when they saw the officers.

"Good morning, sirs," the first sergeant said.

"Good morning, Top," Scott replied.

"I'll tell the captain you're here."

The four officers filled the sparsely furnished orderly room. The dominating feature was a wall-size map of Yellowstone Park, next to a mounted shelf that held the sign-out book in which the enlisted men entered their names anytime they left the fort. An Underwood typewriter was on the company clerk's desk, and at a nod from Lieutenant Scott, the clerk sat down and resumed typing, the keys making staccato popping sounds as they struck the paper.

"Sirs, Captain Anderson will see you," the first sergeant said.

The commanding officer's office was utilitarian, consisting of one desk, one chair, and the US flag on a stand in the corner. A picture of President Grover Cleveland was on the wall, next to the flag.

"Stand at ease," Captain Anderson said, and the officers relaxed their positions.

"Who took the formation this morning?"

"I did, sir," Cade said. "All present or accounted for."

"Good." Captain Anderson drummed his fingers on his desk for a moment before he spoke. "Gentlemen, the mission of the Sixth Cavalry is to protect the park, but everywhere I look, tourists are chipping off souvenirs, and names of the vain are glaring at us from anywhere they can possibly scribble them."

"Captain, even when we catch someone in the act, all we can do is escort them out of the park," Nance said.

"I've got a plan to change that. Effective immediately, anyone found guilty of marking his name on one of the formations will be ordered back to the scene of the crime, and with his fellow tourists looking on, taunting and chiding, we will by force of arms require him to obliterate the supposed imperishable monument to his folly, with the aid of soap and a brush."

"Ha! I like that!" Forsythe said.

"I'm glad you do, Bill, because that's your assignment. If you find any unsightly markings, I want you to locate the perpetrator and administer the punishment."

"Yes, sir. I'll organize a patrol immediately."

Anderson smiled. "I expect no less. Now, for you three gentlemen. You take details out as you would ordinarily do. But keep your eyes peeled for any kind of vandalism, and if you see any new incidents, report them to Bill."

"Yes, sir," the three lieutenants replied.

"That's all, gentlemen, carry on with your duties."

The four officers saluted, then left the office.

After returning from the patrol that afternoon Cade checked his mail: he'd received a letter from James Moss and a package from Libbie Custer. He was certain that he knew what was in the package, and he wanted to open it in private, but he opened the letter from Moss right away.

> *Dear Cade:*
>   *For some time now, I have had in mind a proposal which, I am certain you will agree, is quite bold. I wrote to General Nelson Miles, requesting that I be allowed to equip*

*a number of my soldiers with bicycles for a
test of my theory.*

*Bicycles move quietly and can be
hidden easily when trying to advance
on a suspected foe. Unlike the cavalry,
which, as we all know, must assign one
man in four to tend to the horses when we
fight dismounted, there would be no such
requirement for soldiers on bicycles. Thus a
quarter of the men would be automatically
added to the eligible fighting force.*

*It is my intention to ride from Ft.
Missoula to St. Louis, in an attempt to prove
the worthiness of the wheel as a method of
transportation for the U.S. Army. I believe
my Buffalo Soldiers, with their proven
endurance, capability, and willingness—no,
eagerness—to perform any duty assigned
them, to be perfectly suited for the task, and
such a long trip, successfully completed, will
more than validate my theory.*

*I am pleased to tell you that I have
received approval from General Miles to
undertake the project. I am now provisioning
for some training rides as preparation for
the long ride to St. Louis.*

*Oh, and reference our game, bishop to
queen's rook five.*

*Your friend,
Daig*

When Cade got to his room, he looked at the
chessboard to apply the move.

"Damn!" he said aloud. "He's about to put me in check."

Cade studied the board, trying to figure how to save his king. He had to admit, James Moss was a good tactician, much better than his last-place rank at the academy would indicate. It would take some thought before Cade made his move.

He turned his attention from Daig's letter and the chess game back to the package he had received in the post. Knowing what was in it, he had delayed opening it because he wanted to savor the moment. He studied it, as it lay on his cot, with Aunt Libbie's neat, cursive letters spelling out his name and address. Finally he picked it up, then opened it as if it were some cherished gift. When the paper was pulled away, he took a deep breath, purposely waiting another moment before he turned the contents over. When he did, he saw the picture of him and Marci at the Great Chain, and beneath that was the one of Marci on the barrel of the cannon. He set the two pictures on his bedside table, moving them to get the best angle as he looked at them from his cot, and the memories of that near-perfect weekend came flooding over him.

When he had moved the frames three or four times, he stopped, and sitting back on the bed, he put his head in his hands. What was he doing acting like a lovesick cow?

He had written to Aunt Libbie requesting that she send the photos to him, and now that they were here, he thought it was a pointless thing to have done. What was this woman to him? A will-o'-the-wisp? A fantasy that would forever be unrequited?

Lifting his head, he looked again at the pictures. The photographer had posed them so that they were looking toward each other, not at the camera, and the resulting picture, with its diffused light, showed two people who appeared to care deeply for one another. Miss Farnsworth had been meticulous in placing their hands exactly where she wanted them to better illustrate the line of the poetry she had chosen.

Cade had never met anyone quite like Marci, and sometimes he searched his mind for words to describe her. *Vivacious, intelligent, charming, witty, thoughtful,* and *pretty,* of course, but that went without saying. And, unbidden, the last word popped into his mind. *Unapproachable.* Yes, he would have to face that. She was a member of the social set in Washington, DC, America's most discriminating society. How could he compete with that?

Then Cade saw the inscription on the matting, *as in love they fondly twine.* He was embarrassed, because that was a misrepresentation. As much as he might wish it to be true, it was a lie.

Removing the picture from his table, he slipped it into his trunk. That picture would have to be kept out of sight.

But the other picture—the one of Marci and the Armstrong—was perfect. He picked it up and read the line inscribed, and it fit this picture perfectly: *See! contrasted beauties shine.*

Cade smiled as he looked at the picture. Her black braid hanging loosely to the side of her face, her dark eyes flashing, her smile beguiling—Marci Winters was perfect. Why had he let her get away from him?

Putting the picture back on the table next to his bed, he gathered the brown paper to dispose of it—and saw something else.

Picking up a tintype, he recognized his mother, Aunt Libbie, and General Custer. Another man was there, whom he didn't know. Turning the tintype over, he read, *Edward and Margaret, Autie and me, at the Big Blue River, 1867.*

Cade took the picture to the light on his table and looked at it closely. Could this man be his father? His mother had told him over and over how much he looked like his father, but he could see absolutely no resemblance between the stocky, broad-shouldered man with light hair in this picture, and his own dark hair and tall, slim body. He would have to ask Aunt Libbie about this.

He decided to step out onto the porch one last time before he went to bed. When he did, the brisk night air was so cold he could see vapor clouds from his breath, which, catching the moonlight, seemed almost luminescent.

For the first time, he questioned his decision to become an army officer. What was he doing here? At West Point he had studied tactics, he had read of great battles and crusades that altered nations, and he had walked the hallowed halls of history, touching the captured cannons, battle flags, and memorabilia of a hundred campaigns. That had been all the incentive he needed to keep him focused.

But now he was here, at Yellowstone, answering questions from tourists, looked on by the civilians as little more than a park interpreter. A couple of lines came to him from Tennyson's "Charge of the Light Brigade."

Theirs not to reason why,
Theirs but to do and die.

Well, all right, that was probably a bit of an over-statement. But this was his assignment, he had taken the oath upon the Plain, so if he had to be a glorified park attendant, he would be the best he could be.

As Cade stood out on the porch, lost in such contemplation, he heard the first note of "Taps." He leaned against one of the supporting posts of the porch roof as he listened to the bugle call that put the soldiers to bed at night. This haunting melody was very much a part of his life.

Day is done, gone the sun
From the lakes, from the hills, from the sky
All is well, safely rest
God is nigh.

Cade could still hear the faint sound of music, and the distant laughter, from the hotel, but as he looked around the garrison, he saw that all the buildings, the officers' quarters, and the soldiers' barracks were dark and quiet. Turning, he went back inside, then climbed the stairs to his room. When he sat down on his bed, he picked up the picture of Marci and held it in his hand. As he sat there, he knew what he would do. He would not let his queen get away.

He rose from his bed and composed a letter.

Dear Miss Winters,

I hope that you remember me, as my memory of you is, and perhaps shall ever be, green. I am Lieutenant Cade McDowell, though when we met, I was still a cadet. It was my good fortune to draw your name and thus act as your escort at the Spring Hop held at West Point in March of this year.

That was six months ago, and much has happened in the interim. You have returned for your last year at Wells College, whilst I have been posted to Fort Yellowstone, Wyoming, a military reservation located within the boundaries of Yellowstone National Park.

There are many wonders to see here, the most well-known of which is Old Faithful, a magnificent geyser that erupts every hour, shooting water some 150 feet into the air. But other things are just as memorable. There are mountains, hot springs, reflecting pools, waterfalls, and even a cliff made of obsidian. The black glass is every bit as beautiful as a waterfall. There are also many flowers, bears, mountain sheep, elk, moose, and more kinds of birds than you can count, all arrayed in beautiful colors.

My particular interest is in the great American bison. The numbers are rapidly dwindling, and it is the fond hope of our commanding officer as well as the

*Department of the Interior, that we can bring
this animal back from the brink of extinction.*

*It may sound as if I am waxing poetic
about the park, and I confess my guilt. In
doing so, I would hope to entice you to plan
a visit to this beautiful place. And if you
choose to do so, I hereby tender my offer
to, once again, be your faithful escort and
guide.*

*Should you find it in your heart to answer
the letter of a soldier in the service of our
country, and perhaps even to engage in an
exchange of correspondence, I would forever
be in your debt. If this meets with your
approval, you may post your letters to:*

> *Lieutenant Myles Cade McDowell*
> *Sixth United States Cavalry*
> *Fort Yellowstone, Wyoming*

Your obedient servant,
Cade McDowell

Cade folded the letter and placed it in an envelope, addressing it to Marci at Wells College.

Then he looked over at the chessboard, and in an
instant he saw an opening for his queen that would
take him out of check. Taking his pen in hand, he
wrote, *queen to bishop four*. He was so confident in
his move that he decided he would send James a
telegram tomorrow.

He climbed into bed and, with one last glance at
Marci's picture, turned off the bedside lamp.

Paris, France, December 1895

Although she'd lived in Paris for only a few months, already the walls of Marci's room were covered with sketches she had done at the Académie Julian, one of the most famous art ateliers in the city. The beginning course of study for the nouveau artist was to copy some of the famous paintings in the Louvre, and when the masters deemed a student competent, she would graduate to drawing, and then painting from a live model.

For the last couple of weeks, Marci had been in the drawing phase of her course work, and she was pleased with the caliber of her work and the comments she had received from Monsieur Bouguereau, who was the master in her particular atelier. In the previous week one of Marci's drawings was so good she had won the weekly *concours,* enabling her to choose her seat in the class. This was a coveted honor because the stools were placed in a semicircle around the posing model. Some of the seats gave a poor angle of the model, while others placed an artist too close to the stove, the heat becoming unbearable.

When she walked into the cavernous art studio, several other students were already there assembling their supplies. The seat in the center and to the left had not been taken, this being the preferred spot. Marci made her way to the spot and sat down, putting her charcoals in place. This would be an exercise in shading.

All the girls were chattering when their master, M. Bouguereau, entered the room.

"*Bonjour, mademoiselles.* Today we begin a new phase in our learning. I expect to see detailed drawings of the hands and feet this morning. Concentrate on the texture of the skin and the shading. Tomorrow we will move to the muscular structure of the legs and then the genitalia. The genitals are a particularly interesting work because the folds of the skin must be shaded exactly right or the penis looks grotesque."

When Marci heard the word *penis,* she inhaled sharply. She looked over at her friend Irena. Their subject today would be a man, and he would be nude. Marci felt apprehension, mixed with curiosity and excitement. Since arriving in Paris, she had seen statues and paintings of nude men, and at the *académie,* she had seen drawings, but those had been nothing but inanimate objects, and lines on paper. She had never seen the real thing.

"Ladies, I'd like to introduce you to Leopold, our model for the week." M. Bouguereau turned toward the door and called out, "*Léopold, nous sommes prêts pour vous. Voulez-vous venir maintenant, s'il vous plaît?*"

Leopold entered the room wearing a dark robe, but before he stepped up onto the platform, he slipped out of it and draped it across a stool. He was totally nude.

All sound in the room ceased. There were no creaking stools, no movements of supplies, no twitterings among the students. All eyes were trained upon Leopold and, to be perfectly honest, upon his member.

Marci had never seen a penis, and she was both fascinated and discomfited by it. A good girl did not look at a man unless he was her husband. But here in front of her, without the slightest bit of embarrassment, was a naked man standing as nonchalantly as if he had stepped in for a chat.

Leopold stepped up onto the platform, his penis moving freely as he did so. Not once, since he'd entered the room, had he made eye contact with any of the students. Marci marveled at how detached he could keep himself, looking off as if studying something in the distance, though the confines of the room limited the distance.

When Leopold was comfortably seated, M. Bouguereau posed the model by word and action, moving an arm here, and a leg there, until he had him in the exact position he wanted. Leopold would have to maintain this pose for fifty minutes; then he would have a ten-minute break, and he would be expected to return to this pose for the entire week.

Then the master turned to the ladies, all of whom were trying to keep their expressions as detached as the expression on the face of their model.

"All right, ladies, I expect to see feet by noon."

Marci worked diligently throughout the morning and was surprised that she could indeed concentrate on the feet and ignore that part of the body that had so drawn her attention initially. At lunchtime, Leopold jumped down from the platform and walked out of the room, this time not even bothering to put on his robe.

When he had gone, the lunch lady entered the room, offering hard-boiled eggs and an apple to each of the girls.

"Did you think it would be that big?" Irena asked.

"By *it,* I suppose you mean his penis," Marci said as a smile crossed her lips.

"Of course that's what I mean."

"This is nothing," a French girl who was sitting nearby chimed in. "Wait until he is aroused and his little worm jumps to the size of a flagpole. Then you will see big."

"Babette, have you lain with a man?" Irena asked, her eyes opening wide.

Babette dropped her head and looked at the two young women with a coy expression. "That is a question you never ask a lady, but if you must, I think you should ask the esteemed Miss Gardner. She has lain, as you say, with old Bouguey for all these many years. Why do you think her work gets such acclaim? Could it be that our master, M. Bouguereau, favors her services?"

"Babette, I don't think you should say such things when you don't know they are true," Marci said.

"Ah! What I say is true. Just ask her."

Just then M. Bouguereau and Leopold stepped back into the atelier, and the women returned to their stools and easels, concentrating on the hand for the afternoon session.

When the day was over, Marci was exhausted, both mentally and physically. She walked home alone through the winding streets of the Latin Quarter, avoiding the shop vendors who were out hawking their wares, trying to get one more coin before closing for the night. She had been in Paris for less than four months and she felt comfortable getting around in the areas where she needed to be, but except for the people at the Académie Julian and her pension, she had not met anyone.

M. Julian had more than six hundred students at his nine studios, but he kept the sexes segregated. Five ateliers were for men and four were for women, and except for the masters, the paint vendors, and the models, no men were allowed contact with the women.

Marci laughed. When she had told Stanton where she was going, he had warned her about the debauchery that was Paris, but until today when she had seen a nude man for the first time, she'd felt as if she were living in a cloister. But that was fine. She would be here only until spring, and she wanted to learn as much as she could before leaving.

When Marci arrived at the pension, she stepped into the salon, which was a long room with a roaring fireplace at one end. The room was comfortable with faded old-gold, plush furniture and Turkish rugs seemingly placed at random over the polished wood floor. The walls were covered with drawings and paintings from art students who had been previous residents, and Marci decided after having won the *concours* for the week, her efforts might compare favorably to some of the other work that was on display.

When the meal was over, Marci climbed up to her room and took out her sketch pad. As Bouguereau had stressed, she would do a detailed pencil study and then an oil sketch before she began her actual painting. Because most of the subjects of the paintings in the pension salon were Madonnas or nymphs or goddesses or scenes in and around Paris, Marci decided she would paint something uniquely American.

She began sketching a scene of Washington, putting in the dome of the Capitol and the Washington Monument and the White House, but she couldn't make it come together, so in a fit of whimsy, she put in some cows grazing on the White House lawn. Hadn't Bouguey told them, "If you make a landscape, you must seek a place with cows."

She wadded the sketch into a ball and put it into the little heater in her room, then stepped onto the balcony of her pension overlooking rue de la Huchette. It had rained all morning and well into the afternoon, not a downpour, but a monotonous shower that had sent pedestrians hurrying by under dripping umbrellas, while coachmen sat miserably upon their high seats, hunkered down in their slickers. Finally, in midafternoon, the sun appeared and made an effort to dry the sidewalks and pavement, though little pools of water still stood in the low places.

She watched the people as both foot and vehicle traffic crossed back and forth across the river on Pont Saint-Michel.

Beyond the river she could see the terrace of the Tuileries Garden, the obelisk in the Place de la Concorde, and the now bare-limbed trees that lined the Champs-Élysées. To the west was the Eiffel Tower, one of the most distinctive pieces of architecture to grace the skyline, but the Île de la Cité, with its great cathedral, Notre Dame de Paris, was the focal point from her balcony.

The rain and the chill of the air caused Marci to shudder, and she stepped back into her room, closing the doors to the balcony.

Taking a fresh sheet, she picked up her charcoal and began sketching the reclining figure of Leopold.

She worked into the night, first on the texture of the skin and the shading, then the muscular structure of the legs and the genitals, paying particular attention, as M. Bouguereau had told them, to the folds of the skin.

When she thought she had a credible drawing, she put her easel near the window so that she could examine it at first light and then retired for the night.

When she awakened, she walked to her drawing to examine it with a critical eye. It was not the genitals that took her breath away, but the face she had unconsciously drawn.

It was the face of Cade McDowell.

SIX

Fort Yellowstone, December 1895

The view from his window in the BOQ could have been a Currier and Ives lithograph, perhaps with a name like *Winter Wonderland*. A solid mantle of snow was on the ground from the buildings of the fort, across the parade ground, where mounted drills trained the soldiers and entertained the park visitors in the summer, all the way across to Mammoth Hot Springs Hotel. The Terraces, which in the summer stood out by their alabaster white, now blended in unobtrusively with the rest of the landscape, with only the constant cloud of steam rising from the hot-water springs to mark their location.

It was near zero outside, and during the night just passed, it had dropped to below zero. Because of the cold, and the snow, the routine formations held in the summer were suspended, the troop carrying out its duties with little pomp. One of the winter duties was to patrol the park against poaching, that being a particular problem. Because of the cold and snow, which stood from one foot to fifteen to twenty feet deep depending on where in the park it was measured, the animals' ranges of wandering were greatly reduced. Also, they tended to gather in bunches in those areas where they could paw through the snow to get to forage.

The snow made it easy for poachers to sneak up on the animals, and it made it more difficult for the soldiers to patrol, first because the park boundaries were laid out to correspond to the changing outlines of bodies of water, and second because in many places horses couldn't be used. Cade had just returned from a four-day scout. He had conducted the patrol on horseback where a horse could be ridden, and on snowshoes where it wasn't practical to ride a horse. On this scout he caught, red-handed, three poachers taking elk. The poachers were brought back and put in the guardhouse for further disposition.

At first, Cade couldn't understand why these men would risk a $1,000 fine or two years imprisonment to poach game in the park when there was plenty of game in their own neighborhoods. But Captain Anderson had explained that the real prize was a buffalo. It was estimated that fewer than a hundred buffalo were left in the United States, and a buffalo head would bring thousands of dollars, especially for a European collector. The park herd had now dwindled to fifty animals, and the soldiers had to get an accurate count of them and even round them up for the winter, putting some of them in the middle of Yellowstone Lake on Dott Island.

On the morning after Cade and his detail had caught the poachers, Cade was invited to have breakfast at the Mammoth Hot Springs Hotel. He was to meet George Grinnell, a frequent visitor to the park, who was an anthropologist, zoologist, and a naturalist, as well as the editor of the influential magazine *Forest and Stream*. Along with his friend Theodore Roosevelt, who was now the New York City police commissioner, Grinnell was a cofounder of the Boone and Crockett Club, which had taken on as one of its main causes the saving of the buffalo from extinction. He was here now for the upcoming trial of James Courtenay.

"Good morning, Lieutenant," Grinnell said when he saw Cade enter the dining room. Grinnell stood and pulled out a chair for Cade.

"Thank you, sir." Cade slid into the chair beside Grinnell.

"I see that Courtenay has a whole parade of witnesses here to testify on his behalf," Grinnell said.

"I've been told that he's enlisting his brother, his daughter's father-in-law, the plumber, the bread maker—anybody he can come up with that may back up his story that he wasn't in the park when he got those buffalo scalps. More than anything, we need the boundaries set."

"You're right, but . . . money. That's what it's really all about." Grinnell shook his head. "I hope Judge Meldrum comes to the right decision."

"I have every confidence in the judge."

"My boy, Captain Anderson tells me that you've done a fine job rounding up some of the buffalo over by Heart Lake."

"We did find a few."

"And you took them to Dott Island?"

"Yes. I know that some people don't look very favorably on keeping the buffalo contained in the middle of Yellowstone Lake, but when you see what this Courtenay fellow did, and then last year when Ed Howell was caught in the act of killing six buffalo, I thought something had to be done," Cade said.

"There may be more people that think like you do than you know. Besides being here for the trial, I'm here on behalf of Mr. Langley. He's the head of the Smithsonian Institution, and he's proposed that some of these buffalo should be brought to Washington to the National Zoological Park. If we have about twenty or so, we could start a breeding program and introduce buffalo to other zoos around the country. What do you think?"

"If you want my honest opinion, I don't think it would work."

"Why not?"

"I think the animals that run wild are used to wild grasses, and you wouldn't have that back East."

"If that's the case, we'll just have to bring hay from the West to the East. Congress has already approved this, and we want to bring in a shipment of buffalo in the spring. Captain Anderson has suggested that you might be the best one for the job. Can I count on you?"

"If Captain Anderson tells me this is what I'm going to do, then of course that's what I'll do," Cade said, an easy smile on his face.

New York, March 1896

As the RMS *Etrunia* passed by the Statue of Liberty, many of the ship's passengers crowded to the port side for a good view, including Marci, who was returning from her study at the Académie Julian in Paris.

"That, my dear lady, is the lamp that fires the hope of the world." The speaker was a distinguished-looking older man who was standing beside her.

"It is a welcoming sight for someone who is returning home from abroad," Marci agreed.

That night, on the train to Washington, Marci thought about home. She hadn't missed it as much as she had thought she would—Paris had been too exciting and the art school too interesting. She did wonder how she would be received when she got home. She had corresponded regularly with her friends at Wells, and a few of the young women whom she knew in Washington.

And then, of course, she'd heard from Stanton.

His letters were a constant enigma to her. He wrote detailed accounts of his fund-raising campaigns, references to who was running for which office and who was not, which government appointees had switched to what position, and what scandals were making the rounds of society. All of this was newsy, but that was just it—she could have read the same information from any American newspaper. What she had craved was some personal sentiment, something that told her she and Stanton had a sustainable relationship. But that had never happened. She had come to accept that this was how couples who were comfortable with one another behaved.

One person Marci had never heard a word from was Cade McDowell, and she was a little disappointed about that. But how could he have written her? He would have no idea where to send the letter. She had thought about contacting him after the weekend they had spent together, but the fiasco over the sally-port incident had made her hesitant to do so. A part of her didn't want to know if she caused his dismissal from the academy. Her dismissal from Wells had been embarrassing, but his dismissal from West Point would be devastating.

It had been just about a year now since she had met Cade, and yet he was still on her mind.

Why did she continue to think about him? Even fantasize about him? Didn't she and Stanton have an agreement? Or if not an agreement, at least an understanding? She would be seeing him soon, and she was determined to get a definite commitment from him.

Fort Yellowstone, April 1896

Captain Anderson had assigned one entire cavalry troop to round up the animals to be sent to Washington, and it had taken the better part of the winter. Besides twenty buffalo, Samuel Langley had requested that beaver, elk, and bear be included in the transport to the National Zoo. As Sergeant

Dawes explained, it wasn't like herding cows, and it tried Cade's patience to get the animals ready to go. They were loaded onto specially outfitted wagons and transported to holding pens at the depot in Cinnabar, where part of his troop was assigned to guard them. The buffalo, especially, were vulnerable to theft, because they were outside the boundaries of the park, and all laws protecting them were invalid.

But the beaver were the most troublesome. Cade had to have his men capture specimens at least three times because they kept escaping. Finally he had an iron plate installed around the bottom of their pen so they couldn't gnaw their way out.

When all the animals had been gathered and secured, including the early loading of the beavers into their special car, Cade reported to Captain Anderson.

"Here are your orders," Captain Anderson said, handing a typed sheet of paper to Cade.

April 27, 1896

>*Headquarters*
>*6th Cavalry, United States Army*
>*Ft. Yellowstone, Wyoming*

>*Special Orders*

>*Lt. M. C. McDowell is herewith detached
>from duty at Ft. Yellowstone and ordered
>to accompany representative animals*

*to be transferred to the National Zoo in
Washington, D.C.*

*Time allotted for this duty is one month
from above date.*

*Sergeant Elias Dawes and Private Leon
Hawkins are herewith assigned to Lt.
McDowell for this duty.*

*Funds for rations to be furnished by U.S.
Army.*

*George S. Anderson
Captain, Commanding*

"You're authorized per diem is a dollar for each of
you," Captain Anderson said. He counted out ninety
dollars. "I chose Dawes and Hawkins to go with you
because they're good men, and I don't expect they'll
give you any trouble."

Cade accepted the money, then, with a salute,
returned to his quarters to pack for the trip. As he
was packing his valise, he picked up the photograph of Marci Winters and remembered that she
had said she lived in Washington. It would be good
to look her up. He didn't know her address, but she
had said her father worked at Treasury, and there
couldn't be that many Winterses who worked there.
He would see if he could track her down.

But then he thought of the letter he had sent her
at Wells College. She had not responded to it, so she
undoubtedly didn't want to hear from him. "Marci,
girl, we were ships that passed in the night," he
said as he returned the picture to its place on the
table.

A special train, put together by the Smithsonian Institution, would take the animals to Washington. It consisted of six stock cars as each of the species being transported had its own car, and the buffalo had three. A Pullman car was also attached to the train for the passengers. Cade, Dawes, and Hawkins, plus two representatives from the National Zoological Park, Ned Boutelle and Jacek Murkowski, were making the trip to Washington. With just the five of them in the car, they had a lot of room, so the trip was not uncomfortable.

That didn't mean that it wasn't busy, though, because every time the train stopped for water, Cade and the others would check on the livestock to make certain that they had water and had not been injured in any way.

Because it was a special train, it made no stops except to service the train with water or coal. Thus it made good time, taking but three days to go from Yellowstone to Washington, DC.

Once they reached Washington, the cars were shuttled off to a side track, where they would remain until Boutelle made arrangements for wagons large enough and strong enough to handle the animals. The first night after their arrival in Washington, Cade and the other two military men stayed on the Pullman car, each taking his turn walking guard to see that the animals were secure.

Washington Arsenal, May 1896

Marci, along with three other young women, was bicycling through Rock Creek Park with wheel instructor Gaston Moreau.

The young ladies were all wearing short jackets and Turkish trousers, long, full garments that drooped over gaiters covering the leg and ankle. Gaston had insisted that his students wear the fashionable French costume as a safety measure, as the sport *faire la bicyclette* was rapidly gaining favor in both the United States and abroad.

"*Mademoiselles*, the bicycle is a machine that must be mastered, but, once mastered, it can be an instrument of great joy and utility," the instructor said. He was an unusually handsome Frenchman who moved with an easy grace and stood as if he were well aware of his good looks.

"Isn't he the most handsome man you've ever seen?" Julia Stevenson whispered.

"Oh my, does Reverend Hardin know you have eyes for another man?" Ella Herbert asked jokingly.

Marci laughed.

"*Mademoiselles*, attention to me, *s'il vous plaît*," Moreau said in an exasperated tone.

The four ladies stopped talking and turned their attention to him.

"When riding, the balls of your feet must be on the pedals, and as you pedal, do so with equal force from either leg. Grasp the handlebars firmly, but do not grip them tightly. Sit comfortably upon your seat, with your back straight, though you should lean forward slightly from the waist. Your shoulders must be square, your head up, your chin slightly drawn in, and your eyes fixed straight ahead. Please observe my form as I ride to the curve in the path."

Moreau mounted his bicycle and, assuming a very deliberate pose, rode to the corner and back. Returning, he dismounted. "Now, let's all ride with at least a bicycle's length between each of us, lest someone encounter a problem and cause the whole caboodle to tumble upon one another. I would not want to answer to the Reverend Hardin, or most of all to the vice president, should his daughter be forced to process down the aisle at her wedding sporting a scrape or bruise upon her beautiful person."

"We'll not let that happen, but if it does, we'll make certain Julia is the last one to fall," Letitia Scott said. "And we'll put Marci on the bottom."

"That will never happen," Julia said, addressing her cousin. "Marci will be so far ahead of us, she won't even know if one of us takes a fall or not."

The ladies mounted their wheels, Letitia and Ella with obvious difficulty, but once started, they rode alongside a swift-running stream that formed eddies and falls as it tumbled over the large, water-polished rocks that gave Rock Creek its name. Marci took the lead, and Gaston took the rear so that he would be available should there be a machine malfunction or an accident.

"Miss Winters, please stay with the group," Gaston called as Marci began to separate herself from the others.

"I'll make my own way home," Marci said, the

shouted words floating back as she took off, quickly opening space between herself and the others. Marci had enjoyed her time with her friends this morning, but she had also arranged a meeting with Stanton, a meeting that she didn't particularly want to share with the others.

Gaston Moreau watched as the beautiful young woman sped away on a bright red bicycle. Her black hair was flowing down her back, and the cloth of her trousers was moved in such a way that more of her leg was exposed than conservative society would deem acceptable.

Frustrated because she paid no attention to him, the Frenchman turned to the others. "*Mademoiselles,* here you have a perfect example of the wrong way to ride a bicycle. Do you see her form? Everything about it is incorrect. She is bent over her crossbars and she is riding much too fast. What will happen when she hits loose gravel along the path? She will likely fall and injure herself." Gaston made the sign of the cross. "But as God is my witness, I am not responsible for that one. Come, ladies. Let us continue our lesson without Miss Winters."

Marci was going fast now, and she could feel the wind blowing in her face, see the ground zipping by quickly, and hear the humming of the wheels.

The sight of a beautiful woman on a bicycle turned many heads as she whizzed by at such a rapid pace. Her destination was the National Zoological Park, and once there, she dismounted from her bike and began pushing it over the path that led to the bison park.

෨෨

Cade had come to help introduce the animals he had brought into the park, and he was checking the perimeter of the bison enclosure when he saw a young woman standing by the fence. He took a second look. It couldn't be, could it?

Yes, it was! It was Marci Winters! He knew it was her, because even though it had been more than a year since he'd last seen her in person, he had looked at her photograph over and over.

With a broad smile, he started toward her.

Marci sensed someone coming toward her, and thinking it might be Stanton, she turned to greet him. It wasn't Stanton; it was a man in a military uniform. She gasped in surprise when she recognized him. It was Cade McDowell, the man she had met at West Point!

"Mr. McDowell! Or, I suppose it's Lieutenant McDowell now, isn't it?"

"No, it's still Cade," he said with a disarming smile.

"What in the world are you doing here?"

"I was in charge of bringing some animals here, to the zoo."

"Not the buffalo, I hope. Look at them. From all I've read about them, they're supposed to be such noble beasts. These poor creatures are ghastly."

"That's because you haven't seen them in the winter. When they have their full coat, they are quite handsome."

"I suppose I'll just have to take your word for it,"

Marci said. "So, how have you been since you left West Point?" She was glad to see that he was still in uniform. That meant he was not expelled because of her. "Is the army what you envisaged?"

"Not exactly. Most of us who went to West Point expected to be on the field of battle, but right now there aren't any dragons to slay anywhere in the world. At least not for the US Army. I imagined myself with saber held high, leading a company of soldiers in a ferocious charge against the enemy, and winning untold tributes for my heroic action."

For just a second, Marci didn't know how to react to Cade's comment, then when she saw his smile broaden, she knew he was joking. "I've seen you as a hero."

"Yes, you have, haven't you? When I saved your life by keeping that rock from falling on your head," Cade teased.

Marci felt her cheeks flush. "No, I wasn't talking about Flirtation Walk. I was talking about when you saved the horses the night of the dance."

As Cade started to say something, he saw Sergeant Dawes coming toward him quickly, so he turned his attention toward him.

"I beg your pardon, Lieutenant," Dawes said, saluting as he approached. "Ma'am," he added with a nod toward Marci.

"Yes, Sergeant, what is it?"

"It's Mr. Peabody, sir. He won't sign the receipt unless you're there."

"What about Mr. Boutelle?"

"He ain't there right now."

"All right, Sergeant, I'll be right there." Cade

turned toward Marci. "Please excuse me, Miss Winters. I'm afraid duty calls."

"Of course."

Marci watched Cade and the sergeant walk away at a brisk pace. She was struck with how different Cade looked now. Well, not different in his physical appearance; he was still, she thought, a handsome man. But he looked more mature now . . . not just older, but mature. When he was a cadet, he looked as if every waking moment belonged to someone else. Now, he had a sense of self-confidence about him.

"Cade," Marci called out. "How long will you be in Washington? Will I see you again?"

"I'd like that very much. I'll be right back."

Marci stared after Cade, a warm feeling enveloping her. It was strange how this chance meeting could so reawaken the feeling she had for him for that brief weekend they spent together. Just then she felt a man wrap his arms around her waist and plant a kiss on the back of her neck. The kiss jarred her out of her reverie.

"Stanton, don't do that. I didn't see you when I arrived."

"That's because I wasn't here." Stanton kissed her on the tip of her nose. "But I did see you riding down on the road. You were riding by so fast that you and your machine were almost a blur. You know that's dangerous, and I beg you to stop this nonsense. Don't you get enough of a thrill from playing tennis?"

"You should take up the wheel," she said, placing her hands on his chest. "Perhaps if you rode, too, you would find out how liberating it is to feel the brace of the wind brushing your cheeks. Besides, I think it would be great fun for us to ride together."

Stanton pointed to the bicycle. "You'll never get me on one of those infernal machines."

Marci tried, without success, to suppress a giggle. "If you won't ride a bike, I suppose it comes without question that you're not interested in Professor Langley's flying machine?"

"Don't tell me you watched that charade? You know it's just the secretary's way of conning the Smithsonian's foundation out of more money. They say Langley's spent more than sixty thousand dollars on this fool idea already."

"Well, even if that's what it was about, it was exciting. I was right there on the riverbank when the catapult launched his machine from his boat. Father says it flew more than three-quarters of a mile, and that's ten times longer than any other heavier-than-air flying machine has ever stayed aloft."

"Next thing I know, you'll be telling me some person was idiotic enough to want to sit on the thing."

Marci smiled. "You know man will fly, and who's to say it won't be Samuel Pierpont Langley who does it first?"

"You may be right, but as for me, I'll just keep my feet planted on good old terra firma."

"You're such an old stick-in-the-mud!"

"Ooooh, that's an awful thing to say, especially when we're standing in front of a buffalo wallow. Let me push your wheel and let's get out of here."

Just then Cade walked around the shed housing the hay for the buffalo, hurrying to return to Marci. He had told Sergeant Dawes that he and Hawkins could have the rest of the day to enjoy Washington—that Cade would meet them at the depot at 7:00 a.m. What he saw was like a blow to the stomach. Quickly, he ducked behind the building. He had no intention of approaching Marci when another man was holding her in his arms.

Stanton Caldwell enjoyed Marci's company for two reasons. First, she was a delightful, forward-thinking young woman who was attractive and well educated, and as a plus for Stanton, her connections among the elites of Washington society were invaluable. She had unknowingly passed along many tidbits of gossip that Stanton had been able to pass on to his boss, Mark Hanna, who was the moneyman behind William McKinley's bid for the presidency. Even now, Stanton knew that Marci had been cycling with the daughters of the vice president and the secretary of the navy, and the niece of the vice president's wife.

They walked through the zoo, Stanton pushing the heavy bicycle along beside them, not really noticing any of the animals. He did notice Marci's glancing around as if looking for something, or someone.

"What are you looking for?"

"Nothing," Marci said, covering her disappointment that Cade had not returned.

"What did you girls talk about today?" Stanton asked as innocently as he could.

"We were discussing Julia's wedding. I'm so proud of her. Do you know what she did?"

"No, what?"

"Everybody knows it's supposed to be bad luck for a bride to wear her wedding gown before the day of her wedding, and if she tries on her veil, well, she's just tempting providence, but guess what? Yesterday Julia called on Frances Benjamin Johnston and sat for a series of portraits in all the gowns in her trousseau, and when Frances suggested she put on her wedding gown, she did it. I think that's so sensible. She and Martin are leaving right after the wedding for Kentucky, so when else would she have time for the portrait?"

"You're right. Now, just when is the wedding?"

"It's on June second, and I think she chose the date out of spite."

"Why would you say that?"

"Because it's ten years to the day that President and Mrs. Cleveland were married in the White House. Do you know that Mrs. Stevenson isn't even sure the Clevelands will attend the wedding? They don't get along at all, you know. The vice president is never invited to the White House, and the president hardly passes the time of day with him. I think it's awful the way this free-silver issue is dividing the country."

"Perhaps if Mr. McKinley is elected, everything will be better."

"But he's a Republican, and I don't want that. Father would lose his job and we'd all have to move back to the Catskills. Do you know how I would hate that?"

"My dear, maybe you won't have to leave Washington."

"What do you mean?"

"Who knows? But you should pay particular attention to how Julia's wedding is done."

"Oh, Stanton." Marci threw her arms around his neck, causing him to drop her bicycle.

"Now, Marci, don't go there yet. It will all depend on Mr. McKinley."

"I think I will become a Republican." Marci picked up her bicycle. "I may even try to convince my father to become one, too."

"You'd best be getting home, before he sends a posse after me." Stanton leaned forward and kissed Marci gently as he turned and walked away.

Marci rode back along the path by the buffalo exhibit, stopping for a while to watch the big bull that stood before her, his long beard nearly touching the ground. His matted hair was peeling off in sheets that were still clinging to his sides, giving him the appearance of an animal clad in rags. For a moment Marci empathized with the animal. Someone had put him in a position that she knew he had not chosen.

Was that what was happening to her? She thought Stanton was on the verge of asking her to marry him, and she should be happy, but why was she standing here watching a mangy beast stare at her with a forlorn look? She knew the answer. She was hoping Cade McDowell was still in the vicinity and would suddenly appear, just as he had done when she'd first arrived. But he did not.

Reluctantly, Marci got on her bicycle and slowly wound her way through the paths of the park. She had much on her mind.

Marci stored her bicycle in the shed behind the rose garden in the rear of her family's home, then hurried down the path to the back door.

"Lordy, lordy, child, where have you been? Your mama's near 'bout cried her eyes out worryin' 'bout you," Fanny Turner said as Marci slipped through the kitchen.

"Is Father home yet, Fanny?"

"I expect he is. You'd better hurry on up and get dressed for dinner 'fore he sees you in that garb. I'll slow down the dinner as much as I can, but you know he's gonna be mighty irritated if he has to wait long."

"Thanks, Fanny. I'll hurry."

Marci ran up the back staircase taking two steps at a time. Quickly she stepped out of her cycling costume. Without putting on a petticoat, she stepped into a plain skirt, topping it with a full-sleeved waist with a big bow at the back of the neck. She knew she should pin her hair up, but she didn't have time.

Running back downstairs, she stood at the door to the drawing room to listen to a smattering of conversation. As usual, it seemed Fanny had exaggerated Marci's mother's consternation.

"How was your day today, dear?" Marci's mother asked her husband.

"It was most unpleasant," DeWitt replied, settling into a leather-upholstered chair as Rosemary Winters poured him a cup of green tea. "Why do people think I can convince John to give his support to William Jennings Bryan?"

"What do you tell them?"

"I tell them I have no intention of doing that. Just because Bryan is a Democrat doesn't mean Secretary Carlisle will automatically support him. This free-silver idea of Bryan's would be the ruination of this country."

"Then, perhaps McKinley's support of the gold standard is the right way to go," Marci said as she entered the room, embracing her mother.

"Don't let Mr. Stevenson hear you even breathe that thought if you want to stay friends with his daughter. I'll bet Caldwell's been filling your head with such nonsense," Dewitt said.

"Stanton doesn't discuss his business with me—at least not very often."

"Both of you, stop this right now. A proper young lady shouldn't even know what either Mr. Bryan or Mr. McKinley think about monetary policy," Rosemary Winters said. "Come, shall we enter the dining room and enjoy our meal without talking politics?"

"Yes, dear," DeWitt said, rising from his chair. He winked conspiratorially at his daughter.

"Thank you. I've asked Fanny to prepare her chicken pilaf tonight. I think the rice will be comforting for your digestion. How were your cycling instructions today, Marci?" Rosemary asked, turning her attention to her daughter.

"Monsieur Moreau is a delightful teacher. I think all his students are hopelessly enamored in his presence."

"Surely not Julia! She's to be married within a week."

"I didn't mean it literally, Mother. We all have our special beaus."

"Humph," DeWitt snorted. "I hope that's not what you call Caldwell."

"Father, why do you dislike Stanton so? He's very smart, and everyone I know is keen on him."

"There's something about him, Marci. Something about him that bothers me. I have an instinct about these things. Trust me, Stanton Caldwell isn't the man for you."

"Father, would you forbid me from marrying him?"

Just then Rosemary sputtered on her chicken and rice. "Are you engaged and the man hasn't even spoken to your father?"

"He's not asked me in so many words, but I think it will happen before too long."

DeWitt looked directly at his daughter. "Marci, I feel that Stanton is a man who thinks of himself first. I know his kind. He values relationships only as to how he can profit from them. I think he is applying that same standard to you, believing that your obvious social connections will accrue to his benefit. If he does ask you, I will be very disappointed if you say yes."

For the rest of the meal, no words were spoken.

SEVEN

The Hotel Normandie, Washington, DC, June 1896

As there was no official residence for the vice president, the Stevenson family lived in a suite at the Hotel Normandie. The wedding reception for the Reverend and Mrs. Martin Hardin was held at the hotel, and the guests, numbering some three hundred, overflowed the ballroom and spilled out into the lobby.

"You look absolutely radiant, Julia. I am so happy for you."

"Oh, Marci, wait until this happens for you. I can't even describe what it feels like, because this is the happiest day of my life," Julia said. "And now I am so happy for Letitia. I wanted her to make the announcement that she and Lieutenant Bramwell will be married next week, but she won't do it. She says it's my day."

"Your cousin is very considerate. You know everyone would be speculating why her wedding has to be held so quickly."

"I'm not sure even I know why it was moved, but my guess would be Charles has been assigned to some duty that will take him away for a long time."

"Marci, my dear, I have a favor to ask of you," Mrs. Stevenson said as she approached the two young women. "Would you please go up to our suite and retrieve one of my headache powders from the medicine chest? I fear one of my migraines is approaching."

"Oh, Mother, you've been standing too long. Please sit here until Marci returns," Julia said as she steered her mother to the side of the room.

Marci hurried across the elegant lobby of the hotel, stopping only long enough to request a key from the concierge. She opted to take the stairs instead of the elevator, thinking she could reach the Stevenson living quarters more quickly. When she reached the third floor, she hurried down the hallway to the vice-presidential suite.

"Let me help you," a man's voice said as she inserted the key into the door.

Startled by the unexpected sound of the familiar voice, she turned abruptly. "Stanton!"

"Are you surprised to see me?" He gave her a chaste kiss on the cheek. He took the key from her hand and deftly inserted it into the door.

"Yes, I am, but what are you doing here? You weren't invited to Julia's wedding."

"No, but this is a public place, and Mr. Cake kindly allowed me to use his office to watch for everyone who was invited to the wedding."

"I don't understand why you would want to

do that. That's a little sinister, isn't it? Spying on people?"

"My dear, I don't look at it as spying, I look at it as acquiring knowledge that I may be able to use. You know that my business depends upon gathering information about prominent people."

Once inside, Marci hurried to the bedroom and then into the adjoining bath, where she retrieved the medicine for Mrs. Stevenson.

When she returned to the bedroom, Stanton caught her and pulled her into his arms.

"Not so fast. I can't let you go without a proper kiss." Stanton lowered his face toward Marci's.

"No, Stanton," Marci said as she looked around Mrs. Stevenson's bedroom. "This is not the proper place."

"Ah, my dear, what better place for a stolen kiss? I do believe this is the first time I've ever been alone with you in a bedroom." He began to run his finger against the fullness of her lips.

Sensations coursed through Marci's body, and with his coaxing, she raised her lips toward Stanton.

He took advantage of the opening Marci had given him, and he kissed her, releasing the passion that he knew was a part of her. When he raised his head to look into her face, he could see the desire that he had awakened.

"Come." He led her toward the bed just inches away.

"The medicine. I must get it to Mrs. Stevenson."

"We'll only be a moment. I know you, Marci. You

are a very passionate woman and you want this as much as I do." Stanton sat on the side of the bed, pulling Marci onto his lap.

"Just one more, and then I must get back downstairs, before someone comes to find me." Marci began to giggle.

Stanton lay back across the bed, pulling Marci down with him. He started showering her with kisses as she protested playfully.

"No, Stanton, no, I have to get downstairs."

"One more, just one more."

"Miss Winters!" a voice boomed from the doorway.

Immediately, Marci rose from the bed and looked toward the voice, seeing the vice president's mother, who was also a resident of the suite.

"I—I—I'm so sorry, Mrs. Stevenson. I didn't mean . . ."

"I would hope not. Young man, I don't know who you are, but I think you should vacate these premises as rapidly as possible before I call the authorities, and, Marcia, I expect your parents to reprimand you in a most forceful manner. You have sullied my daughter-in-law's bedchamber, and on the occasion of my granddaughter's wedding. The girl whom you describe as your best friend. How could you do this?" The woman turned and stomped out of the apartment.

Marci buried her face in her hands as the impact of what had just happened hit her.

"I'm ruined," she said softly. "I can never show my face in Washington society again."

"It's going to be all right." Stanton drew her

to him. "You still have me. We'll get through this together."

"Thank you. Those words will be something for me to hang on to. I do love you, Stanton, and just knowing that you love me, too, means a lot."

Stanton continued to hold her, but he said nothing. His mind was racing. What would happen if Mark Hanna found out what he had done, and in the vice president's suite? It was perfectly acceptable to dally with women, but to compromise a lady of society was unthinkable, especially if one's position was based upon raising money from the well connected.

"We need to get out of here before the old lady really does send someone. There's a way through Horace Cake's office that leads to the back of the hotel. Come on."

"I can't just run away. I was sent to get medicine for Mrs. Stevenson and I will deliver it."

"That's insane. Don't show your face down there."

Marci turned and headed for the door, leaving Stanton alone.

"I'll go over to the square and wait for you. Meet me on the back side of McPherson's statue," Stanton said as he headed for the elevator.

Marci nodded, then took the stairs, descending slowly, choking back tears. Maybe Eliza Stevenson would be discreet. Maybe she would remember what it was like to have been a young woman in love. Maybe she wouldn't say anything.

When Marci entered the ballroom, the worst thing

possible was taking place at that very moment. She watched as the elder Mrs. Stevenson was encircled by a bevy of women, and the woman in the center of the confab was Rosemary Winters.

"Marci, there you are," Letitia Scott said, coming toward her. "I don't think you have met Charles yet. Marci Winters, may I introduce you to my future husband, Lieutenant Charles Bramwell."

"I'm very pleased to meet you," Marci said without taking her eyes off Eliza Stevenson. "I have something for your aunt. Will you see that she gets this?" Marci handed the little packet of medicine to Letitia. "I'm feeling sick."

"Oh . . ."

Marci didn't wait for a response, but fled from the room and the hotel, crossing the street and entering McPherson Square. She hurried to the equestrian statue and stepped behind it.

"Stanton?" she questioned quietly, but there was no answer. "Stanton, where are you?"

She stood anxiously for a few minutes, but clearly, no one was in the park. How would she get home?

She would walk. She knew that the distance from her home on V Street was no more than a mile and a half, having ridden it many times on her bicycle. It made no difference that she was dressed in a heliotrope satin dress with a train that was now dragging on the ground. She reached for her neck and removed her diamond necklace and slipped it into a slit in the side of her skirt. She had been foolish enough tonight without further tempting fate.

What would happen to her? She slowed her steps, dreading what lay ahead.

When she reached her home, the iron gaslight that hung above the door, usually so welcoming, was anything but. She assumed the hour was past ten, but she wasn't sure how long it had taken her to walk from McPherson Square. Taking a deep breath, she opened the door and entered the house.

No one was around. Surely her parents weren't still at the reception?

Then she smelled the distinct aroma of pipe tobacco. Her father was here, and more than likely in the library. She walked to the wood-paneled door and, grabbing the handle, jerked it open, ready to take his tongue-lashing. She stepped into the room, and stood quietly waiting for her father to speak first.

DeWitt Winters did not raise his eyes from the newspaper he was reading. He said nothing.

Marci stood at the door for several minutes, watching the muscle in his jaw twitch as he clenched and unclenched it. There was no doubt her father knew exactly what had happened in Letitia Stevenson's bedroom, or at least Eliza Stevenson's telling of the tale.

Marci cleared her throat, but still her father did not look up from his paper.

"I'm so sorry," she said at last.

Her father put his paper down and stared toward Marci, looking hurt and angry, but still he did not speak. It was withering, and for the first time tears began to stream down her face as the impact of what had happened bore down upon her. She so wanted her father to invite her to come to him so she could explain, and then he would reassure her that everything would be all right. That he would take care of whatever she had done this time.

But his furious glare never left her face.

This was one thing that her father couldn't make right.

Lowering her head, she backed out of the library and closed the door behind her.

The knot in her throat was getting larger and larger as she climbed the stairs. Her mother must be in her room. Marci had to talk to someone, so she went to her mother's room, and as she raised her hand to knock, the door opened and Fanny stepped out into the hallway.

"Missy, you really stirred up a ruckus tonight. I say, leave the poor woman alone." Fanny closed the door behind her as she turned her back on Marci and proceeded down the hall. Marci started again to open the door to her mother's bedroom, but decided against it and turned toward her own room.

Once in her room, Marci undid her dress and slipped out of it, allowing the bloodred garment to puddle on the floor. When she was free of it, she kicked the dress, sending the satin fabric across the floor, as the diamond necklace that she had put in her pocket fell out onto the rug. She didn't bother to pick it up.

Marci spent a sleepless night. For the first time in her twenty-two years she didn't know how to get out of her predicament. And if the previous evening was any indication, her parents were not going to offer any help.

She went to her writing desk and sat down. She had to pen three notes this morning: one to Mrs. Stevenson apologizing for her lapse in judgment, one to Julia for taking away some of the glow from her wedding, and one to Stanton.

The first two were easy, but the one to Stanton . . . What could she say? He was the person most responsible for her problem. She had not asked him to come to the Stevenson suite . . . he had followed her.

And then he had told her to meet him in McPherson Square, but he had not kept his part of the bargain. A niggling thought crept into her mind as her father's words came back to haunt her.

Something about him bothers me. I have an instinct about these things. Trust me, Stanton Caldwell isn't the man for you.

"Oh, please, God, don't let Father be right," Marci said as she picked up her pen:

> *My dear Stanton,*
> *Since the unfortunate intrusion of the vice president's mother into what could best be described as an "indelicate" situation, my life has been in a state of turmoil. I have disgraced myself, I have brought shame upon my family, and I may have done irreparable damage to my friendship with Julia, a relationship that I hold very dear.*
> *You are now my island of tranquility in a tumultuous world, and I am so thankful for your love and support. I am sure there is but*

one way out of this cauldron of shame and
personal dishonor, and that would be for us
to marry. I do not propose a public wedding
of pomp and fanfare, for that would only add
fuel to the gossip that Washington society
finds so titillating. A small, quiet marriage,
perhaps in my father's home, would, I think,
quiet the wagging tongues. And as the
measure of our love need not be determined
by the magnitude of the wedding, we would
be able to begin our life together as man and
wife.

    With much love,
    Your Marci

P.S. I'll be on the bridge near Peirce Mill at
2:00.

Marci folded the three letters and put them in envelopes. Because she wanted to make certain they were in the morning post, she dressed quickly and slipped out the kitchen door, retrieving her wheel from the shed. She rode through the streets of Washington on her way to the post office, and as she did, she imagined that anyone who cast a glance her way was condemning her for her transgression.

A burst of laughter rang out through the Metropolitan Club, the most fashionable men's club in all of Washington.

"Ha! I would like to have been a fly on the wall when DeWitt Winters took his daughter to task!"

Alfred Barney said. "There's not been that much excitement at a wedding since Cleveland married his ward."

"What could possibly have been going through that girl's mind?" Arthur Gorman asked. "She had to know she'd get caught. The very idea, up there diddling while her best friend was marrying a preacher, no less."

"I hear that wasn't the half of it. She wasn't just banging the poor bastard; she was in the act of fellatio," Daniel Lockwood added.

"Just a minute, who's to say that's a bad thing? If she can do that, I'd like to see her teach my wife a thing or two," Barney added, and a round of guffaws ensued.

"Does anybody know who the lucky stiff was?" Mark Hanna asked.

"Not a hint. My wife says the new parlor game will be trying to guess which man had stepped out during all the folderol."

Stanton Caldwell sat silently. He had accompanied Mark Hanna to the Metropolitan Club with the intention of telling him that he was the man at the center of the scandal. He had contemplated offering his resignation if Hanna thought his presence on the team would hinder William McKinley's chance of capturing the nomination for president. But now, listening to these men talk, Stanton knew no one was connecting him to what had happened at the wedding. He let out a long breath, not even aware that he had been holding his breath during this whole conversation.

"No one can deny Miss Winters is some kind of

woman. Who here has not turned his head when she's whizzed by on that red bicycle?" Lockwood asked. "Just more reason to keep women off those contraptions. They should just tend to their knitting, as far as I'm concerned."

This brought another loud burst of laughter, to which Stanton added his own guffaws with as much enthusiasm as any of the others.

When Marci returned from her ride, she slipped into the kitchen, where Fanny Turner was setting bread dough to rise.

"I'd think you wouldn't have the nerve to show your face this morning," Fanny said.

"Is Mother up yet?"

"No, and like as not she'll be abed for quite a while. Your nan's heart gave out from age—your mom's is likely to fail from ache. Girl, why did you do that to her? I know you've been raised better than that."

"Not one person has asked me what happened. Why can't I tell my side of the story?"

"Honey, you're a woman, and nobody cares what your side of the story is. You're going to have to learn to live with that."

"That's not right," Marci said, but in her heart she knew Fanny was right. Marci grabbed a cold flannel cake and headed up the back stairs.

She knew she had to talk to her mother. Maybe no one else would care, but surely her own mother deserved to know what her daughter had done or, in this case, not done. Marci knocked lightly, and when there was no answer, she turned the knob and opened the door.

Marci stepped into a room that was as dark as the dead of night. She tiptoed over to the side of her mother's bed, trying not to awaken her should she be asleep. What she saw caused her to gasp. Her mother's hair was like that of a madwoman, and her eyes were swollen to the point where Marci didn't know if she was sleeping or not.

"Oh, Mama, I did this to you, and I am so sorry," Marci whispered. She took her mother's hand in hers, and for an instant she thought she felt a movement, perhaps a squeeze, but nothing else. Marci stood there for several minutes, hoping for some recognition of her presence, but it didn't come. She left the room with a heavy heart.

For the rest of the morning, Marci stayed secluded in her room. She wondered what Mrs. Stevenson had reported when she left her daughter-in-law's bedroom. More than likely, Marci would never know what gossip was being told about her.

Marci paced back and forth on the wooden bridge that spanned Rock Creek. She kept checking her watch, flipping the gold lid off the porcelain face. It was now half past two and no Stanton. As she ran out of excuses for what could possibly be delaying him, she finally accepted that he was not coming. Closing the lid with a snap, she turned the watch over. There in an elegant scroll read the name *Lulu Matilda LeDuc*. Her own nan.

When Marci was a child, she used to love to

say her grandmother's maiden name, sometimes singing it over and over, much as other children repeated nursery rhymes. She fingered the scroll-work and then put the watch in her pocket. Pushing her bicycle, too dejected to even attempt to ride, she moved down the path toward the gristmill.

"Pssst, Marci. I'm over here."

Marci turned toward the sound, and down by the turning waterwheel, she saw Stanton standing in the shadows. "Oh, Stanton, you came!" Marci exclaimed, dropping her bicycle on the path and hurtling over the rocks toward him. She threw herself into his body, almost dislodging him into the creek. "Didn't you see me on the bridge? I've been waiting for over an hour."

"I saw you, but I thought it would be better if we met over here. I knew you would come this way sooner or later."

Marci cocked her head, wondering why it would be better not to meet on the bridge, but she didn't ask. She was so relieved to see him. "Did you get my note?"

"Of course. How would I have known to meet you here? Now, what happened when you got home last night?"

"It's just terrible. Neither my mother nor my father has so much as spoken a word to me. Mother has not risen from her bed, and it's our fault. Will you come to our house tonight and confront Father with me?"

Stanton removed himself from Marci's embrace, putting some distance between them. "I'd love to, but I can't. I'll be leaving for St. Louis very soon.

The convention starts the sixteenth, and I'll need to make certain everything is in place for Mr. McKinley's nomination."

"Did you read my note?"

"Yes, and I think it's a wonderful idea, but not right now. I don't think our getting married would solve anything, and if by chance Mr. McKinley wins the presidency, then I am sure to have a very high level position in any McKinley administration. As my wife, it wouldn't make any difference what anyone said about you. They would have to accept you in Washington society."

"But, Stanton, that's the future. What am I going to do now? This afternoon, when I get home to a family that won't speak to me, or when I want to go to tea with my friends and no one will have anything to do with me? If you will recall, I was merely going up to the suite to get Mrs. Stevenson some powder for her headache. It wasn't I who initiated anything untoward."

Stanton lowered his head. "I know. It is I who was the improper one, but you have to understand my position. Should we marry right now, I would be without employment, perhaps to be blackballed from ever working for any campaign again. You do understand."

"I'm a woman and nobody cares," Marci said, remembering the words Fanny had said to her this morning.

"That's not true, and to prove that, I have something for you." Stanton reached into his pocket and withdrew a small velvet, drawstring bag. "Here, take this."

Marci took the bag and slipped the cord. She withdrew what she thought was a plain gold ring, but turning it over, she saw some sort of a design on one side.

"Oh, Stanton, yes! But I thought you said you didn't want to get married."

"This isn't a wedding ring. It's a *fede* ring, and these two interlocking right hands mean we've made a bargain to wed. *Fede* is an Italian word meaning 'trust,' and that's what I'm asking you to do. Trust me. Will you wear it until the time is right for us to marry?"

"Yes, I will wear it."

Were things moving too fast here? She wanted to marry Stanton, she needed to marry him because getting married right now would solve her problems. Was that reason enough to marry someone? Shouldn't the woman be in love with the man? She was in love with him, wasn't she? She had been trying to convince herself of that for more than a year now, but she wasn't sure. It didn't matter. She would cope with whatever she had to do.

Marci threw her arms around him, in an attempt to bolster her decision, and Stanton held her to him, all the while nervously watching to see that they were not being observed.

EIGHT

Marci was in her room when the she heard the tinkle of the dinner bell. Although she had not seen her father, she assumed he had returned from the Treasury Department, and the summons to the dining room was encouraging.

This evening, she had taken great pains with her appearance. She was dressed in a most conservative aquamarine house gown with a high neck and tight-fitting sleeves. The foot of the skirt, the wrists, and the yoke were trimmed with black ruching that complimented her black hair. She had pulled her hair straight back, caught in a smooth bun, with no errant ringlets escaping. Her intention was to portray the most reserved picture of womanhood possible.

When she entered the dining room, her father was standing by the window, his back turned to her. He was looking intently at the dark moreen curtains.

"See to it that Fanny directs the changing of the

wool to the cotton draperies," DeWitt Winters said, turning from the window and approaching Marci.

"Yes, sir."

Marci waited until her father pulled out her chair to seat her in her regular place at the table. He then seated himself at the head of the table.

"Will Mrs. Winters be taking supper?" Fanny asked as she entered the room, this time dressed in a crisp-starched gray uniform with a white apron.

"No, perhaps a cup of broth would sustain her. You can take it to her after you have served my daughter and me."

"She does need nourishment," Fanny said as she went through the swinging door to the kitchen.

The two sat in silence, DeWitt examining his nails, while Marci fixed her gaze upon the corner cabinet, as if a knickknack that had sat in the exact same spot for the last ten years might suddenly have found itself in a different spot.

Fanny returned with an oyster pie and fresh asparagus. She served the steaming morsels, ladling extra cream on the succulent crust as she placed the vegetables beside it.

"Thank you, Fanny," Marci said with a heartfelt smile. Fanny knew that oyster pie was one of Marci's favorite foods, and by preparing it tonight the faithful housemaid and cook seemed to be trying to make Marci feel less uncomfortable, if that was possible.

The meal was passed in silence except for the clink of silverware hitting the china. When dessert was offered, Marci declined.

"Sir, may I be excused?" She looked toward her father for the first time during the entire meal.

"Yes." DeWitt pulled his watch from the pocket of his vest. "I expect to see you in the library in fifteen minutes."

"Yes, sir."

Marci went to her room and attended to her toilet, cleansing her teeth, smoothing her hair, and applying just a hint of rose powder to her cheeks to take away her chalky coloring.

She paced the room, thinking no fifteen minutes had ever drawn out more in her entire life. With two minutes to spare, she descended the stairs and stood at the door of the library waiting for the clock to announce the hour. With its first chime, she opened the door.

When she entered, her father rose from his big, brown leather chair, which was positioned next to the fireplace. He motioned with his hand for her to sit on the settee some four feet away from him.

Marci took her seat, lowering her head and clasping her hands in front of her. She waited for the first word to be said, but when none came, she raised her face to see her father standing at his desk. He filled his pipe with tobacco and busied himself for a long moment, tamping it down, then striking a match and holding it to the bowl. He drew several puffs until the tobacco gleamed, and his head was wreathed in an aromatic, blue smoke.

Deliberately he moved toward the big leather chair, still puffing on the pipe, holding it by its bowl, and staring at Marci through the smoke. She took some solace in that he was staring, and not glaring, at her.

Finally, he pulled the pipe from his mouth. "In all the years your mother and I have been married, I have never seen her this distraught."

The words were quietly spoken, but they hit Marci with the impact of a blow from a club. Tears began to well in her eyes, trailing down her cheeks, but she wasn't weeping aloud.

"I'm so sorry."

"I've never seen such a lapse in judgment—from either man or woman—in my entire life. A common whore doesn't do what you were caught engaging in, let alone a respectable young woman in Washington society. And worst of all, you were in the bedroom of the wife of the vice president of the United States. And on the day of your supposed best friend's wedding. I have only one question: How could you do such a thing?"

"Father, I don't know what Mrs. Stevenson said, but nothing happened! Absolutely nothing happened!"

"Were you in the home of the vice president, in a bedroom with a man?"

"Yes, and Mrs. Stevenson walked in at the exact moment when I was kissing Stanton." Marci ran her thumb nervously over Stanton's ring, which she had placed on her left hand.

"Stanton Caldwell. I should have suspected as much. Did you arrange this little tryst, or did he?"

"It wasn't like that at all. Julia's mother asked me to retrieve some of her headache powder from her suite, and when I was at the door letting myself in, Stanton came up behind me."

"And you permitted him to follow you into someone else's home? And then you allowed him to dictate to you whatever act he wanted you to perform? For the first time in my life I can empathize with Richard Olney."

"Are you going to banish me?" Marci asked in a voice so quiet she could barely hear the words herself.

"As much as I am tempted to follow in the secretary's footsteps, you are my daughter, and this, too, will pass. But I am forbidding you from being in the company of that man ever again. Do you understand me?"

"Father, there is something I should tell you. Stanton and I have plans to marry."

She could not honestly say Stanton had asked her to marry him in so many words, but wasn't the ring on her finger a visible symbol of a pledge to do just that?

DeWitt put his pipe down, and drumming his fingers on the arm of the chair, he twitched his mouth and narrowed his eyes as if he were weighing her comment. At last he said, "And when do you expect this marriage to take place?"

"That's the problem."

DeWitt's eyebrows shot up questioningly. "Problem?"

"Stanton doesn't want to get married . . . at least, not right away. You see, he is working with Mark Hanna trying to get the nomination of William McKinley for president. And if his candidate is elected, Stanton is sure to get a high position in the government. But if we were to marry right now with all this—this gossip going around, he might lose his influence and wind up without a job of any kind."

"What an—honorable—man you've chosen," DeWitt said, setting the word apart sarcastically. "And just what do you plan to do until Mr. Caldwell deems it acceptable for his career to marry you?"

"I propose to just go on with my life, as if nothing has happened."

"No."

"What do you mean, no?"

"I mean you will not go on as before. This scandal can do nothing but intensify, and I don't think your mother could survive it."

"But I told you, nothing more than a kiss happened."

"And I told you once that perception can be as damning as the truth."

"Then, what am I going to do?"

"You're leaving Washington," DeWitt said.

"I don't want to leave. Stanton is here, and I can't leave him."

"You'll not be welcome in this house under these conditions."

"Then, I'll find another place to live."

"And what will you use for money? Because if you stay in Washington, you can't count on any help from me."

"I'll draw on the money from Nan's trust."

"I don't think so. I'm the executor of that trust

until you are twenty-five, and I'll not release one dime unless you leave Washington and this man."

Marci took a deep breath as she tried to think of some acceptable plan of action. "I could go back to Paris."

DeWitt shook his head. "I don't think so."

"All right. What is it you want me to do?" Marci asked, shouting the words in frustration.

"You're going to have a job, a job that will provide an income for you, should you be forced to stay a maiden lady for the rest of your life, thanks to your wonderful Mr. Caldwell."

"And I suppose you've made arrangements for this job?"

"I have. You've met Mr. Johnston, my clerk at the Treasury Department."

"I know him."

"And you've met his daughter. In fact you were in her company when you accompanied Julia for her wedding portraits. Frances Benjamin Johnston is Andy Johnston's daughter. She's planning a photographic trip through the West, and she's in need of an assistant photographer. I've volunteered you for the position."

"Father, that's insane! I don't know anything about photography."

"I don't believe there's any need for further discussion," DeWitt said, and rose from his chair.

NINE

1332 V Street NW, Washington, DC, June 1896

Marci wasn't sure how Frances Benjamin Johnston would receive her. By now the word of her "assignation" with a strange man in the bedroom of the vice president of the United States was all over the city, or, at least, all over the social set of the city. Marci knew that Frances traveled in that network and had a portfolio of photographs of the most prominent women in Washington society, including the wife of the vice president. That meant Frances Johnston had certainly heard the stories about Marci, so, with no little anxiety, Marci strolled up the walk through the rose garden that led to Miss Johnston's studio behind her parents' home.

Marci's father had told her that it had already been set up for her to work with Frances, but the question in Marci's mind was, how would Frances treat her? Would she regard Marci as soiled property in need of rehabilitation? Taking a deep breath, and squaring her shoulders, she knocked on the door.

"Oh, good," Frances said with a broad smile as soon as she opened the door. "You're right on time!"

Marci saw a woman that she took to be in her early thirties, rather small, but Marci thought, quite attractive.

Stepping back from the door to invite Marci in, Frances had a quickness about her, portraying a woman of great energy. "I have to tell you, Marci, you've made a very good opening impression on me. I value punctuality and dependability above almost every other virtue. Come in, come in, I've made tea."

Just inside the studio was a neat sitting room with comfortable-looking chairs and a sofa, and Marci started in that direction, but Frances called out, "No, no, I do my work downstairs." Again she displayed an almost restless liveliness as she led Marci down the steps.

In direct contrast to the neat sitting room upstairs, this room looked messy, but as Marci examined it, she realized that she had, too quickly, reached that conclusion. It wasn't messy, it was cluttered, and the clutter had some structure. The walls were plastered with magazine covers: *Scribner's, Harper's, Lippincott's,* the *New York Ledger,* among others, and when Marci examined them closely, she realized that they were all covers that featured Frances's work, using the halftone method of reproducing her pictures.

"Do you take sugar with your tea?" Frances asked.

"No."

"Neither do I. We seem to be hitting it off quite well, don't you think?" Frances poured two cups

from a kettle that set on a small gas burner. "Now"—
Frances sat in a chair in front of a cubbyhole desk
in the corner—"before we start talking about what
your duties will be, let's get rid of this thing that's
hanging here in the room between us."

"I beg your pardon?"

Frances chuckled. "I was trying to be subtle, but
you're right. Let's get it in the open. I know that
there has been talk about you, and you are concerned about what I might think."

"Miss Johnston—"

"It's Frances. Actually, my friends and family
call me Fan. And I know exactly what Mrs. Stevenson saw because she told me. And I know that she
didn't see what some of the gossip alleges. So, to
keep you from worrying about things, let me tell
you that I think nothing at all about it. And unless
you specifically want to talk about it, though God
knows why you would want to, it will never come
up between us.

"I think our working relationship will depend
upon mutual trust, understanding, respect, and,
most of all, friendship. What do you say, Marci?
Shall we be friends?"

These were the first noncondemning words Marci
had heard spoken to her in the five days since the
incident in Mrs. Stevenson's bedroom. Her face,
which had been somewhat taut with concern, now
spread into a huge, welcome smile of relief.

"Oh, yes, Miss—"

"Huh, uh-uh." Frances waved her finger back and
forth. "Not *miss*."

"Yes, Frances—Fan. Yes, we will be great friends!"

"Good, good. Now, I'm told that you studied art at the Académie Julian."

"Yes, I did."

"Wonderful. So did I. That means you already have an eye for composition, light, and shadow. The talent you need to be an artist will serve you well as a photographer. Let's get started on our first lesson, shall we? Suppose you were to take a picture right here, right now. How would you set it up?"

"I would prefer to take the picture upstairs in the sitting room."

Frances chuckled. "Is this room too cluttered for you?"

"No, it isn't that. I want to compose the picture, and I think there will be more opportunity there."

"All right." Frances picked up the camera, then led Marci upstairs. When they went into the sitting room, Frances gave the camera to Marci.

"This is a Kodak camera. All you have to do is look through here to compose your picture, then push the button. All right, Marci, make a picture."

Marci smiled. "You said *make,* rather than *take.* So I shall take you at your word. I intend to *make* a picture."

"Good, good, what do you have in mind?"

Marci walked over to the fireplace and studied the mantel. She saw a clock, several photographs in frames, a bronze plate on its edge leaning against the wall, a beer stein, and a wooden box. When she looked in the box, she saw several ready-rolled cigarettes. She picked one up, then looked back at Frances.

"I don't smoke," Frances said, "but when I have

gentlemen here who may become photographic subjects, I like to have them available."

"Fan, just to take a picture of this room would be bland and uninteresting, even though you do have it beautifully decorated. I need to make the room come alive, and for that I need to take a picture of you."

"All right, where do you want me to stand?"

Marci shook her head. "Huh, uh. You aren't going to stand anywhere. You're going to sit right here on this ottoman."

Frances sat down and Marci looked at her for a moment. "Turn to your right, so that I see you in profile."

Frances responded.

Marci continued to look, then smiled, walked over to the mantel, withdrew a cigarette from the box, and took down the beer stein. She gave them both to Frances.

"Now, this is what I want you to do. I want you to cross your legs, but not normally. Cross your legs as a man does, so that the ankle of your right foot is resting on your left knee. Then, hold this cigarette in your right hand and lean forward so that your elbow is resting on your knee. Hold the cigarette between your fingers like this." Marci positioned the cigarette. Then she pulled Frances's skirt up, revealing her petticoats. "Grasp the beer stein in your left hand and hold it just here, on your thigh, with the arm crooked, and your elbow pointed slightly back, just enough to interrupt the flow of your back. And, finally, jut your face forward, as if you are in conversation . . . no, not merely a conversation, as if you have just given someone a piece of your mind, and you are daring them to disagree with you."

Frances laughed, and perhaps because she was an artist herself, she was a good subject and was able to assume just the pose Marci wanted. Marci took two or three pictures, winding the film forward after each snap.

"There," she said when finished.

"Good, good, let's go develop the film now. I'm anxious to see how you did."

Half an hour later, Frances and Marci emerged from the darkroom with three eight-by-ten prints.

"Oh! Oh my!" Frances gasped as she looked at the photo. "Oh, even though I am the subject of this picture, I have to say that it is an absolutely beautiful study! Notice the compositional grids, the visual balance, the alignment of the vase on the mantel with the back of my head and the back of the stein! What a wonderful eye you have, Marci! Yes, yes, you'll be a great assistant, though I suspect you'll be doing a lot less assisting than you'll be photographing."

Marci beamed under the praise. After the last several days, she desperately needed something to lift her spirits, and Frances had done just that.

"Have you ever been West, Marci?"

"No farther west than Pittsburgh."

Frances smiled. "Then, what an exciting summer you have ahead of you. We are going to visit Wonderland."

"Wonderland?"

"Yellowstone National Park," Frances said enthusiastically. "Here, I have some photographs of the place taken by Mr. Haynes and Mr. Jackson."

For the next several minutes, the two women looked at the photographs. Then they came to one that caught Marci's attention right away, showing a large, perfectly round, unusual-looking object. "What is this?"

"This is the crater of Castle Geyser," Frances explained. "This smooth area here is crystallization, and in the middle, a hot spring. It is said that the water in the spring is a beautiful turquoise blue."

"Oh, what a sight that must be. I would love to see the colors."

"You will, Marci, you will. For now, I suggest that you visit the Capitol Building." Frances put away the photographs. "Look at Thomas Moran's paintings. Some of them are of these very scenes. Through the paintings, you'll be able to see the many marvelous colors of the oddities of the park."

"Oh, it sounds most exciting." Marci realized that, though she had been forced into this position by her father's insistence that she leave Washington, she was actually looking forward to the adventure. "When do we leave?"

"We leave in a few days. We'll be going through St. Louis, then on up to Minnesota and across to St. Paul, where we'll catch the Northern Pacific and go by train as far as we can."

"St. Louis? When will we be in St. Louis?"

"June fifteenth and sixteenth. I have a photographer friend who lives there, and since we'll be traveling across the country anyway, I've told Mattie Hewitt I'll stop by to see her."

Marci smiled. "I look forward to visiting St. Louis." Marci knew that the Republican National Convention was being held from the sixteenth to the eighteenth in St. Louis. That meant that Mark Hanna would be there, and so would Stanton Caldwell. Stanton had told her that, under the circumstances, it wouldn't be good for them to be seen together in Washington, at least not until after the election. But, surely, they could be seen together in St. Louis.

"I'm told you're a good bicycle rider," Frances said.

"Yes, I enjoy it very much," Marci replied, not sure why Frances had broached the subject.

"You wear trousers when you ride bicycles, do you not?"

"Well, yes, in a manner of speaking. But they aren't trousers such as men wear. They're actually called Turkish trousers. They're what everyone was wearing in Paris when they were on the wheel."

"But do they give you mobility?"

"Yes. They're long, full garments that droop over gaiters and cover the leg and ankle."

"Good, good. Bring several such outfits, as well as dresses, and you might want to invest in some men's trousers. I find they are most convenient sometimes, when a woman is crawling over rocks and such. Oh, and even though it's summer now, where we're going can get quite cold. I'm not exactly sure how long we'll be staying. Does it make any difference how long you're away from Washington?"

"No, ma'am. My plans are very . . . fluid right now."

"You've forgotten already. If you call me ma'am

all the time, I'll think I'm your mother. We'll be leaving Sunday afternoon at two o'clock. Meet me at the B and P Depot by one thirty."

"All right, I'll be there."

From Frances's studio, Marci went by trolley to the Capitol Building and, there, studied Thomas Moran's painting *Grand Canyon of the Yellowstone*. A printed sign hanging beside the painting said that it had been purchased from the painter in 1872, for the grand sum of $10,000. The painting was huge, seven feet by twelve feet, so large that it almost gave Marci a sense of actually being there.

At the center was a waterfall that was naturally and perfectly framed between rocky cliffs. The artist had created a perspective of light and shadow, and of color, tone, and tint, so that it offered a remarkable sense of depth and altitude. Standing there looking at the painting, Marci could almost experience an illusion of wind and the scent of pine.

She felt a tiny thrill just looking at the painting and, at that moment, realized she was very much looking forward to the adventure.

On the day she was to leave, Marci was busy packing when there was a light knock on the door to her room.

"Marci?"

It was her mother's voice, and Marci quickly opened the door. When she did, Rosemary Winters took her daughter in her arms and the two women embraced, holding each other for a long moment.

"Marci, I—"

"Mother, I'm so sorry."

"No, child, it is I who should be sorry for the way I have deserted you these last few days. I had no right to turn my back on you. You are my daughter, and no matter what happens, I will never lose sight of that. I love you so. "

"You have every right to be upset with me. Even though I swear to you nothing happened, I allowed myself to be compromised. I should have been more careful, more aware of the hurt my carelessness could cause others."

"I don't want you to leave thinking that I am upset with you. In fact, if you really don't want to leave, I'll talk to your father. I believe I can get him to withdraw his demand."

"No, Mother, I think it would be best if I did go. As long as I stay here, the scandal will never go away. Once I'm gone, once I am no longer here to feed the frenzy, there will be no need to continue the gossip. Besides, I had a most interesting visit with Fan, and—"

"With who?"

"Frances Johnston. She prefers to be called Fan. Mother, I think photography will be a wonderful outlet for me, and Fan thinks I have a talent for it. And I must say that I'm anxious to see the West and the Yellowstone National Park."

"I'm going to miss you." Rosemary smoothed an errant strand of hair from Marci's face.

"And I'm going to miss you, too. And I'll miss Father as well, though I feel that won't be reciprocated."

"Your father loves you, Marci. Right now he's

hurt and confused. I think he has heard some talk that he won't share. He knows it isn't true, but he's having a hard time. The truth is, darling, he's hurting for you."

"I've gotten our family into quite a mess, haven't I?"

"It will pass," Rosemary said. "Do you need any help getting ready?"

"No, I'm ready to go."

Rosemary and her daughter hugged again, then when they went downstairs. Marci looked into her father's study. He was standing, facing the fireplace, his hand on the mantel.

"DeWitt, Marci is leaving now," Rosemary said.

DeWitt hesitated for a second, then he came to the door and embraced his daughter. "Whatever happens, know that your mother and I love you, and we will always love you." He gave Marci an envelope.

"What's this?"

"It's five hundred dollars."

"Father, that isn't necessary, I have a job."

"It's good to have a job. It's even better to have a little money."

"Thank you, Daddy. I know I've disappointed you and Mother, and I'm so very sorry for that. I'll never again stretch the limits of your love as I've done."

"This time," DeWitt said with a deep rumble. "I don't know what parents do when they have a dozen children."

"You must write, child," Rosemary said, barely able to hold back tears.

"I will, I promise, and thank you for being my parents. I love you." Marci hugged both of them in a long embrace, then walked out to the waiting hackney.

Fort Yellowstone, June 13, 1896

It was a pretty day, a Saturday afternoon, and except for the soldiers on patrol duty within the park, the troop was enjoying some time off. A baseball game was under way between the soldiers and the civilians who worked at the park.

The soldiers were behind by one run when Cade came up to the plate in the bottom of the last inning. One runner was on base. Cade swung at the first pitch, connected solidly, and lofted it high over the center fielder's head. Cade easily rounded all the bases before the ball was retrieved, securing victory for the Fort Yellowstone nine.

Amid cheers and congratulations from the other soldiers, Cade started back across the parade ground toward his quarters. When he got up onto the porch, Nance congratulated him on the home run.

"Thanks," Cade said.

"Look at that!" Nance pointed. Turning in the direction Nance was pointing, Cade saw two men riding bicycles. "Damn, they're fast. I'll bet they're going faster than a galloping horse."

"Probably not," Cade said. "In a short sprint, a horse is faster. But a good bicycle rider would beat a horse in a ten-mile race."

"Yeah, and you don't have to feed them or stable them. Say, didn't you tell me your friend Lieutenant Moss has permission to take a corps of

Buffalo Soldiers on a bicycle trip from Montana to Missouri?"

"Yes, he has permission from General Miles to make the run next spring. The Spalding brothers supplied his men with wheels, and he's setting up some trials right now. If it works, who knows? We may all be riding bicycles."

Nance chuckled. "Better not let Sergeant McKay hear that. If he didn't have his horses to take care of, he'd leave the army."

"The cavalry better not get rid of horses—at least not my horse."

"Nobody's going to take Rowdy away from you, I can bet on that," Nance said as he stepped off the porch and headed for the commissary storehouse.

Cade continued inside, then went upstairs to take a shower and change clothes in time for supper.

As he was dressing, he mulled over his conversation with Nance. Maybe there was a place for bicycles in the army, especially at Fort Yellowstone.

Sitting down at his desk, he took paper and pen from the drawer, dipped the pen into the inkwell, and began to write.

> *Lieutenant James Moss*
> *25th Infantry Regiment*
> *Fort Missoula, Montana*

> *Dear Daig:*
> *I have been thinking about your idea of equipping soldiers with bicycles. I think it is such a good idea that I would like to make*

a suggestion to Captain Anderson that we equip some of our soldiers at Yellowstone with bicycles. As I have told you, our duty here at the park is not like it is at other army posts. Most of our duty consists of riding through the park, playing nursemaid to the tourists who, generally due to their own fault, find themselves in some kind of difficulty or even real danger.

We have to keep these same tourists from desecrating the park when they try to leave their names or initials carved in the mineral formations, or when they chip off souvenirs. But we are also charged with preventing poaching, and I think that we could approach poachers on bicycles, at least in the summer months, more silently than we can on horseback, and thus be more effective.

It is with that in mind that I want to make a proposal to you. You said that you will be making some shakedown rides before undertaking the 2,000-mile ride to St. Louis. Might I suggest that one of your preliminary bicycle trips be made from Fort Missoula to Fort Yellowstone? That would certainly be a long enough trip to both prove the value of the wheel, and to train the men for such a journey.

Sincerely,
Cade

He folded the letter, then put it in an envelope. Before he mailed it, he would have to get Captain

Anderson's approval for the use of bicycles within the park, as well as make provisions for the housing of Lieutenant Moss and his troop of black soldiers, but if the captain approved, it would be great to see Daig in person.

St. Louis, June 15, 1896

Frances Johnston and her friend Mattie Hewitt were discussing some mutual business venture, and though Marci was invited to stay and listen, she demurred, saying that she would just be in the way. She told Frances that she would take a tour of the city since she had never seen St. Louis before. In truth, she intended to go to the convention so she could find Stanton.

Marci smiled as she envisioned the look on Stanton's face when he saw her. How surprised he would be! How excited! She could barely suppress her own excitement as she hailed a hack to take her to the site of the convention.

"The St. Louis Exposition and Music Hall, please," Marci said.

"Are you sure that's where you want to go?" the hack driver asked.

"That is where the nominating convention is being held, isn't it?"

"No, ma'am. Last month we had a tornado that tore through here. Didn't you read that 280 people were killed?"

"I did read that, but I didn't think that would affect the Republican Convention."

"The building was badly damaged, so the powers

that be wanted to move the convention out of St. Louis, but our folks got together and put up a temporary building on the grounds of the City Hall. Do you want to go there?"

"Yes. Please take me wherever the delegates are meeting."

The driver cracked his whip and the hack rolled through the streets of St. Louis. When they reached the grounds of the City Hall, he pointed to the building that would house the convention. The grounds were crowded with people, many of them wearing ribbons with the name of their candidate inscribed. She saw a lot more McKinley ribbons than any other, and she was pleased about that because she knew that Stanton was working hard to get McKinley nominated. Marci wasn't sure how she would be able to locate Stanton, but she thought it might be best just to wander around in the building.

When she passed through the front door, though, she was stopped by a man in a police uniform. "Miss, nobody is allowed in except for delegates or specific guests of a delegate."

"Oh, I don't want to stay. I'm just looking for someone."

"Is he a delegate?"

"No, I . . . I don't think he is. But he would be with Mr. Mark Hanna."

"What's his name? I can't let you in, but I can send a messenger to fetch him for you."

"Oh, would you? Thank you, that would be wonderful. His name is Caldwell. Stanton Caldwell."

The police officer held up his hand and summoned a boy of about sixteen. "Go to the headquar-

ters for the McKinley delegation, locate Mr. Mark
Hanna, and ask for . . ." The policeman glanced
back at Marci.

"Stanton Caldwell," she said.

"Have you got that?" the policeman asked.

"Yes, sir, Mr. Stanton," the boy repeated.

"No, no," Marci said. "Mr. Stanton Caldwell. Wait
a minute and I'll write a note."

Marci dashed off a note telling Stanton she had
a few hours in St. Louis on her way to Yellowstone
National Park, and she was excited to see him.
When she was finished, she folded the paper and
handed it to the young messenger, who took off at
a run.

"You can sit in one of those chairs if you wish."
The policeman pointed to a row of chairs over to
one side.

"Thank you, you have been most kind."

A few minutes later several men came in wearing
straw hats with hatbands with McKinley's name on
them. "Whoop, whoop, whoop! McKinley, McKinley,
McKinley is our man! McKinley against the bosses!"
they shouted. "Gold as the standard!"

Marci smiled at their enthusiasm.

"Maine, for Speaker Reed!" another group shouted.

Marci watched all the activity while she waited.
Was the boy having a hard time finding Stanton?
Had he not come to St. Louis?

But her worry was for naught when she saw the
young messenger come running back from the audi-
torium. She watched as the boy said something to
the policeman. The policeman pointed to her, and the
boy came over. But why wasn't Stanton with him?

"Couldn't you find him?" Marci asked.

"Yes, ma'am, I found him."

"Are you supposed to take me to him?"

"I don't know, ma'am, but he asked me to give you this note." The boy held out a folded piece of paper.

"Thank you." Marci opened the note.

> *Marci,*
>
> *You have no business being in St. Louis. Your presence here, at this time, can only cause difficulty for me. Trust me. Please, make no more attempts to contact me. I will contact you when I think the time is right. Go on your way and wait.*
> *Stanton*

With tears of rejection and humiliation stinging her eyes, Marci got up and walked quickly from the building.

TEN

En route to Yellowstone, June 21, 1896

Marci had fought tears from St. Louis to Minneapolis. She was overwhelmed with hurt, betrayal, and disillusionment, though those feelings of rejection competed with anger. By the time she and Frances transferred to the Northern Pacific, heading for their ultimate destination, anger had become the dominant emotion.

The more Marci thought about it, the angrier she became. She began to enumerate all the times Stanton had disappointed . . . no . . . *disappointed* wasn't a strong enough word. He had *betrayed* her.

Last summer, she had practically begged him to marry her after she had been dismissed from Wells, but he ignored her. Stanton had initiated the debacle in the vice president's suite, but he didn't even meet her at McPherson Square as he'd promised, forcing her to walk home alone. He had vowed to be her bulwark, but from the moment of her "indiscretion" he had avoided her, insisting that their meetings be held in secret.

But the final straw was what had happened in St. Louis. Between St. Louis and Minneapolis, every time she read the note he had sent her, she was overcome with depression. But after she left Minneapolis to embark on the long train ride into what was for her uncharted territory, the note no longer fed into her misery; it fed her anger. *Please, make no more attempts to contact me,* the note had said.

"All right, Mr. Caldwell," she said quietly. "You shall have your wish. I will make no more attempts to contact you . . . ever."

Marci tore the note into little pieces, then lifted the window and, holding her hand into the airstream, let the pieces blow away.

"Good!" Fan said.

"What?"

"I'm not sure what that note said, but I know it was upsetting you. You've made the right decision by getting rid of it."

Marci smiled, pleased with herself that she could smile again. She felt her spirits renew. "I know I've made the right decision as well."

Shortly after that exchange, Frances leaned back in her seat and went to sleep. For the next several minutes, as Frances napped, Marci played with the ring on her finger, rotating it with the thumb of her left hand. She held up her hand to examine it.

Stanton's words came back to her.

Fede *is an Italian word meaning "trust," and that's what I'm asking you to do. Trust me. Will you wear it?*

Trust me, he had said, and now those words

seemed like a mockery. *Will you wear it?* he had asked.

"No, I won't wear it," Marci said quietly, so as not to awaken Frances.

Marci took the ring from her finger and dropped it beside her seat. Let the porter find it when he cleaned the car. Like destroying the note earlier, removing the ring from her finger gave her an uplifting sense of freedom.

She spent the rest of the trip enjoying the scenery. Through North Dakota and eastern Montana, she couldn't help but contrast what she saw with what she had known for her entire life. She had traveled rather extensively by train through New York, New Jersey, Pennsylvania, Delaware, Maryland, and Virginia. In those states many towns were along the railroad, all close together. And between the towns were many farms, so that one was always within sight of civilization.

And even after coming on this trip, there were towns and farms between Washington and St. Louis, and then between St. Louis and Minneapolis. But since leaving Minneapolis, the towns became fewer, and what ones she saw were much farther apart with only an occasional sign of life. Now and then she would see fields of grain waving in the breeze, or some cattle standing listlessly in the noonday heat, and even more rarely a few houses, weathered, small, and so terribly remote that Marci wondered how anyone could possibly live here.

❦

Fort Yellowstone

"You wanted to see me, sir?" Cade asked, reporting to Captain Anderson in response to a summons. Cade had been conducting the monthly quartermaster inventory.

"Yes. I want you to take a detail and go to Cinnabar tomorrow to meet a train."

"All right, sir," Cade said, not questioning the order.

Captain Anderson sighed, picked up a piece of paper, looked at it for a moment, then put it back down. "You'll be meeting F. Jay's private car and a couple of photographers. I don't understand why Mr. Haynes shouldn't be the one to shepherd these folks around, but I'm following this missive from on high. Listen to this direct order. It comes through the Secretary of the Interior, Hoke Smith, by way of Secretary Lamont. These photographers are to be given, and I quote"—the captain picked up the paper again and read from it—"'unrestricted access, within the bounds of safety, as to areas they wish to photograph anywhere in the park.'"

"I thought Mr. Haynes was the official park photographer."

"He is, but these two must have some kind of connections in Washington." Captain Anderson continued with Cade's instructions, "The train will arrive at eleven forty-three tomorrow morning. The Yellowstone Park Transportation line is providing them with a dedicated coach from Cinnabar, and you're to provide the coach with a military escort until it reaches its destination."

"We'll meet them at eleven forty-three? That's very nearly noon, Captain. Do I provide lunch for the photographers and my detail?"

"Lieutenant, you attended West Point, and as you know, I was for a while an instructor there. So I'm going to answer that question as if you had asked it in my classroom. I have no idea as to how you are to handle lunch. Therefore I suggest you keep yourself flexible enough to respond to the—"

"—situation and terrain," Cade said, interrupting with a smile, stating one of the most oft-used clichés of military tactics.

"Good for you, Lieutenant, you just earned yourself a number one merit in my class on strategy and tactics."

"I will be prepared for any contingency, sir."

"Good. And I'm sure that, over the next several days, or weeks, as you continue your escort duty, you'll adapt even further."

The smile on Cade's face was replaced by a questioning look of protest. "I beg your pardon, sir? Did you say several days or weeks?"

"I did. We don't know how long these people are going to be here, but I expect you to be with them for as long as they're here."

"When you say several days or weeks, do you mean several days that could stretch into a week, or do you mean several weeks?"

"Perhaps I should read the rest of the order as I received it from the secretary of war." Again, Captain Anderson read from the paper: "'From the Fort

Yellowstone garrison, you will furnish a line officer who will, *for the duration of the photographers' stay,* be charged with attending to their logistical needs, seeing to their safety, and providing liaison where needed to enable the photographers to complete their mission.'"

Captain Anderson put the paper down and looked up at Cade again. "As you can see, it says 'for the duration of the photographers' stay' and is nonspecific. You, Lieutenant, will be that line officer."

"Yes, sir," Cade said, his tone of his voice indicating his displeasure with the assignment.

"Look at it this way, Cade. As long as you are assigned to these photographers, you'll be exempt from any collateral duty. You won't have to pull officer of the day, you won't have to take any formations, you won't be riding around looking for campfires that haven't been extinguished, and you won't be slapping people on the wrists for writing their names on one of the geyser formations. And, the photographs may actually call attention to the park and help the Department of War and the Department of the Interior to work together, to give us more appropriations for policing the park."

"Yes, sir. I can see that."

"Good." Captain Anderson smiled. "Cade, don't look at this task as one performed by the officer most junior, look at it as a task that might garner good results."

"I'll do that, Captain," Cade replied, returning Captain Anderson's smile.

∽∞∾

Livingston, Montana

Marci and Frances stood on the brick platform of the Livingston depot with their luggage and belongings stacked up around them.

"Do you see Mr. Haynes?" Marci asked.

"No." Fan looked around, trying to find her friend. "F. Jay is usually very reliable. I got a telegram from him assuring me he would be here to meet us when our train arrived."

Behind them the engineer blew two short toots on the whistle, then with a gush of steam from the outlet of the cylinder, a clanking of the piston rod with the crankpin, and a series of chugging sounds, the train began to leave the station. Marci could hear the wheels of the cars as they passed over the rail joints, and she felt a slight apprehension.

For the last five days the train had been her home, and she had become comfortable with her accommodations. Now she was standing on a depot platform with Fan, and the person who was to meet them was nowhere in sight. Marci's mind began to focus on alternative plans, even though she knew Frances would make any decisions.

Just then, from the direction of town, a buckboard approached, pulled by a galloping horse.

"I'm coming! I'm coming!" Marci heard a man calling as he waved his hat wildly.

Frances laughed. "That's him." She shook her head as she pointed to the buckboard.

The buckboard halted and a rather tall, slender man with a sweeping mustache hopped down from the wagon. He placed his bowler hat on his head and gave the driver some money.

"Thank you, Mr. Haynes," the driver said, then he turned the buckboard around and drove off at a much slower pace.

"I'm sorry, Fan," F. Jay said as he approached, taking her hand in his and raising it to his lips. "Lily had some errands for me to do while I was in Livingston, and I was certain I could get my business done and be back in time to meet the train." In the distance could be heard the whistle of the train that was just departing. "But, I can see that I'm not terribly late, as the train is still in sight. Now I can say, Fan, my dear, welcome to Yellowstone. Or, rather to Livingston, but we'll get to Yellowstone tomorrow morning."

"Oh, I thought we'd get to the park tonight. I'm anxious to see Lily and the little ones again."

"Little ones. It's been a while since you've seen my children. Jack is twelve already, and George is ten. And Bessie, well, she married a young lieutenant last year and is now at Fort Custer. But tell me, Fan, who is this lovely young woman with you?"

"Oh, I'm sorry. Yes, this is my new assistant, Marci Winters. She's new to our profession, but she has a wonderful eye, and I believe very soon she will be my associate rather than my assistant. I know you're going to enjoy having her around."

"F. Jay Haynes, my dear." He extended his hand to Marci, and she took it with a firm grip.

"I'm very pleased to meet you, Mr. Haynes."

"While we're here, should we go on into the depot and get our tickets for tomorrow?" Fan asked.

Haynes laughed. "My dear, there are distinct advantages to being in the employ of the Northern Pacific Railroad Company. One perquisite is that I have a universal railroad pass, and the other advantage is . . . look to your left."

Haynes pointed to a railroad car that was painted in a glossy green, with yellow trim. It looked different from any other railroad car Marci had ever seen. In addition to the normal train windows, it had three oversize windows in the center, and under the center window, in yellow letters, was written:

PRIVATE CAR OF F. J. HAYNES
OFFICIAL PHOTOGRAPHER
NPRR

"Now, that is impressive!" Fan said with a big smile. "How long have you had that?"

"For a while now. Wait until you see the inside. You'll be so jealous. I can do all my work from that car. It has a studio and a darkroom right on board, so all I have to do is find a place to park and I'm in business."

"It can't get there by itself, can it?" Fan asked.

Haynes laughed. "No, of course it has to be pulled by an engine. Tomorrow morning we'll be attached to the Yellowstone Special, which will leave for Cinnabar at about eight thirty, if it's on time."

"Then, Marci and I will get a room in a hotel and meet you in the morning."

"You don't have to do that. This car has four private bedrooms, though one has been converted to my darkroom. I want you to see it. Come on, let's go inside."

The private car was roomier and much better appointed than Marci's pension in Paris had been. In the main salon, two comfortable sofas faced each other with ample room in between.

"Oh, how nice," Marci said. "This is like a little house on wheels. You have a table and chairs, and a stove for heating and cooking, and, oh, what beautiful photographs. You've been everywhere."

"Thank you," F. Jay said. "I've been very fortunate to get to go wherever I want and do the work that I love. And now it's so much easier to take quality photographs than it used to be. Isn't that right, Fan?"

"Well," Frances said, drawing out the word, "I'm not as quick to adopt new ways as you are."

"Don't tell me you're still using eikonogen as a developing agent?"

"I am." Frances laughed. "But I did bring my new Kodak that George Eastman sent me."

"For your sake, Marci, I'm glad she's done that. You could be running up and down the mountains to the dark boxes carrying the wet plates."

"Now, my dear friend, I'm quite proud of my product, and I prefer to think I get good results by doing the ordinary exceptionally well."

"That you do. Shall I get your belongings?"

"Please do," Frances replied.

On the overhead storage bins, the undersides were lined with landscape photography that Marci knew without being told were pictures of Yellowstone. On the walls between the windows were portraits of children, of beautiful young woman, sedate-looking older women, serious-looking young men, and dignified-looking older men.

F. Jay made several trips back and forth with the luggage for the two ladies.

"My God, ladies, how long are you planning to stay? You have enough to outfit the Sixth Cavalry."

"We don't know how long we'll be here, but it's better to be prepared than to be sorry."

"I suppose you're right, but I for one am starving. May I treat you ladies to the finest meal in Livingston?"

During dinner Marci spoke little, listening instead to what she now knew were two of the nation's top photographers exchanging questions, ideas, and tidbits of knowledge that Marci was able to gather and store. On the walk back to the car after dinner, she was surprised at how cold it was this late in June. She looked up at the sky and thought she had never seen a night sky so brilliantly arrayed with stars.

At first she had difficulty getting to sleep without the rocking motion of the train. But once she did fall asleep, she slept soundly.

Cinnabar, Montana

Cinnabar was the end of track for the spur railroad, so here the train would discharge the tourists it was delivering and pick up those who had already enjoyed their visit to Yellowstone. After taking on the returning passengers, the train—not having the use of a roundhouse—would make a wide circle that would put it back on the track properly pointed toward Livingston.

When Cade and the three men with him reached Cinnabar, three YPT coaches were pulled up at the depot, waiting for the Yellowstone Special to arrive from Livingston.

"Sergeant, stand by the horses," Cade said as he dismounted. "I'll check with the drivers and see if one of them is the dedicated coach."

Cade had been stationed at Fort Yellowstone for nearly a year now, so he knew almost all of the drivers, and as he walked up toward the coaches, he found the three drivers sitting at an outside table having their lunch.

"Hello, Lieutenant McDowell," Tommy Clark said. "I'll bet you're here for me."

"Is your coach for Mr. Haynes and the other two photographers?"

"It is."

Cade smiled. "Then, yes, I'm here to be your escort."

"Huh," Larry Overstreet said. "How come me 'n' Jimmy ain't gettin' a military escort?"

"Because nobody cares what happens to either one of you," Tommy Clark teased. "Lieutenant, if you 'n' your men ain't et yet, best you do that. I've picked up Haynes before. He's always rarin' to go, soon as gets here."

"I thought that might be the case."

Cade walked back to Sergeant Dawes. "Sergeant, Mr. Clark says we'd better eat now, so let's break out the rations."

"Yes, sir."

Cade and the three men with him had brought canned beans, canned peaches, and a cloth bag of biscuits. Opening the cans, they sat on a bench at the far end of the depot platform to have their lunch, finishing it just as they heard the whistle of the approaching train.

Cleaning up the empty cans and paper, the men stood by their horses as they watched the train come in, with gushing steam and the steel-on-steel squeal of braking wheels. Finally the train came to a halt and began disgorging passengers, and Cade looked for F. Jay Haynes.

"There he is, Lieutenant," Sergeant Dawes said. "His car's way back there at the rear of the train."

Cade looked toward the back of the train, but a sudden burst of steam completely blocked his view. He stared into the steam until it drifted away, then he saw Haynes. Cade smiled and started toward him, then stopped abruptly.

Two women were with Haynes. And one of the two women was either Marci Winters or someone who looked exactly like her.

"Oh!" Marci gasped, covering her mouth with her hand when she saw an army officer coming toward her. "Oh, it can't be!"

"What is it?" Frances asked, concerned about Marci's unexpected outburst.

"It's him! It's Cade McDowell!"

Cade and Marci both started quickly advancing toward one another. Marci, who had been walking behind Haynes, passed him in her eagerness to reach Cade.

The two met halfway between Haynes and Frances and the soldiers who made up Cade's detail.

Marci wanted desperately to embrace him, but she knew that it would be embarrassing to both of them if she was that undisciplined. As it was, she knew her reaction would require her to explain to Frances.

They reached each other, but stopped just short. Though it seemed woefully inadequate, Marci extended her hand. Cade took it, not to shake it, but to hold it, and as they stood there, he didn't let it go.

"What are you doing here?" Marci asked, though even as she asked the question, Cade was speaking the same words.

They laughed, then Cade said, "You first."

"What are you doing here?"

"I'm here to meet you."

"You're here to meet me? But how did you know I was coming?"

Cade smiled. "I wish I could say that it was my brilliant deduction and reasoning, that I perceived you would be here. But the truth is, I had no idea it would be you. My orders were merely to meet Mr. Haynes's private car and escort him and his guests to their destination."

By now Haynes and Frances Johnston had come even with them, and Cade, realizing that he was still holding Marci's hand, let it go.

"Well, Lieutenant McDowell, apparently you and Miss Winters are already acquainted," Haynes said.

"Yes, sir. I had the distinct honor and privilege of being Miss Winters's escort last year when a group of young ladies from her college honored the cadets of West Point with a visit."

"Oh!" Frances said. "This could be interesting."

Marci flushed slightly, and Frances reached out to lay her hand on Marci's arm. "Now, don't get flustered."

"I understand we are to have a dedicated coach. Do you know which one is ours?" Haynes asked.

"Yes, sir, it's here," Cade said.

"Who's the driver?"

"Mr. Clark."

"Good, good, Tommy Clark's a good man." Haynes turned to the two ladies. "If you'll go with the lieutenant, I'll make arrangements to have my car separated, and I'll get someone to see to our luggage."

When Haynes started into the depot to make arrangements for the car, Frances looked at Marci. "Aren't you going to introduce us?"

"Oh, of course. Frances Johnston, this is Cade," Marci started, then she corrected herself, "Lieutenant Cade McDowell."

"I'm very pleased to meet you, Lieutenant. Are you stationed at the park?"

"Yes, ma'am." Cade looked at Marci. "I've been at Fort Yellowstone since I graduated from the academy." He nodded his head in Marci's direction as a smile curled his lips.

Marci looked away, not wanting to deal with her recollections of that memorable weekend she had spent at West Point.

She saw the arriving passengers clambering onto

the other two coaches, which were now overflowing. Both men and women were climbing up on the top to find a place to sit for what would be a long ride to the Mammoth Hot Springs Hotel.

"Those coaches look very crowded," Marci said. "Will there be room for our baggage?"

"You don't have to worry about that," Cade said. "You'll be riding with Mr. Haynes, and he has a coach all to himself."

"Good old F. Jay," Frances said.

The two passenger coaches left, leaving a cloud of dust, while Haynes's coach waited for F. Jay.

"I'd better check to see what's keeping F. Jay," Frances said as she started toward the depot building.

Marci smiled as Frances walked away. "She did that just to give us a moment alone."

"That's very thoughtful. It's too bad we aren't actually alone."

Marci lowered her head as she felt her face begin to flush. She, who was usually so sure of herself, felt almost shy at what was a simple, uncontested statement. With people standing around, they weren't alone, but her mind was conjuring up other places and other times. She searched for a witty response, but no words came to her.

"I can't tell you what a shock it is to see you, but what are you doing here?" Cade asked. "Oh, wait, I know. You're here to take pictures for the Department of the Interior."

"I had no idea you were here."

"When we ran into each other at the National Zoo, I thought you knew the animals had come from Yellowstone. I should have told you, but you were . . ." He stopped in midsentence as his mind flashed back to the scene of Marci in the arms of another man.

"I didn't know."

"Well, it doesn't matter. You're here now. Do you know how long you get to stay?"

"No, I'm to be Fan's"—Marci started to say *assistant,* but amended it—"associate. And how long I'm here will depend on her. I hope we'll get to see one another again."

"Careful what you wish for," Cade said with a chuckle.

"Everything's been taken care of," Haynes said as he returned to the coach, while a handful of men made quick work stowing the baggage on one of the seats and on top of the coach. "What do you say we get on our way to Wonderland?"

"Will the ladies be going to the hotel, Mr. Haynes?" the driver asked.

"No, they'll be staying with Lily and me at the studio." Haynes glanced into the coach. "Say, Tommy, do you mind if I ride up top with you? I forgot my friend brought everything she owns."

"You stop that," Frances said good-naturedly. "Not every photographer has a traveling darkroom to go with her everywhere."

"I guess that's right, but you know you can use anything I have." F. Jay used the spokes of the front wheel to climb up to the driver's seat.

Cade opened the door for Marci and Frances and offered his arm to both ladies as they climbed into the coach. Once they were settled in the coach, he

mounted his horse, then nodded at the driver. The
driver let out a loud whistle, then popped his whip
over the heads of the team, and the horses started
forward with a jerk. Cade and one of the privates
rode in front of the coach, Sergeant Dawes and the
other private rode behind, and with the wheels of
the coach throwing up rooster tails of dust, they got
under way at a brisk pace.

ELEVEN

All right," Frances said as the coach got started, "I've been waiting and this is the perfect time."

"Perfect time? Perfect time for what?"

"You know what. The lieutenant. Tell me about him."

"There's really nothing to tell. We met at West Point when he was a cadet. Several of the women from Wells College were invited to the campus for a dance, and while we were there, he was my escort. That's all. End of story."

"Hah! I saw the way you two greeted each another. There was more there than 'Oh, he was just my escort.'"

Marci smiled self-consciously. "All right. Maybe it was a little more than a casual meeting. But it doesn't matter now."

"What do you mean, it doesn't matter?"

"When I met him at West Point, I was . . . involved with someone else."

"Really? This other person you were involved

with, did it have anything to do with the confetti I saw you scattering to the winds?"

"Yes, I'm afraid it's one and the same."

"Then, you aren't involved with that skunk anymore, are you?"

"No, at least as far as I'm concerned."

"It's obvious to me you've not put the lieutenant out of your mind all this time. Am I right about that?"

"Yes, you are."

"Well, then, it looks to me like you've been given a second chance. And my advice to you would be not to let this chance pass you by."

"Oh, Fan, you don't know how much I would like that to happen, but there's more to it than that. You know what I'm trying to run away from back in Washington. This man is one of the most honorable men I've ever met, and I seem to have a knack for messing up everything."

"Do you think he's heard the rumors about you?"

"Oh, surely not!" Marci gasped.

"That's my point. He doesn't know what you've done, or even what people say you've done. Marci, I consider myself a good judge of people's character, and so far, I like you. In fact, I like you very much. If he's as honorable as you say he is, give him a chance to make up his own mind about you."

"I hope you're right."

"I know I am. I saw the look on his face when the two of you were standing together. I'm a photographer. It's my job to read people's faces."

"I don't know, Fan."

"What is it you don't know?"

"What if I'm misreading this? What if you're misreading this? I've already been . . ." Marci stopped in midsentence.

Frances reached over and took Marci's hand into her own. "You've already been hurt once. I figured as much when I watched you tear up the letter. But, honey, you can't let your life just stop altogether. You've taken the first step; you've put the man and the hurt behind you. Don't let whoever it was hold sway over you any longer. You have your own life to live . . . live it to the fullest."

As Cade led the coach down the road from Cinnabar to the Yellowstone Gate, his mind was whirling in disbelief. Ever since he had met Marci Winters, she had been his fantasy.

Would she live up to his fantasy? She was certainly as pretty as he remembered, and as friendly. She did appear to be a bit more mature, though. Had their time together at West Point, more than a year ago now, been nothing more than the exuberance of her youth? He thought she had greeted him effusively enough when she had first seen him, but then when her friend had gone into the depot, she had seemed more reserved, and he wondered about that. He had to question, if they were going to spend time together here, in a totally different environment from that of their first meeting, where would it lead?

Was this an opportunity dropped into his hands by fate? Or was this likely to be the end of the fantasy he had created? He would just have to wait and see what would happen, accounting for situation and terrain.

Situation and terrain.

He laughed as he applied the old military maxim to this situation. He had to face it. He lived, breathed, and bled army blue.

When they reached the entrance to the park, the other two coaches were stopped and the passengers had been off-loaded and were standing nearby. Sergeant Peabody and the three soldiers in the sergeant's detail were checking the tourists in, getting their names, and ascertaining where they were going, and how long they planned to be in the park.

In addition to checking them in, they were also checking for weapons.

"Hey, I got a right to carry a gun," one of the passengers said when the soldier asked for his pistol. "You've got no right to confiscate it."

"We aren't confiscating it," the soldier said. "We're just marking it."

Reluctantly, the passenger handed over his pistol, and the soldier tied a red cord around it, then sealed the knot with red wax.

"Be prepared to show your weapon at any time while you're in the park," the soldier said. "And when you show it, this seal better not be broken."

Cade walked over to the table where the soldiers were checking in the passengers, and seeing him approach, Sergeant Peabody stood and saluted.

"Sergeant, I'm on a special detail escorting that coach." Cade pointed to the one that Tommy Clark was driving. "I'll be personally responsible for the occupants."

"Yes, sir, Lieutenant. Just go on through."

"Thank you, Sergeant."

As the coach went into the park, passing the other two coaches, a great deal of good-natured shouting came from those who were still at the inspection point, who had to remain behind until all the passengers were processed.

"Don't you go getting the best rooms now!"

"What's the hurry? The geysers will wait for you!"

"Hey, who are the soldier boys guarding that they're so important they can go on through? Is that the queen of England?"

From the time the Haynes group left the depot at Cinnabar until they reached their destination took just under an hour, including the brief stop at the entrance of the park. Although they were now within sight of the Mammoth Hot Springs Hotel, that wasn't their destination. Instead, they pulled up in front of a large, white building with a wraparound porch. Its fence was most unusual, being made of hundreds of elk horns. When the coach stopped, it sat there for a moment as the dust thrown up by the wheels drifted slowly by the windows of the coach.

"Here we are, ladies!" F. Jay Haynes called. Before he could climb down from the seat, Cade dismounted and hurried over to open the door for Marci and Frances.

He helped the two ladies down, and Marci stood there for a long moment, staring at the building. The stately structure was two and a half stories high. Hanging just under the roof of the front porch was the sign HAYNES PARK VIEWS. To the right of the house was an L-shaped addition that looked big enough to be a house in itself.

Haynes pointed to the extension. "That's my studio."

"I like your fence," Marci said as she walked over to touch one of the antlers.

"Can you believe all those horns were collected within thirty miles of here? What do you think of my place?" F. Jay asked, taking in the house with a sweep of his arm. He was clearly proud of it.

"It's . . . very—" Marci started to say, but she was interrupted by Haynes.

"Oh, there's my Lily. Come out here and meet our guests. You remember Fan, of course, and this is her associate, Marci Winters. Miss Winters, this is my wife, Lily."

"It's so good to meet you, Mrs. Haynes," Marci said, extending her hand.

"Oh, please, we aren't very formal here in the park. It's Lily." Lily ignored Marci's offered hand and embraced her. "You're about our Bessie's age, I'll bet. How old are you?"

"I'm twenty-two, ma'am."

"And still not married? Bessie married a very nice lieutenant last year, and now she's moved off to Fort Custer. She just wrote me telling me I'm going to be a grandma, and I can hardly wait. Every woman wants a grandbaby, you know."

"Yes, ma'am." Marci didn't know exactly what to say to Mrs. Haynes, a tall woman with an oval face and flashing blue eyes. These features were somewhat overshadowed by an ample bosom, which was her most prominent physical attribute.

"Sergeant Dawes, you and the men are dismissed from this detail," Cade said. "You may return to the garrison."

"Yes, sir." Sergeant Dawes saluted.

Cade returned the salute as the three men turned their horses and started toward the fort.

"Tommy, if you'll toss things down, I'll help F. Jay get the ladies moved in."

"All right." Clark set the brake and tied off the horses, then climbed on top of the coach and started handing things to Cade.

"Now, Mar—Miss Winters, if you'll tell me which pieces belong to each of you, I can separate them before we take them in." Cade had decided midsentence that, in front of the others, it might be a bit forward for him to call her Marci.

When all the pieces were unloaded and divided, Cade picked up bags that belonged to Marci, and Clark and F. Jay picked up Frances's belongings.

"Gentlemen, I thank you," F. Jay said. "It would have taken me all afternoon just to get these two into the house. Lily, have you decided where we're going to put 'em?"

"Put Fan in the guest room, and then put Marci in Bessie's room. That'll get her as far away from Jack and George as she can be."

"I've never had any brothers or sisters, so I'm sure I would welcome the company of two young men," Marci said.

"Not these two," F. Jay said. "What one doesn't think up, the other one does, wouldn't you say, Lieutenant?"

"I wouldn't say that," Cade said. "They're just

good, red-blooded American boys who have the rare opportunity to live at the most beautiful spot in the country."

"That's what I think, too," Lily said as she led the way to the bedrooms.

Marci's room was upstairs at the front of the house, isolated from the other rooms, and as she started toward it, Cade followed.

"You did bring a lot with you," Cade said. "Where do you want me to put this stuff?"

"Put it over here," Marci said as she moved over by the window.

Cade took the bags to the spot Marci had indicated, and after setting them down, he turned to her. For a long moment they looked directly at one another, neither saying a word.

Finally, Marci turned her face to the window. "It really is beautiful here."

Cade stepped up behind her, standing just inches away. More than anything, he wanted to turn her around and hold her in his arms, just to feel her body next to his. Over and over in his mind, he had re-created the kiss he had shared with her under Kissing Rock, but he wasn't sure that kiss had meant as much to her as it had to him. After all, she had not responded to his letter when he had tried to contact her. He closed his eyes and breathed in the scent of her, then buried his need deep inside. He knew he would be devastated if he attempted to kiss her and she turned him away.

When he knew he was in control of his emotions, he moved the curtain back from the window and pointed.

"That's Fort Yellowstone—where I live. The first white building over there with the red roof is my building, and this is the parade ground right in front of us. You won't see anything like you saw on the Plain, but for what it is, it can be impressive."

"Is there a Flirtation Walk?"

"With 3468.4 square miles in the park, I'll bet there's one someplace, but I just haven't found it yet. Now that you're here, we'll have to look for it together."

"Oh, Cade, I don't know how much time we'll get to be together. You see, I'm not here as a tourist. I have a job working for Frances Johnston, and we'll be going all over taking photographs."

Cade smiled. "I know we will."

"We will?" Her eyebrows rose in question.

"According to orders Captain Anderson has received from the Department of War, the Fort Yellowstone garrison will furnish a line officer who will, for the duration of the photographers' stay, be charged with attending to their logistical needs, seeing to their safety, and providing liaison where needed to enable the photographers to complete their mission." Cade smiled. "I am that line officer." The smile broadened. "And I will be with you for the duration of your stay."

"Oh, Cade! That's wonderful!" Marci said as she threw her arms around him.

Cade's smile turned to a chuckle. "I have to confess, I wasn't too happy when I drew this assignment, but that's not the case now." He pulled her tighter against him.

"I seem to remember that you proved to be an exceptional escort once before."

"I was, wasn't I?" Cade's lips were now only inches away from Marci's.

She knew he was going to kiss her, and even though a part of her told her she shouldn't allow it to happen, the smoldering flame in his eyes pulled her toward him, and she moved her mouth toward his. When his lips touched hers, she felt a tingling in the pit of her stomach.

The kiss began innocently enough, soft and tentative, as if he were exploring the bounds, but when she offered no resistance, the kiss deepened. She felt his tongue trace the soft fullness of her lips. Then, as it had when they had kissed under Kissing Rock, a kiss that she had relived in her memory many times, his tongue slipped through her lips to explore the recesses of her mouth.

She felt new spirals of ecstasy racing through her, leaving her mouth burning with fire. When his tongue withdrew from her mouth, she followed it with her own, returning the kiss with reckless abandon.

"Marci!" Frances called from down the hallway. "Are you about through in your room?"

The unexpected sound caused Marci to jump back, separating quickly from Cade's embrace.

"Just a minute," Marci called.

"Come down when you can and we'll make plans for tomorrow. F. Jay has some ideas for us to discuss."

"I'm on my way."

"I guess I should be a part of this planning session as well, since I'm to be your bodyguard," Cade said.

"Bodyguard? Cade, there's nothing for us to be afraid of, is there?"

"Things happen in the park, but for the most part the danger comes from wild animals, not from wild men."

Marci grinned mischievously. "Would a wild man kiss somebody in the park?"

"He might." Cade kissed her on the nose. "Now, we'd better get down there before they send one of the hellions up here."

"Do you mean one of the boys?"

"Yes, and more specifically, George. We've rescued a tourist or two from one of his pranks."

Marci reached up to touch her hair. "How do I look? I mean, can you . . ."

"Tell that you've just been kissed? Oh, definitely so."

"What?"

Cade laughed. "I'm teasing, Marci. You look just fine."

The door to Marci's room hadn't been fully closed, and Cade pushed it open, then followed Marci down the steps.

"There you are," Lily said when she saw Marci and Cade. "F. Jay and Fan stepped into the shop, so just go on through that door."

When Marci stepped into the commodious room attached to the side of the Haynes house, she saw it was filled with books, papers, cameras, tripods, boxes, and overflowing shelves.

In the middle of the room was a table, and spread out on the table was a map.

"I think we may as well start here, tomorrow,"

Haynes said. "These are the Mammoth Terraces that you could have seen when you came in if you'd been on the outside of the coach. I think the Terraces are one of the most photogenic features in the park. It's very close by, and its hot-spring formations are excellent subjects for photography. Imagine, if you will, exquisite buildups of white travertine that hang like exquisite stalactites on the roof of a cave. Then add half a dozen fanciful colors that are formed around the thermal springs, and you have a spectacular site. It makes me think of waterfalls that are arranged like giant steps going from one terrace to another."

"You make me wish we had color film," Marci said.

"My dear, if you set up the picture just right, even though it be in black and white, the colors will just sing," F. Jay said. "That is, if we can get a picture without any tourists in it."

"People in scenic views aren't necessarily bad," Frances said. "I find putting figures in my work serves a purpose. A single figure can highlight the grandeur of the site quicker than anything else."

"Of course, you're right, Fan," F. Jay said as he swept his hand around the room. "If it weren't for people wanting their pictures taken next to the scenery, I wouldn't have much business, but my busiest studio is at the upper geyser basin. That's where Old Faithful is. In season, I know I must take two or three hundred pictures a day down there."

"Do you take them all yourself?" Marci asked.

"Not always. I have a man who works for me, and when he has to be away, I send Jack to do it."

"Your son?"

"Yes, he's developed quite a photographer's eye. You'll meet him at supper tonight."

"I'm looking forward to it," Marci said.

"F. Jay, if you're going to visit with your guests tonight, I'll go back to my quarters," Cade said.

"Oh, Lieutenant, you may as well join us for supper. I'm sure Lily will have more than enough."

"Not tonight, I'm afraid. Captain Anderson will be expecting my report." Cade glanced toward Marci. "What time do you want to move out in the morning?"

"I want to be at the Terraces at first light, so I'd like to be at Minerva Terrace by six thirty. Do you think you can be here?"

"Yes, sir. You hear the wake-up just like I do," Cade said with a chuckle as he turned to Frances and Marci. "Miss Johnston, Miss Winters, it has been my pleasure to meet you."

"Let's get one thing straight. You may be in the army, but I'm not. I want you to call me Fan, and since I've been told you've met 'Miss Winters' before, I would bet my bottom dollar you didn't call her Miss Winters when it took you so long to get her settled in her room. So from now on, you are Cade and I'm Fan and this is Marci."

"Yes, ma'am," Cade said as a wide smile crossed his face.

The next morning Marci awakened early and was dressing when she heard a bugle call. Thinking it must be the "wake-up" that Cade had referred to, she stepped to the window and, drawing back the curtain, looked out over the parade ground. Men in blue uniforms were coming from a rather large building set back several hundred yards from the gravel road. When they reached the middle of the field, they assembled themselves in orderly lines. Then a lone figure came out from one of the two identical red-roofed buildings that were set apart from the big building. When the man stepped in front of the group, she saw one man raise his hand in a salute, and the man in front returned the salute.

There was so much about the army she didn't understand. How had Libbie Custer ever become so much a part of her husband's career that she could write multiple books about army life? If Marci was going to be a part of Cade's life, she would have to learn about all this ceremony that surrounded the military.

"Marci Winters. Stop it. Stop it right now!" she said emphatically. "You fool. You have no right to think you'll ever be a part of that man's life."

As soon as the words were out of her mouth, she saw a rider and a big, black horse approaching. Her heart began to race wildly as soon as she recognized Cade. How would she ever be able to concentrate on photography when he would be with her every second of the day?

When Marci was dressed in a light traveling suit, she went down to the parlor, where she heard voices coming from the porch that stretched across the front of the Haynes home. When she stepped out, Frances, F. Jay, and Cade were sitting in some rocking chairs, each drinking a cup of coffee.

"There you are," F. Jay said upon seeing her. "If you hadn't come down in the next five minutes, I was about to send the cavalry up to see what happened to you."

An impish expression crossed Marci's face. "Will you promise to do that if I go back upstairs?"

Cade sputtered when he heard Marci's comment, spitting coffee everywhere as he went into a coughing fit.

"Look what you've done to poor Cade," Frances said as she began to slap his back. "Are you all right?"

"I think I just swallowed my coffee wrong," Cade said as tears began to build from his coughing.

"I'm so sorry," Marci said, barely containing her own laughter.

"Get in there and get a bite to eat," Frances said.

When Marci had stepped back into the house, F. Jay shook his head. "I think my George won't be getting anything over on that one this summer. It's going to be fun having her around, don't you think, Lieutenant?"

Cade didn't answer as he took another sip of his coffee.

As F. Jay had wanted, they arrived at the Terraces just at daybreak. The sun's rays began to color the ledges of the Terraces in the most beautiful shades of orange with a mix of pinks shining on the alabaster falls. For a while Marci sat in the wagon, mesmerized by the scene.

"Pssst. Marci," Cade said in a whisper. "Do you want me to set up a tripod for you?"

"Oh! Oh, yes, I forgot."

Cade stepped up to help her out of the wagon, and as she was standing, she placed her hands on his shoulders to steady herself. When she did, their faces were within inches of one another.

"I would have done it," Cade said.

"What?"

"Come up to get you out of bed."

Marci shook her head. "I really am sorry I said that this morning, but it just slipped out. I hope you weren't embarrassed."

"Were you?"

She looked at him for a long moment, her eyes widening. "No," she said at last.

"Would you be embarrassed if I kissed you right here?"

"Yes," she said much too loudly.

Cade laughed as he lifted her out of the wagon and placed her feet on the ground, relishing the feel of her body against his.

"Marci, look at the sun hitting the peak of Sepulcher Mountain," F. Jay said, ignoring what repartee between Cade and Marci he may have overheard. "Set your tripod up right here, and I think you'll get a good shot."

Cade took the tripod to the spot that F. Jay had indicated, and Marci got her camera and attached it. Soon she was shooting multiple shots, moving from place to place, trying to get other angles of the Terraces.

"Let's move on up Capitol Hill and shoot back

toward the fort. It will give a good perspective where we are," F. Jay said as he began to put his equipment back in the wagon.

Cade heard F. Jay's words, but he attached his own meaning to giving "a good perspective where we are." If this morning was a precursor to what the summer was going to bring, he was looking forward to a wonderful experience.

He was watching as Marci made her way off the Terraces, and he wanted to hurry to her and help her, but he thought better of it.

Don't rush anything. Take it slow and easy. She'll let me know when she's ready. Ready for what? He wished he knew, because he felt that the answer to that question could affect him for the rest of his life.

TWELVE

Frances was excited about her pictures and was anxious to see her work, so she convinced F. Jay to return to his studio by early afternoon so she could spend the rest of the day in the darkroom.

"I guess you're through for the day, Cade. Maybe you could show Marci around Mammoth so she'll know where to go if I want something—that is, if it is still part of your duty," Frances said.

"The order clearly states that a line officer is at your disposal, so I would assume being Marci's escort would be a part of my duty."

"Good, and, Cade, do plan on joining us for supper this evening?" F. Jay said.

"Thank you." Cade turned to Marci. "Where would you like to start our tour?"

"I'd like to see where you live."

"All right, but before I show you, let me take Rowdy back to the stable." Cade stepped up to the hitching rail where his horse was standing quietly.

"He doesn't seem like a Rowdy to me," Marci said

as she patted the horse's neck. "Why did you name him that?"

"I didn't. Someone who had him before I did named him that."

"Then, he's not really your horse."

"Now he is. I bought him from the army." Cade untied the reins. "Come on, old boy, let's get you to the stable."

Marci could see a broad area separating F. Jay's house from a row of buff-colored buildings, all with tall, red chimneys and red roofs. Though the buildings didn't resemble West Point in any physical way, they had a regimen to them, all aligned and similar in appearance.

As they crossed the parade ground, Cade pointed to the row of buildings that were the closest to them.

"That's the officers' quarters over there. And that's my window on the right." He pointed to the first building.

"That's a big house. How many people live there?"

"Just me and three other lieutenants. I'm the most junior officer so they try to give me a hard time, but I don't let them get away with it."

Marci smiled. "I'm sure you don't."

"Really, we've got a good bunch of men here. Fort Yellowstone is a small post and everybody gets along well. It's like we're all family."

When he said that, Marci recalled that Cade had told her he had no family. She could see how the military could become so important to him.

Just then a squad of soldiers came into view. They were marching back and forth, carrying rifles on their shoulders. One man was marching alongside and barking out words that were so clipped that Marci could not understand what he was saying.

"That man—the words—they don't make sense. 'Hip, hoop, hireep, harp!' What is that?"

Cade chuckled. "It makes perfect sense if you're a soldier. He's counting cadence, one, two, three, four."

"You mean you have to learn a new language when you join the army?"

"Sort of. Come on. While we're right here, I'd like you to meet my commanding officer."

They stopped in front of a building that was a little different from the officers' quarters. It was made of stone but still had the same red roof. Cade tied Rowdy to the hitching rail and they climbed the steps into the building.

When they entered, a man was sitting behind a desk that had papers strewn all over it. A sign on the desk read FIRST SERGEANT, and he stood when Cade and Marci stepped inside. "Lieutenant, ma'am."

"Sergeant Gilbert, this is Miss Marci Winters. She's a photographer, and she's going to be here for a while. I'll be showing her around."

"Gee, sir, that looks like awfully tough duty." The first sergeant smiled.

"What can I say, Top?" Cade sighed and shook his head. "Somebody has to do it. Is the old man in?"

"Yes, sir, I'll tell 'im you're here."

The first sergeant went into the CO's office and Marci turned to Cade. "Won't you get into trouble calling him an old man?" she asked quietly.

"Not *an* old man, *the* old man. It's what everyone calls the commanding officer."

Just then Captain Anderson stepped into the outer office, smiling broadly. "I'm George Anderson." He extended his hand to Marci.

"Captain, this is Miss Marci Winters," Cade said.

"So, Miss Winters, you are one of the people in the lieutenant's charge, are you? I hope he's treating you well."

"Oh, I couldn't ask for anything better, Captain."

"I thought I'd show her around the company area this afternoon," Cade said.

"Can't you do better than that, Cade? With all the wondrous sites in the national park, I hardly think she'd be interested in an army post."

"Oh, but I am interested. The time I spent with Cade at West Point was a most enjoyable experience, and I'm sure my time at Fort Yellowstone will be equally so."

Captain Anderson's eyebrows shot up in surprise and he looked at both of them with a smile on his lips. "Cade, why didn't you tell me you knew Miss Winters?"

"Sir, it is purely coincidental that our paths should cross again. When I was a fourth classman at the academy, I was honored to be her escort at the Spring Hop. We've not been in contact since that weekend, so neither of us knew the whereabouts of the other."

"That's true, Captain. I've been abroad studying art. Now I'm sorry I didn't bring my paints and brushes as well as a camera. I can already see the park has untold opportunities for some unbelievable work."

"That's quite true. Have you by chance seen any of the works of Thomas Moran?"

"Oh, yes, sir. I saw the *Grand Canyon of the Yellowstone*, at the Capitol Building, and now I can't wait to see the real thing."

"Mr. Moran was here before my tenure, but I'm told many of his paintings used William Henry Jackson's photographs as templates. When you're making your pictures, you might want to keep that in mind."

"I will, thank you."

"It's been my pleasure to meet you, Miss Winters, but I'm afraid I have to finish my morning report. Lieutenant McDowell, I will expect to be kept apprised of your activities. Now carry on," Anderson said. "Oh, Miss Winters, can the regiment count on your participation at the Fourth of July festivities?"

"It will be my pleasure, sir."

After they left the headquarters, while Cade was untying Rowdy, Marci was watching several soldiers stretched out in a long line, walking across the parade ground. "Don't tell me that's some sort of drill?" Marci watched one man after another bend over and retrieve something. "What are they doing?"

"They're on police-call detail, and somebody gets to pick up every day. That's why with all these tourists in and out of the park you don't see a speck of trash anywhere."

"I suppose that would be a problem." Marci and Cade moved away from the headquarters building toward the line of officers' quarters. "Now, which window did you say was yours?"

"It's that one. Do you want to get a ladder and climb up and see me?" A devastating grin crossed his face.

Marci laughed. "I'd better not. But I don't think Fan would treat me like Miss Nash did, when I went to your quarters at West Point."

"What are you talking about? You didn't go to my quarters."

"No, but I went through the sally port, and Miss Nash saw me do it. She convinced Dean Smith that I had gone into your room, and that was enough to get me expelled from Wells."

Cade stopped abruptly when Marci said that. "What?" he gasped. "You were expelled from college just because you stepped through the sally port?"

"That's right. I didn't get to go back for my senior year."

"That's stupid, and it's all my fault! I'm the one that asked you to wait there for me!"

Marci laughed and put her hand on his arm. "It isn't your fault. We both know nothing happened, and it may have worked out for the best. I didn't get to go back to Wells, but I spent a term in Paris studying art at the Académie Julian, and I wouldn't trade that experience for anything."

"Then, that's why you didn't answer my letter."

"What letter?"

"I sent you a letter, but I posted it to Wells College."

"Oh, no, I couldn't have received it. I'm sorry."

"I'm not sorry," Cade said with a broad smile.

"You're not?"

"If you didn't get my letter, that means you weren't ignoring me."

"I assure you, Cade, I wouldn't have ignored you."

"Well, that's encouraging." Cade's mouth quirked into a smile. Then his expression changed as he sobered. "I'm not sure I would have been as forgiving if I'd been asked to leave the academy."

"It's different for you. West Point was the springboard for your life, your career, but the whole purpose of going to Wells is to make some man a trophy wife." Marci screwed up her face and in a mocking voice said, "'Now, girls, what would Mrs. Cleveland do? You know she's a Wells girl.'"

"Somehow, Marci, with your talent and personality, I can't see you as a trophy wife for anyone. A wife, yes, and it will be a lucky man who gets you, but I see you as a full and equal partner in a marriage. You'd never be a woman whose only purpose was to boost your husband's social standing."

What Cade might have thought was an innocent comment about a wife boosting a husband's social standing resonated with Marci. It put her relationship with Stanton in perspective, because now she realized that was exactly what he had wanted from her. He didn't love her, he never had. He had wanted her only for what she could do for him. How glad she was that her father had intervened and that she had not married Stanton last summer.

She turned to Cade and took his hand in hers. "You know, Cade, sometimes things work out for the best."

Cade liked the feel of her hand in his. He did not drop it as they continued on toward the stable.

"Oh, oh," Cade said, and lowered his head.

Marci saw someone coming toward them, walking briskly and smiling broadly. "What's wrong?"

"It's Lieutenant Nance. Jeff shares my BOQ." Cade dropped Marci's hand. "This might get a little strange, but, please, just go along with it. I'll explain it all later."

The lieutenant stopped in front of them, then, it appeared to Marci, he actually stared at her with an appraising eye. She looked up at Cade and saw a strange expression on his face, an expression she hadn't seen before. What was it?

"Cade, my boy, you didn't tell us Marci was coming to visit." Nance looked pointedly at Marci. "I'm Jeff Nance, in case this junior second lieutenant here hasn't mentioned me."

"Lieutenant Nance, Marci Winters," she said, extending her hand as she glanced over at Cade. The strange look she had seen on his face now seemed to be something between embarrassment and apprehension.

"I bet you're here for the big dance Saturday night." Nance looked over at Cade. "You're not going to get jealous if Marci dances with any of your friends, are you? You will let her do that, won't you?"

"No, I, uh, it's all up to Marci what she wants to do," Cade said.

"I'll be glad to dance with any of Cade's friends."

"Good. May I be the first to ask for the privilege? That is, after Cade, of course."

"Of course," Marci said.

"Carry on, Lieutenant," Nance said with a smile as he continued on his way.

"We'd better get Rowdy back to the stable," Cade said. "That building is the barracks for the enlisted men."

"Cade?"

"There are sixty men housed there." Cade pointed to one of the buildings.

"Cade?"

Cade stopped and found something to examine in Rowdy's halter. "What?"

"Aren't you going to explain?" Marci asked with a bemused grin.

"Explain what?"

"Explain how it is that Lieutenant Nance recognized me and called me by name, even though we've never met."

"Oh, that."

Marci was tickled by Cade's discomfort. "Yes, that."

"It's complicated. I'm not sure you'll understand."

"You explain it, and we'll see if I understand."

"All right. Do you remember the pictures that were taken of us at Trophy Point?"

"The ones the photographer took?"

"Yes. Miss Farnsworth sent them to me before I left West Point, and now"—Cade took a deep breath—"the one of you sitting on the cannon is on the table by my bed, and the one of the two of us by the chain is on my desk. I haven't lied to anyone, but neither have I corrected anyone's misconception. All the men who live with me have seen those pictures, and they've made the assumption that you are . . ."

"That I am your girl?"

"Yeah. And like I said, I haven't said anything to make them think anything else."

"I see."

He pointed to another building. "That's the post office over there."

Marci hadn't said anything else, but she did continue to look at him, her smile broadening.

"Marci, if it embarrasses you, I'll tell them the truth and take the pictures down."

"You don't have to take them down. I'm actually quite flattered."

Little did Cade know that while he was looking at her innocent picture every night before he went to bed, she was doing the same thing, only the picture she looked at wasn't as innocent. She had placed her nude drawing with Cade's face on it beside her bed as well. She wondered which of the two had the more prurient thoughts.

"That's the quartermaster building, where all the supplies are kept."

Marci shook her head. It was so like a man to move on to something else when she was envisioning what his real body would look like transposed onto her drawing.

As they were ambling slowly toward the stable, two soldiers overtook them. One of them looked to be barely a boy, while the other seemed much older.

"By your leave, sir," the two said, saluting Cade as they passed.

"Carry on," he said, returning the salute.

Marci waited until the two soldiers were beyond hearing. "What does that mean? 'By your leave'?"

"When an enlisted man overtakes an officer, they salute and say, 'By your leave, sir.'"

Another soldier was approaching, and as he drew closer he saluted. "Good afternoon, sir."

"Good afternoon," Cade replied, returning the salute.

"How come he didn't say 'by your leave'?"

"He didn't have to. He was approaching, not overtaking."

Marci threw her hands up in the air. "How in the world does anyone ever understand the army?"

They approached a long, low building, which Marci recognized as the stable, but it had none of the unpleasant odors that she expected from a facility that held between one and two hundred horses.

A soldier carrying a length of rope came out to meet them. He saluted, and Cade returned the salute.

"Sergeant McKay, I'd like you to meet Miss Marci Winters. If you ever need anything and I'm not around, this is the man you want to look for. He's a good soldier."

"Ma'am," Sergeant McKay said with a slight nod. He seemed to stand taller when Cade praised him.

"I'm pleased to meet you, Sergeant."

"Yes, ma'am. Are you putting Rowdy up for the night, sir?"

"Yes." Cade patted his horse on the neck. Rowdy neighed and shook his head.

"We'll get him rubbed down right away," McKay said as Cade handed him the reins.

As Cade and Marci left the stable, he pointed out

the fire station, the grain storage, the infirmary, and a host of other buildings that were necessary to support the operation.

Marci noticed a row of identical houses set several hundred yards away from what she would consider the fort.

Cade saw her looking toward them and explained, "Soapsuds Row."

"I can just imagine what that means." Marci raised her eyebrows. "Is that where the women who follow the troops live?"

Cade roared with laughter. "Not under Captain Anderson's watch, and especially not at the national park. You'll not even see a bottle of alcohol here—I take that back—the captain keeps his own private supply, but only for medicinal purposes, you understand."

"Well, that's good to know. So I am to assume, then, that those houses really are for laundresses?"

"Yes. It's a very lucrative position, and noncommissioned officers compete to have their wives chosen for the duty. When you add their pay to what their wives make, they draw more money than any other officer on the post, and that includes Captain Anderson."

"I'm glad you told me that. If my job as a photographer doesn't work out, I'll have to apply."

They were just heading for the Mammoth Hot Springs Hotel when there was a loud, booming noise.

"What was that?" Marci asked.

"Remember when we saw the cannon up on Cap-

itol Hill? It's six o'clock and they're firing it to signal 'Retreat.' There'll be a moment of silence while
every soldier faces the flag and salutes as 'Retreat'
is played."

Marci watched Cade come to attention, then with
the first notes of the bugle call, he saluted, holding
the salute while the music was played. Unexpectedly, she felt a little thrill as if, somehow, she had
become a part of all this . . . a part of the life that
was so important to him.

That evening following dinner, F. Jay took everyone into the studio for a showing of the pictures that
had been taken on the Terraces.

"The light was just right this morning, and the
gathering storm in the background added a lot of
texture." F. Jay displayed one photograph and then
another. "I am particularly proud of this one. Look
at the dramatic elements it has working for it."

On the horizon lay the peaks of the Gallatin Range,
above which were the dark clouds of a distant thun-
derstorm. The mountains were visible through a
shroud of steam rising from the hot springs. The
Terraces lay parallel with one another, rising in
steps from snow-white, through varying shades of
gray, to dark.

"It's hard to believe all that can be captured with
black-and-white film," Frances said. "What lens
were you using, F. Jay?"

"Oh, no, Fan. As much as I would like to, I can't
take credit for this work of genius. It was done by
our young protégée." F. Jay turned to Marci. "I think

there is no doubt you have a photographer's eye. I'm proud of you."

Marci beamed under the praise.

For the next few days F. Jay, Frances, and Marci concentrated on getting wildlife and vegetation pictures as they rode in an open carriage, with Cade riding alongside, always keeping a watchful eye. They were in the northwest quadrant of the park in view of Bunsen Peak when they ran into a herd of mule deer that numbered in the hundreds, and all three photographers got a significant number of outstanding pictures.

When they moved their operation, Marci was disappointed when traveling along Upper Glen Creek because she saw huge corrals and sheds marring the view. "Why do they put those there? Those buildings just ruin the scenery," Marci said to Cade.

"Did you have milk and butter on your table this morning?"

"Of course."

"Right here is where it came from. It's a dairy farm. You have to remember we're a long way from everything out here, and we have to do with what we have. Back at the fort—I didn't show you the root cellars and the icehouses and the greenhouses that are heated with steam from the thermal pools. It's not so bad in the summertime when all the people are in and out, but in the winter, we become our own little microcosm."

"I'd love to be here then. Back in the Catskills where I was raised, I loved the snow, and in the winter this would be a true wonderland."

"Has Fan given you any idea when you're leaving? Maybe she plans to spend the winter."

"She has mentioned staying until September, so we'll be here at least until then."

"So we only have two months for sure," Cade said.

"Two months for what?"

"Two months to—oh, I don't know. Two months to get lots of pictures."

"Cade," F. Jay called. "Do you think we can get to Bighorn Pass? The larkspurs and the clematis should be blooming, and we've not had the opportunity to get many flora shots."

"I'll find a place where the wagon can cross the river, and I'll be right back." Cade jumped up on Rowdy and urged the horse to a gallop.

"What was that all about?" Frances asked when she brought her equipment to the carriage.

"I don't know. He just asked me how long I thought we were going to stay."

"Oh dear, is he getting tired of having us here? We haven't even seen the best scenery yet!"

"I don't think that was it." As Marci began taking her camera off the tripod, all the while she kept her eye on the retreating figure.

THIRTEEN

The next morning when Cade showed up at the appointed time, he saw, instead of the larger carriage, a much smaller buggy with a single horse tied off to one of the elk antlers. F. Jay was standing by the fence with folded arms.

"That poor little horse is going to have a hard time if he has the three of you and all your equipment to pull." Cade dismounted and tied his horse beside the buggy.

"There won't be three of us today. Only two are going out."

"All right, I can look out for two as well as three."

"Lieutenant, I've been in the park since the seventies, and I know it like the back of my hand. So, there's really no need for you to follow me around all the time."

"Mr. Haynes, until I get orders from Captain Anderson to the contrary, I think—"

"Hold on." Haynes raised a hand. "Let me finish my comment. What I was about to say is, there's no need for you to follow me around. So I have a proposal. Suppose I take Frances with me and leave Marci in your hands? She's proven, to both Fan and me, that she's a capable photographer. I see no need for the three of us to be taking the same pictures. I think this project would be better served by having us separate, at least into two teams. I know that's asking a lot of you to take a novice in hand, but I do think it would be more productive."

"Let me get this straight. You want me to be a personal guide for Marci?"

"Yes, that's the idea, or if you would prefer, you can go with Fan and I'll go with Marci."

Cade could barely contain a smile and fought hard to keep his expression neutral. "I don't see that it would in any way be contrary to my orders if the two women went their separate ways."

"I think you should go up by Indian Creek, maybe as far as Dome Mountain, but, Cade, I don't have to tell you, watch out for the grizzly bears. It's a little late for mating season, but there may be a stray sow someplace, so be careful."

"If we're going to Dome Mountain, wouldn't it be better if we left the buggy behind and just got a horse for Marci?"

"You're probably right. If you can get an army horse for her, I'll have George load the camera equipment on old Dolly. That little burro knows every inch of this park, and no matter where you go, she'll trail for you."

❧❧❧

When Haynes went back into his studio, Frances was standing at a table examining some of the pictures from the last couple of days.

"So, did you arrange for the young lieutenant to have some private time with our Marci?"

"I did."

"And how did he take it?"

Haynes smiled. "I believe it met with his approval."

Fan chuckled. "You make a good cupid, F. Jay."

Haynes shook his head. "No, no, you are the cupid, I'm just the arrow. If we've made a big mistake, just remember, this was your idea."

"F. Jay said you and I are going out separately today," Marci said a few minutes later when she came outside.

"Yes, I hope you don't mind."

"No." Marci's mouth spread into a smile. "I don't mind at all."

"F. Jay wants us to go over by Indian Creek, maybe as far as Dome Mountain. If we go there, I think we'd do better on horseback—that is, if you would want to ride a horse?"

"I'd love to do that. It seems the only riding I do around Washington is on my bicycle, and it's been years since I was on a horse."

"Good, I'll have the stable sergeant pick a horse for you."

"Would that be Sergeant McKay?"

"It is."

Marci smiled. "Then, I know I'll have the best horse in the stable. But now I should go change clothes. I take it you don't have many sidesaddles."

"That's right."

Cade watched Marci return to the house. He had to admit, he was looking forward to this day having Marci to himself, although he had to remind himself that this was not a pleasure outing. She would be expected to get some good pictures, and he would make certain she did.

As Cade stood out front waiting, Haynes and Frances came out, carrying cameras and tripods.

"We'll miss you today," Frances said when she saw Cade. "But I think Marci needs some time by herself. It will give her confidence in her work."

"Where will you be going?" Cade asked.

"I think we'll go down to Obsidian Cliff and then set up by Beaver Lake," F. Jay said.

Just then George Haynes appeared, leading a burro loaded with parfleches containing film and equipment. The tripod was strapped to the top of the frame. "Good morning, Lieutenant. Mama packed a lunch for you and Marci when she heard you were going off the main road. She said you might not be near any of the lunch stations."

"Thanks, George. Your mama's very thoughtful." Cade took a cloth bag and attached it to his saddle horn.

"All right, Cade. She's in your hands. I expect you to take care of her," Frances said, and she and F. Jay climbed into the buggy that was still standing in front of the studio.

"I will, ma'am."

Just as Haynes and Frances drove off, Marci came back outside, dressed for the day. She was wearing denim trousers and a red flannel shirt with a broad-brimmed hat shading her face. Her hair was hanging in one long braid, just as it had been the day the photographs were made at Trophy Point.

"Where's a photographer when I need one?" Cade asked.

Marci furrowed her brow. "I'm a photographer. Don't you think I'm good enough?"

"Of course I do. It's just that I'd like a picture of you just the way you look right now."

A warmth began to radiate throughout her body as she recalled the time the last picture had been taken, and the kisses they had shared. Two kisses, one under Kissing Rock, and the other in her room.

"Let's head over to the stable and pick up a horse for you. This is Dolly, and she'll be doing all the hard work for us." Cade handed the burro's lead rope to Marci.

"Will my horse be as good as Rowdy?"

"Impossible. You know there is no such animal."

Cade and Marci and the animals walked across the parade ground to the stable. Neither spoke to one another, each aware of what this day represented. They had been together often since Marci had arrived at the park, but they had never been completely alone. Today would be a first.

When they reached the stable, the stable sergeant came out to meet them, saluting Cade as he approached. "Good morning, Lieutenant, Miss Winters."

"Good morning, Sergeant McKay," Marci replied.

"Sergeant, I want you to draw a well-mannered horse for the lady."

"Yes, sir." McKay went back into the stable. He returned a few minutes later, leading a horse the color of copper. "Here you go, Lieutenant, I saddled Cinnamon for the lady. He's about as well mannered a horse as we have in the regiment."

"Thank you, Sergeant."

McKay held the horse while Marci mounted with such ease and grace that Cade saw quickly that she was an accomplished horsewoman.

Once Marci was mounted, Cade swung into his own saddle and, holding the line that was attached to Dolly, nudged Rowdy out of the stable yard. Marci turned Cinnamon toward Cade, then followed him out of the post at a trot.

Indian Creek was about ten miles from the fort, and they covered that distance in just under two hours.

"This is where F. Jay suggested we set up," Cade said as he slipped off Rowdy. He took Cinnamon's reins and held them as Marci dismounted, then he tied the two horses and the burro to a willow that was growing near the creek. "I don't see much to take a picture of, but maybe your artist eye can see something I don't."

"Of course there are things to take." Marci removed her equipment and set it up to start taking pictures. She took her first several pictures of Dome Mountain. "I can't believe it."

"Can't believe what?"

"That mountain, it looks so close, and yet look at all the snow. You would think that, being that close to the snow, it would be cold here, but it's actually quite warm."

Marci moved the tripod several times, getting pictures not only of the mountain, but of Indian Creek and the vegetation.

"What kind of plant is that?" she asked. "Oh, that's silly of me, I don't expect you to know."

"But I do know. Part of my job is to be a park interpreter, answering any question a tourist might ask. I know that this is alpine timothy, and this is yarrow, and this is mule's ear." He picked one of each of the varieties he had named and gave them to Marci.

Marci put the small bouquet in the band of her hat and placed it on her head. "I hope you don't get bored while you're waiting."

"Take your time." Cade reached into his saddle pouch. "If you promise me you'll not wander too far from this spot, I'm going down to the creek and try to catch a fish." He pulled out a piece of string and attached a hook.

Marci watched as Cade walked toward the creek. He found a flat rock and, leaning over the water, began to dangle the string. Marci had to smile. Cade, the strong, muscular man, looked to be enjoying his pursuit with childlike delight. In that instant, she held her camera steady and snapped several pictures of Cade. When he tired of his attempt to catch a fish, he sat back on the stone, keeping a vigilant eye on their surroundings. Marci thought his expression was commanding and masculine. Cade McDowell was a handsome man.

She remembered what F. Jay had said about Thomas Moran using the Jackson photographs as templates. She was sure he meant for scenic studies, but if she could develop these pictures herself, no one would know how many she had taken of Cade. When this excursion was over and she had to go back to Washington, she would paint a portrait. Then she, too, would have a proper picture to set by her bed.

The morning passed quickly, and before long she saw Cade pull out a watch from his pocket.

"Hey, Marci! Do you know it's past lunchtime?" Cade called. "Aren't you hungry?"

"I'm sorry. I guess I got carried away with my work. Pick us out a spot for a picnic and I'll grab the lunch bag from your saddle." She left her camera and ran back to the horses.

Cade looked around and found a grassy spot near some pine trees. As he did, he saw a peregrine falcon swoop by, and he suspected Marci would want to take a picture, so he retrieved her camera and tripod.

"It's too bad we didn't bring a tablecloth," Marci said as she sat down beside Cade, and opened the drawstring on the bag. "What do you think Lily fixed for us?"

"Let me think. A ham sandwich, a hard-boiled egg, and a dill pickle."

Marci pulled out exactly what Cade had suggested. "That's not fair, you looked!"

As Marci was taking out the lunch, Cade stretched out on his side, supporting his head on his hand, his body close to hers. His hat lay beside him, and his hair, dampened by the warmth of the summer day, was forming haphazard curls against his forehead.

She reached out to brush the dark brown hair aside, and when she did, he caught her hand. She was captivated by the dark brown eyes, as his expression changed from one of teasing and lightheartedness to undeniable desire. Her glance dropped to his lips, which were full and sensuous. Without a word being said, she knew he was going to kiss her, and she leaned toward him in expectation, her mouth suddenly going dry in anticipation.

Their lips met in a warm, slow kiss. It was neither demanding nor hesitant, but comfortable and sensual because it was equally shared. After a long moment, during which his lips continued to hold hers by no other means than their velvet sweetness, they separated. An infectious flame in his eyes ignited a growing fire in her own body. He reached for her and pulled her across his chest as he lay back on the soft grass.

He reclaimed her lips, and she returned his kiss with a hunger that surpassed anything she had ever before felt. She opened her mouth on his, giving as much as taking, as she sensed his strength beneath her. Abruptly, he sat up, forcing her to rise also. For a moment she wanted to cry out, to tell him no, she didn't want him to stop.

But her cry was stillborn when she realized what he was doing. He was unbuttoning his shirt with hands that moved purposefully. When he got to his saber belt, he pulled the shirt from his pants and loosened the buckle, allowing the belt to fall to the ground. He took off his shirt and placed it on the ground and then lay back again, once more pulling her to him.

But Marci wanted more. Cade was still wearing the army-issue summer underwear that made the wool shirt bearable as it rubbed against his skin. Before she lowered her body to his, she unbuttoned the union suit and pushed it aside, running her fingers through the chest hair that began at his neck and disappeared below his waistband. Cade withdrew his arms from the sleeves and pulled her to him, as her cotton flannel shirt created a friction on her now-erect nipples that even her thin-gauze camisole did not prevent. His mouth moved to her lips but she withdrew.

"Wait," she said in a whisper. She rose to a sitting position, her legs straddling his body as she began to unbutton her shirt, doing it with much deliberation. She watched as Cade's eyes followed her every move, his breathing becoming more and more ragged. When she unbuttoned the last button, with only her thin camisole to cover her nakedness, Cade grabbed her hands.

"Marci, do you understand that there's no turning back?"

Marci considered Cade's comment. Had she gone beyond the point where she could turn back? It wasn't Cade who was asking for more; it was her own body that was betraying her—urging her to experience an act that was as old as time itself. Here, in this beautiful wilderness, she understood the story of the Garden of Eden. Cade was Adam and she was Eve, the temptress. Sitting astride Cade's body, she began to sense and then feel that he was as powerless to stop this as she was.

There were only the two of them. No one would

interrupt, no one would tell lies about her. Only Cade and she would know what had happened on this grassy spot under the pine trees, and she trusted Cade implicitly. She intuitively knew he would never hurt her, not physically, not mentally. Now was the time to satisfy the hunger—the desire—the ache that was consuming her body.

No, there was no turning back.

"Yes, I want this more than I ever thought possible." Her dark eyes were filled with longing as they locked onto Cade's while she removed her shirt, tossing it to the side. Now only her camisole was in place, and Cade, recognizing the gift she was offering, raised his hands and began untying the lacings that held it together. Marci kept her hands still as the gentle breeze wafted across her bare skin.

When the last of her upper garments was removed, Cade took her breasts in his hands, fondling them as if they were perfect globes. His thumb began a slow, sensuous circular motion, moving ever closer to the now-straining nipple. When he finally reached it, touching it ever so lightly, a ripple of excitement coursed through her body. The light touch was maddening and she thrust her chest outward, hoping he would satisfy the aching she was feeling.

When she did that, a seductive smile crossed his face. "Are you asking for more?"

"Yes, Cade, I want more. I can't describe what is happening to me. It's like there's a tingling in the pit of my stomach."

"Maybe I can make it better." He pulled her to him and with his tongue began stroking her engorged nipples.

When Marci could stand it no more, she lifted her breast, forcing it against his lips, and he took her offering into his mouth and began sucking the nipple. At first it was as gentle as the tongue had been, but it turned into an urgency that caused Marci to collapse on him crying out in agony. He wrapped his arms around her, pulling her to his chest and holding her in an embrace that set her afire.

Marci lifted her head and began to kiss Cade with an insatiable hunger.

"You know there's more," Cade said. "Are you ready for this?"

Marci looked at him, and because she was unable to speak, she responded with a nod of her head.

Laying her down, he began to unbutton her trousers, and when he tried to push them down, she facilitated it by lifting her hips from the ground. She found charges of excitation coursing through her as she thought of what was to come, but before Cade could lower her jeans, he raised his head abruptly. He lifted his finger to his mouth signaling for her to be quiet, and then she heard what had gotten his attention.

One of the horses whinnied, and Dolly hee-hawed.

"Is somebody coming?" Marci asked as she grabbed for her camisole.

Then they both knew what was bothering the animals. They heard a low growl as a big brown bear appeared not a hundred yards from them. They watched in suspended animation as the bear began to slap aside fallen trees, moving them as easily as a man would pick up sticks. When the grizzly had found a cache of ants, it sat back on its haunches, much as a dog would do when begging for a morsel of food. The bear began eating the ants, scooping them up with its claws.

Marci grabbed for her camera and began taking pictures rapidly, the sound of the shutter getting the bear's attention. It stopped and raised its nose into the air, trying to get the scent.

Then both Marci and Cade heard the sound of crashing trees from somewhere in the woods, and the bear, hearing it as well, quickly lost interest in the sound of the camera or the ants. Getting on all fours, the bear started running toward Cade and Marci.

"Let's get out of here!" Cade shouted, more loudly than he had intended, as he pulled Marci along with him.

Almost instantly, they saw the cause of the bear's agitation. Another bear, half again the size of the first one, came charging out of the trees in pursuit of the first one. This beautiful bear had white-tipped fur, giving the animal a blond coat. When it caught up with the smaller bear, there was a growl that was closer to a roar, as both bears plunged into Indian Creek.

All at once the pursuit stopped, and the two bears seemed to prance around one another.

Again, Marci focused her camera and began taking pictures.

"No, Marci, let's get out of here before they get our scent." Cade grabbed their clothes and the tripod and raced across the open meadow to where the horses were tied. Cade was amazed that when he reached the willows, he was somewhat winded;

but Marci was on his heels, hardly panting at all. "That could have been a disaster."

"Why do you say that?"

"The grizzly boar was in pursuit of a sow who apparently hasn't mated yet. If they would have gotten our scent—well, let's just say, I'm glad they didn't."

A broad grin crossed Marci's face.

"I'm serious. It wouldn't have been funny," Cade said more sternly than he intended.

"I was just thinking what would have happened if the bears hadn't come along."

Cade's eyes filled with desire as he returned her smile. "As much as I would love to finish what we started, this is not the time." He placed a tender kiss on her lips. "Put on your clothes. We'd better get back."

They got to the Haynes household before dark at about the same time Frances and F. Jay were arriving.

"I can't wait to get in the darkroom," Marci said as she jumped off Cinnamon. "It was an amazing day and I know I have fantastic pictures!"

"That's what I like to see," F. Jay said. "Enthusiasm for your work sells pictures. But what was so fantastic about Dome Mountain?"

"It wasn't the mountain; it was what happened by the creek. While Cade and I were eating lunch, a brown bear got within a hundred yards of us. She was just sitting there eating ants and I thought she looked like a fuzzy toy."

"Cade, how did you let a bear get that close to you?" F. Jay asked with a sharp rebuke.

"I'm sorry," Cade said as he lowered his gaze.

"F. Jay, nothing happened. They're back safe and sound, and as you said, great pictures sell," Frances said. "It's late, but if you don't mind, I want to see some of my prints, too. Tell Lily that Marci and I are going to be working late tonight and we'll grab a snack later."

"Thanks, Cade, for a wonderful day," Marci said, trying to convey to Cade through her intonation and her expression that she was not referring to her photo outing. "I'll see you first thing in the morning."

"Good night, Marci." Cade took the reins to Cinnamon and began to walk away.

When Marci and Frances were out of earshot, F. Jay called out to Cade, "Lieutenant, let this be a lesson to you. Don't forget that your sole purpose in escorting Miss Winters is to look out for her safety."

"It won't happen again, sir." Cade watched F. Jay turn and walk toward his house. The thought of the bears, especially the raging boar, getting so close to Marci caused him to shudder. He hadn't just said the words. He would not let her be put in jeopardy again. He loved her too much for that.

He loved her too much for that.

There was no denying his feelings. For over a year now, he had fantasized about Marci Winters. Every night before he'd turned off his lamp, he'd looked at her picture, waiting and hoping she would answer his letter. Now he had something better than a letter . . . he had her in his care.

Marci waited for her turn in the darkroom as Frances developed the pictures she had taken.

"Look at this one," Frances said, calling attention to one particular photograph as she pulled it out of the chemical bath. It was of a coach, overflowing with tourists, and a hay wagon meeting on a narrow road. The coach was so close to the edge of a steep incline that a misstep by one of the horses could have precipitated its fall. On the inside, the wagon was so close to the cliff that its wheels were almost scraping the wall. The hubs of both the wagon and the coach were inches apart. Even though the photograph captured only a second in time, tension and drama filled it as the drivers negotiated their passage. The driver of the coach was looking not toward the drop-off, but at the hubs.

"Oh," Marci said. "Those poor people. They had to be scared to death."

"That's what you want your photographs to do—cause people to empathize with their subjects. Now, let's see what you've got with the bear pictures."

Marci looked at her negatives, picking out the ones she thought were the best to print. She hadn't realized how many pictures she had taken of Cade, but she put those aside, wanting to print them in private. She looked carefully at the negatives of the bears, analyzing them for structure and drama. One of the bear eating the ants was particularly good, and the other one she chose was of the moment the larger bear had just stood on his hind legs.

"You're going to like this one," Marci said as she removed the second picture. "I think the person who looks at this will be able to imagine the blood-curdling roar that the bear is making."

Frances had many compliments for the first pic-

ture, of the bear sitting on her haunches eating the
ants.

"The lighting is perfect, the fallen logs counter-
balance the vertical lines of the trees, and the bear
itself looks so lovable and harmless. Yes, Marci, you
did really well."

"And here's my masterpiece." Marci handed the
second picture to Frances.

Frances took one look at it and immediately
handed it back to Marci. "You can't show that to
anybody, at least not the way you've printed it."

Marci took the picture back, somewhat confused
by Frances's reaction. What had she done wrong?
She had used the same exposure in shooting the
picture and the same chemicals in developing it.
She took it in her hand. The bears were perfectly
framed, and the look on the larger bear's face was
exactly what she had wanted to convey.

"I don't understand. What's wrong with this one?"

"A photographer never wants to make what's
going on behind the camera more important than
what's going on in front of it. What do you think
is going through my mind when I see a man's and
a woman's shirt lying on the ground, and if that
isn't evidence enough, what about this?" Frances
pointed to Marci's camisole, shown clearly in the
picture.

"Oh, Fan, I . . ."

With a little laugh, Frances put her hand on Marci's arm. "Far be it from me to condemn you, Marci.
I think it's wonderful that you and your lieutenant
seem to be getting on so well. But, it might be best

to crop these pictures before F. Jay sees them, don't
you think?"

With an embarrassed smile, Marci nodded. "Yes,
that may be best."

As Marci lay in bed that night, she looked at the moon
shadows on the wall, thinking about her bad luck.
What was wrong with her? Every time she kissed a
man, her action seemed to draw controversy.

At West Point. An innocent thing—stepping through
the sally port while Miss Nash was watching—caused
her expulsion from Wells.

At Julia's wedding. A request from Mrs. Stevenson
to retrieve headache powders and the subsequent
fiasco with Stanton had caused her "banishment"
to Yellowstone.

And now today, at Indian Creek. This incident
had been her own doing. Cade McDowell had not
put her in a compromising position. It was she,
Marci Winters, who had removed her shirt and
thrust her breast into his mouth. It was she who
allowed herself to be brought to such an emotional
state that, but for the interruption by the bear, she
would gladly have given her virginity to Cade.

What did she really know about Cade? The only
thing she knew about his family was that both his
parents were dead—his father with General Custer
and his mother in Michigan. The only person in the
world with whom he seemed to have any connection was Libbie Custer.

Then there were his feelings about the army. In
her opinion, the army with all its regulations and

ceremony was his surrogate family. He was first, last, and always a soldier. No, make that an officer. How could any woman compete with an institution if she wanted him to love her?

If she wanted him to love her?

Just by formulating the question, did that imply that she loved Cade? She didn't know the answer. *Faire l'amour* was what she had heard it called in Paris, when a man and a woman had *les relations sexuelles.* But were making love and having a sexual relationship the same thing? This afternoon she would have given herself to Cade with no regrets. By contrast, she had never even considered anything beyond kissing with Stanton Caldwell.

Stanton Caldwell. How easily she had put him out of her mind, as easily as she had dropped the ring and discarded the shredded note he had sent her from the convention center.

Yet she had tried to convince Stanton to marry her. Not once but twice. Both times had been in her attempt to save face. If she fell in love with Cade, would it be true love, the kind that lasts a lifetime, or would it be an attempt by her to once again save face? Thanks to her inattention to details in her photograph, Frances undoubtedly knew exactly what Marci had been doing.

Marci turned away from the moon shadows, closed her eyes, and, troubled, sought sleep.

Cade was standing at the window of his room in the bachelor officers' quarters looking out across the parade ground. In the moonlight, he saw a sentry walking his lonely post, but the sentry wasn't the object of his study. He was looking beyond the sentry, beyond the parade ground, at the house that stood gleaming white in the moon that was three-quarters full and bright on this last day of June.

F. Jay Haynes was right to call him out for his actions this afternoon. Had anything happened to Marci in his care, he would have been subject to dereliction-of-duty charges. And that charge could have led to his court-martial. What was he thinking when he allowed their kisses to go so far?

It had begun so innocently. He was stretched out eating a sandwich when she had brushed his hair off his brow. What had been so erotic about that simple action?

But it was erotic. From the moment she had touched him, he had known. When he looked into her eyes, it was as if she were telegraphing him, *Kiss me, please kiss me.* And he had wanted it, too.

When she'd removed her shirt, he had cautioned her that there was no turning back. She said she wanted this more than she ever thought possible. She had specifically said *this*. She did not say, I want *you*.

Cade turned away from the window and, sitting down on his bed, took his head in his hands. Was this woman trying to use him? Was she wanting him to take her, to punish another man?

His mind was instantly transported back to Washington, to the day he had been delivering the animals to the zoo. He remembered that she had asked him, *Will I see you again?* and when he'd returned to make arrangements, she was in the arms of another man. Then she walked away without looking back. He had been dismissed as artfully as if she were his superior officer.

Just then the sound of "Taps" drifted across the quad. He knew what he had to do, and it would be one of the most difficult decisions he had ever made. Tomorrow, he would go see Captain Anderson and ask to be taken off the detail. Cade took one last look at Marci's picture, then turned off his lamp and crawled into bed.

FOURTEEN

The next morning Marci was dreading coming down for breakfast. Had Frances told F. Jay what she had discovered about Marci's outing yesterday? As it turned out, her fears were unnecessary. The Haynes boys had been told about Marci's encounter with the bears and they had many questions that she was happy to answer, anything to deflect attention from the real mess she knew she had created.

"All right, boys, enough bear talk," F. Jay said. "But Marci's experience yesterday tells me we should take a different route today. If we go east over toward Tower Junction and Pebble Creek, we'll more than likely run into elk and moose. And if we're lucky, we might see a buffalo. Have either of you ever seen one?"

"I've seen buffalo at the Washington Zoo, and I must say, I wasn't impressed. They were dirty and smelly," Marci said, but then she remembered Cade's comment about how majestic they were in their natural habitat. "But I'm sure it's much different when you see them in the wild."

"They are magnificent beasts, and it's in large part because of the buffalo that the army is at Yellowstone. Do you know that there are probably less than a couple hundred animals in this entire country?"

"That just makes our expedition all the more important," Frances said. "If buffalo become extinct, we'll need a photographic record of what they were like in the wild."

"You're right," F. Jay said. "But now we'd better stop lollygagging. You know Cade's out there waiting on us, even as we speak."

At the mention of Cade's name, Marci unconsciously shifted her gaze toward Frances to gauge her reaction. Frances nodded her head slightly but made no other response. Marci took a deep breath and gave Frances a half smile in gratitude. Marci had vowed to herself that she would put some distance between her and Cade for a few days, and she needed to steel her resolve.

Marci found that denim trousers were more practical than a skirt for the places they were exploring, so once again she was attired in the jeans. She chose a more feminine blouse than the red flannel shirt she had worn yesterday. Her main reason for doing it was so neither Cade nor Frances would be reminded of yesterday's transgression.

When she stepped out on the porch, F. Jay was standing by the fence talking to Frances, but there was no Cade.

"What did you do to Cade yesterday?" F. Jay said with a chuckle. "He's always Johnny-on-the-spot, and today he's late."

Marci didn't have to respond because out of the corner of her eye she saw an officer coming from the stable. She thought it strange that Cade was not riding Rowdy. As the officer drew closer, she recognized Lieutenant Nance.

"Good morning, Lieutenant. Where's Cade this morning? I hope he's not in the infirmary?" F. Jay asked.

"No, sir. Captain Anderson asked that I relieve Lieutenant McDowell on this detail."

When she heard the words, Marci was crestfallen. She had made up her mind that she was going to put some distance between the two of them, but she'd never dreamed that it would be this drastic. She was sure Frances had not told F. Jay about Marci's dalliance yesterday, and at breakfast it had been assumed that Cade would be waiting for them.

That meant only one thing: Cade had requested to be withdrawn. She stifled a knot that was forming in her throat. What had she done?

Fort Yellowstone, July 4

The army celebrated Independence Day with much pomp and ceremony. They played "Patriotic Numbers," according to the program, Captain Anderson and Commissioner John Meldrum both gave long addresses, and the cavalry unit presented a "Mounted Drill." Marci and Frances, along with the Haynes family, joined many other civilians—from workers to tourists—to watch the mounted cavalrymen perform.

Cade was the officer in charge of the mounted drill. Marci watched with keen interest as he took center stage, dressed in his finest uniform, as were all the soldiers, and gave the commands in a loud, authoritative voice.

The demonstration continued for half an hour, with horses leaping over obstacles and performing intricate maneuvers, all at a gallop, and the men holding their drawn sabers high. When the drill ended, the men returned to their original position of troop front, in which the men and horses were once again in one long line, side by side, facing Cade.

"First Sergeant!" Cade called.

The troop first sergeant left the formation and rode up to Cade, where he saluted.

Cade returned the salute. "Dismiss the troops, First Sergeant."

Cade galloped off the field before the first sergeant gave the order as Marci watched until he disappeared behind the stable.

"That was exciting," F. Jay said. "I wish we would have thought to get pictures."

"We should have. Lieutenant McDowell has so much bearing about him. It's like he exudes manliness, but it's not an act with him," Frances said. "I like Lieutenant Nance, but it's not the same when he escorts us. Cade made me feel like this detail was every bit as important as anything else he might be asked to do, but Lieutenant Nance—well, for the three days he's been with us, I get the impression he thinks we're a nuisance."

"I noticed that, too," F. Jay said. "I think I'll speak to Captain Anderson and see if we can get Cade back, but before I do, Marci, you don't have any objection, do you?"

"No," Marci said, looking toward the stable for any sign of Cade. "I'd like that. I'd like it very much."

"All right, I'll see what I can do."

For the rest of the day, Frances and Marci watched the activities. There were potato-sack races, tug-of-war pulls, and ball games, but at no time did Marci see Cade after the cavalry drill. It was as if he had disappeared.

Cade had seen Marci sitting on the bleachers watching the horse drill, and he had felt her eyes boring into him. What must she think of him? Did she blame him for what had happened at Indian Creek? Did she know that *he* had asked to be taken off the detail?

More than anything else, he wished he had someone in his life he could talk to about this, but there was no one. This kind of emotional turmoil was not something a man spoke of with another man. He supposed he could discuss it with Captain Anderson, as his commanding officer, but then he would have to tell what had happened between him and Marci. And that was definitely off-limits. He would never divulge that, for the protection of her reputation, and for the possibility of jeopardizing his career.

The regulations and structure of the army exacerbated his problem. At this moment, he could almost wish that he weren't in the army. Things were becoming complicated for him, and being in the army made it even more so.

He needed to get away for a while, from the park, the post, the army, even from Marci. He needed to go someplace where he could think, without external distractions. He knew there really was no such place, but perhaps a long ride would serve the momentary purpose.

Up in his room, Cade opened his trunk and took out a pair of jeans, a brown shirt, and a leather vest. It had been over a year since he'd last worn civilian clothes. He had bought the clothes when he had spent the month with Cass Conrad, right after they had graduated.

"What do you mean you don't own any mufti?" Cass had teased. "You can't go fishing in uniform. Why, no self-respecting catfish would let himself be caught by someone in an army uniform."

Cade smiled as he looked at the big, silver buckle on his Western gun belt. Strapping it on, he removed his pistol from its army-issue holster and took a look at himself in the mirror. The man he saw looking back could have been a cowboy just in off the range.

Thus attired, he decided to go for a ride with no particular destination. He wanted to be by himself for a while to think about what he was going to do about Marci. By the end of the tourist season, she would be going back to Washington, and he would be posted at another fort most likely within a year.

As forts went, Yellowstone was considered a plum assignment, but what if he was posted to Fort Missoula, or Fort Harrison or Fort Custer? These were isolated billets where if he asked her to join him, she would be separated from any of her kind.

If he asked her to join him. What a selfish thought. Why couldn't he voice the words *if he asked her to marry him*? Deep inside, he knew the answer. He had never been around any married couple, and he didn't know how a husband would act. He was scared.

He and his mother had lived in near poverty— she stooping over a board, ironing other men's shirts from morning till night, and he mucking out horse stalls for as long as he could remember. As the wife of an army officer, there wouldn't be much money available. Hadn't he told her that laundress was one of the most sought-after positions because of its pay?

And then there was always the threat of leaving a wife a widow, to fend for herself. Both his mother and Libbie Custer had been left, and until a friend spoke up and demanded a pension, both women were left nearly destitute. Could he do that to Marci?

No, he thought too much of her, but then he amended his thinking. He *loved* her too much to put her through what his mother had endured.

Cade was riding north, and when he reached Gardiner, he decided he needed a drink, the park being dry. He chose one of the many saloons that were friendly to soldiers, and tying Rowdy off outside, he pushed through the bat-wing doors. A large banner was stretched across the mirror behind the bar.

HAPPY BIRTHDAY AMERICA

"What'll it be, cowboy?" the bartender, a towel tossed over his shoulder, asked, coming down to him.

Cade smiled when he heard himself called a cowboy. That was a first for him. "A beer."

"Would you like to try our new Michelob?"

"No, just draw it from the keg."

The bartender put a beer in front of Cade, picked up the nickel, then moved to another customer.

Cade's thoughts were troubled as he took a long draw from his mug. It had been a long time since he'd had a drink, and it tasted good.

"Hello, honey," a woman's voice said.

Turning, Cade saw a woman, scantily dressed and with a painted face. She might have been pretty at one time, before the dissipation of her profession had set in.

"Hello," he said, lifting his glass in a salute. The hello was a courteous response only, implying no interest in anything she might have to offer.

The woman didn't take the hint. "Honey, did you come to celebrate the Fourth of July? We can make our own fireworks," she added with a high-pitched, cackling laugh.

"No fireworks here." Cade took another swallow of his beer.

The practiced smile left the woman's face. "You don't know what you're passing up," she said as she moved on down the bar.

Maybe he didn't know what he was passing up, but he knew one thing for sure. Only one woman could make things better for him, and that woman wasn't a bar girl. Then he saw a large lithograph on the wall. At the bottom were the words *Custer's Last Fight,* and below that, the name Anheuser-Busch Brewing Company.

Cade picked up his beer and walked over to look. Custer was clearly evident in the middle of the picture, which showed soldiers, some standing, some on their knees, many already dead, in a desperate struggle with a horde of Indians swirling around them.

"We just got that. Pretty dramatic, ain't it?" The questioner was sitting at the nearby piano, but he wasn't playing.

"If you like to see a slaughter." For a long time, Cade studied the figures in the picture. He wondered if the artist had been at Fort Lincoln. Did he know the men who followed Custer? If he did, which one of these men was Cade's father?

He would never know. Except for Libbie, no one knew anything about his background, least of all Cade.

He missed his mother. She didn't live long enough to see him graduate from West Point. His mother had always told him that he could be anything he wanted, and he had believed that being an officer in the army was what he wanted. He still believed that, but now he wanted something more. He wanted Marci; he wanted her to be a part of this life.

But what did he have to offer someone who had lived a life of privilege—someone who was personally acquainted with such people as the secretary of war, the vice president, even the president? Was he being foolish?

Then he got an idea, and he smiled. Libbie Custer. She was the only link to his past, and she could also be the link to his future. Why hadn't he thought of her before? Aunt Libbie would give him better advice than anyone else could.

Tossing back the beer, he left the saloon and mounted Rowdy, heading for the depot at Cinnabar. He knew Aunt Libbie was in New York because she was spending the summer at her friend's writers and artists' colony at Onteora. He would send her a telegram.

No trains were due to arrive or leave for several hours, so the depot in Cinnabar was nearly deserted. When Cade went inside, he heard the rhythmic clicking of a telegraph instrument. Cade stepped up to the Western Union window and waited as the telegrapher, a thin, bald-headed man, wearing a visor and garters around his sleeves, transcribed the incoming message. When the clicking stopped, the telegrapher clicked something back, then stood up and approached the window.

"Something I can do for you, mister?"

"I'd like to send a telegram."

"All right." The man handed Cade a pencil and a pad. "Print it very clear, so I can read it."

Cade took the pad and pencil and nodded, then turned away from the window.

"Where're you goin'?"

"To find a place to sit. I've got more than I can say standing here."

"It's your money."

Cade found a long bench over in the corner of the waiting room, and sitting there, he held the pad on his lap and began to write.

> *Dear Aunt Libbie,*
>
> *Don't let the telegram frighten you. I am well, but I need to talk to someone and you're the only family I have. If you recall, I met a woman at the Spring Hop at West Point. Her name is Marci Winters, and by a strange quirk of fate, she is working at Yellowstone as a photographer. My lucky assignment is as her escort detail.*
>
> *Marci comes from Washington society and power, her father being in the Treasury Department, and therein is my problem. Despite our diverse backgrounds, I have fallen in love with her. She has done nothing by word or deed that would suggest that she is even aware of the gap between us: however, it is a gap that I fear may be insurmountable. I am but a second lieutenant, what can I possibly offer her but my love? I seek your advice. I don't know what to do next.*
>
> *I look forward to your post.*
> *Love, Cade*

The telegrapher counted the words, then let out a low whistle. "You sure you don't want to cut this down a bit?"

"No, sir, I want it sent just as it is, word for word."

"All right, if you say so. But that's going to cost eight dollars and ten cents."

Cade winced. That was five days' pay. "Just send it." He handed over the money.

That night as Cade reached the top of an incline on his return to Yellowstone, he could see a pyrotechnic display bursting in the sky. By the time he rode into the company area, the fireworks were over. With nobody on duty at the stable, Cade took care of Rowdy himself, giving him an extra handful of oats before taking the time to rub him down. When he left the stable, he heard the band playing music, and he remembered the dance at the pavilion of the hotel. He had been looking forward to it, before he had . . . before he had lost his head.

If an officer lost his head in battle, it could mean his life, as well as those of every man in his command. The poster in the Gardiner saloon came to mind as a bloody reminder of the truth of his thought.

There was no doubt, he wanted to be at the dance. He wanted to see Marci, to hold her in his arms, but he didn't trust himself. Making his way to the shower room, he took off his clothes and stepped into the stream of water that was piped directly from one of the hot springs. He stayed until the tank of cold water that made the hot water tolerable was exhausted and his skin was pink. Picking up a towel, he didn't bother to dress as he walked down the hallway to his room. As he had done for many nights before, he reached for Marci's picture and held it in his hands.

"You're so stupid. You've spent the whole day

acting like some lovesick fool when you know she's not a quarter mile away." Jumping up, he dressed in a clean uniform and, with hurried steps, walked across the parade ground to the hotel.

Marci was aware the moment Cade stepped into the pavilion, even though the gaslights were turned low. She was dancing with a private who was barely eighteen.

"I've seen you all over the park," the private said, "and I even bought some of your pictures to send to my ma."

"You should get your own camera. Anybody can take a snapshot now with the Kodaks that are available. And here at Yellowstone, you have hundreds of opportunities to take all kinds of pictures."

"Mr. Haynes said you took my favorite. It was a bear sittin' up just as pretty as you please. Looked like he was eatin' or somethin'."

Marci took a gulp of air. "It was just one bear, right?"

"Yes'm."

Just then there was a tap on the private's shoulder. "Excuse me, Private Gilmore, may I cut in? I'd like to dance with Miss Winters."

"Yes, sir." The private came to a complete stop and clicked his heels. His hand rose to salute.

"Not tonight, Private." Cade took Marci's hand in his. "I guess I didn't ask you if you wanted me to cut in."

"I believe I've danced with half the soldiers at this post, so one more won't make any difference."

"Oh," Cade said, taken aback by her comment. "I didn't mean to . . ."

"Lily explained it as being part of the noblesse oblige," Marci said with a lilting laugh. "She said it was every woman's obligation to spread her dances around because the ratio of men to women is so one-sided."

Cade stopped on the dance floor and, displaying an amused smile, cocked his head. "Did Mrs. Haynes suggest that madam should share anything else besides her dances?"

"Why, Lieutenant McDowell, I do believe you're jealous." Marci gently laughed.

Just then the music stopped.

"I believe we should step away from this crowd of peons and give the lady's feet a rest, don't you think?"

"That would be good."

Cade took her hand and led her off the dance floor. They left the pavilion, and crossing the road, they walked in the direction of the lower Terraces, where Cade found a wooden bench.

"I've missed you. It's not the same with Lieutenant Nance."

"Jeff's a good man."

"Cade, tell me the truth. What happened? Did you ask to be relieved from escorting us?"

Cade lowered his head, the moonlight clearly illuminating his profile. "I did."

"Why?"

"Because F. Jay was right. My job was to protect you, and I let my own desires get in the way of my duty. I don't think you understand what could have happened. Bears in heat are dangerous."

"It wasn't your fault," Marci whispered.

"If I remember"—Cade turned toward Marci and lifted her chin with his finger—"you weren't holding a gun to my head."

"I wish I had one now."

"Now, that's not something a man wants to hear from his woman."

Marci was overtaken with giddiness. She had just heard Cade call her "his woman," even though she knew he had said it in jest. Ever so slowly, she began leaning toward him, her lips parted in invitation.

With no other contact but the lips, he kissed her, a lingering, sensuous kiss.

When he broke the connection, Marci went willingly into his arms. They held one another for a long moment with Cade's head resting upon hers. For the first time in his life, he felt contentment, a belonging that he couldn't put into words.

When he kissed her again, it was with all the pent-up hunger he had tried so hard to deny. What would he do when the summer was over?

On Friday of the week following the Fourth of July, Cade and Jeff Nance were called to company headquarters.

"Gentlemen," Captain Anderson said, "I have a dilemma. Haynes and his bunch have expressed dissatisfaction with your demeanor, Jeff. It seems they think you are merely tolerating the photographers. Is that true?"

"I will do my best to modify my behavior, sir."

"That's not what they want. They want Cade back. So I'm relieving you of that detail and returning you to your regular duties."

"Very well, sir."

"All right, Jeff, that'll be all."

Nance saluted, then did an about-face and left the captain's office. Captain Anderson looked back toward Cade. "Now, Cade, that brings me to you. I know that you asked to be relieved of the assignment. Is there some problem with it?"

"No problem, I'll be happy to return to the detail, sir."

"Good, that takes care of that. I understand they're planning an excursion down to the Lower Geyser Basin, which means you'll have to spend the night." Captain Anderson began shuffling through some papers on his desk. "It looks like the soldier station is full, so I expect you'll need to billet at the Fountain. If you'll get a receipt from the hotel, I'll arrange for your per diem."

"Thank you, sir."

"That'll be all. Carry on, Lieutenant."

Cade saluted, then left the office before Captain Anderson could see the smile on his face as he hurried to his quarters to fill a necessary bag for the trip. Seeing Private Seabaugh, he sent him to draw Rowdy.

"Well, if it isn't the missing lieutenant," Frances said when she saw Cade waiting by the carriage. "It's good to have you back. Lieutenant Nance was a real horse's ass. Do you know one day he put a stopwatch on us?"

"The lieutenant is nothing if not efficient."

"Well, you can't put a stopwatch on good gloaming. It happens when it happens, and the time just before sunset often creates the best photographic contrast," F. Jay added.

"I'll try not to hurry you," Cade said just as Marci was joining the group.

"Cade," she said with more delight than she intended. "If I'd known you were rejoining us, I would've been here earlier."

"That'll be the day." Frances shook her head. "You've been the last one out of bed every day this whole summer."

"But I can dress quickly."

"I wouldn't brag about that," Frances said, "or I could bring up a time when you didn't."

Marci's face flushed, but she didn't shy away from the teasing. "Maybe once or twice I could have been faster. Where are we off to today, Lieutenant?"

"I've been told we're off to the Lower Geyser Basin."

"Ah, the paint pots again. I don't understand how the most delicate colors come out of that boiling cauldron. And I can see roses or lilies or whatever I can imagine gets thrown up from them."

"Let's hope you get good pictures today," Frances said.

It was forty miles down to the Lower Geyser Basin where the Fountain Geyser was located. Often, Lily prepared a lunch for them, but F. Jay had persuaded the group to take their noon meal at the Lunch Station at Norris. This large tent was filled with tables and chairs, but the main attraction was the personality of the proprietor, Larry Mathews. He was a rather rotund man with red hair, a freckled face, and a heavy Irish accent.

"Ladies, welcome to my place. Go on upstairs and freshen up a bit, and, by golly, when you return, the best food in the park will be waitin' fer ya. Lizzie, show the pretty ladies the way," he said, beckoning to a little girl about five years old.

She led Frances and Marci "upstairs," which was really only another tent, where tourists were smoothing their hair and removing the dusters many had worn to keep the dust from accumulating on their clothes.

Next to a washbasin, Frances picked up a little bottle that had fallen to the floor. "Look, Marci, someone has lost some eau de cologne." Frances inquired if the bottle belonged to anyone in the tent at the time, and when no one claimed it, she handed it to Marci. "Here, my dear. Use this with discretion."

When Frances and Marci returned to the dining tent, true to Larry's word, the food was ready. And while the elk stew was not outstanding, it was substantial.

Larry circulated throughout the tent. "What can I get for yez? Will yez have anything else? Speak up if yez want somethin' yez don't see." All the time Larry was joking and teasing the guests.

A woman, whom he introduced as Bridget, brought out a platter of cakes that she called kisses.

Marci took one off the tray, and when she did, Larry boomed out from across the tent, "Oh, me Bridget, pass the kisses to the pretty one. We all know one is never enough."

Playing along, Marci took three cakes and handed them to the people sitting at the next table.

"I would have taken one of those," Cade said so low only Marci could hear.

"You'll have to wait."

From the Lunch Station they rode on, with F. Jay stopping along the way, first at the Congress Pool, which threw boiling water thirty feet into the air, and then the Minute Man, which true to its name erupted every thirty seconds. Each time they stopped, Cade waited patiently, never once trying to hurry them.

"Wait until you see the next one," Cade said as he helped put some of the equipment back into the carriage. "It's called the Black Growler."

The Black Growler was close to the road, in a basin about twenty feet in diameter, with three openings in the side. The openings were black, and while this wasn't technically a geyser that threw up water, the holes did emit clouds of steam that rose hundreds of feet into the air, all the while with a loud roaring and hissing sound.

"This is unbelievable! It's so loud!" Marci said, raising her voice to make herself heard over the roar.

"Engineers say if we could harness this steam, it would produce forty-five thousand horsepower," Cade said.

Marci laughed. "I can't fathom how much power that is, but I know it's a lot."

"Before you came here, did you have any idea what Yellowstone was?" Cade asked.

"I can see why the railroad advertises the park as Wonderland. People can write about it, talk about it, and take all the photographs they want," Marci said, "but until someone actually comes here and sees for themselves, they won't have any conception what it's really like."

For the rest of the afternoon they continued to ride along the road, and each sight they came to was just as impressive as the one before it.

At last they arrived at the Fountain Hotel, a two-story building with a colonnaded porch along its length. Cade made arrangements for the carriage and the horses as Haynes and the women checked into the hotel.

Before Marci went to her room, she came out under the guise of going to see the Fountain Geyser, but in actuality she was looking for Cade.

"Will you be staying at the hotel?"

"Yes, the captain says the soldier station is full, so for the night I'll get to act like a civilian."

Marci looked at Cade with a puzzled expression. Did all soldiers think of nonmilitary people as somehow being different?

Just then, a few steps away from where Cade and Marci were standing, a great gush of water began coming from a well-like opening that was nearly thirty feet across. The water didn't rise that high, but it began spreading out in a fanlike plume of water that was dissipating into droplets. From Marci's viewpoint, the droplets transformed the sun into a multitude of brilliantly colored rainbows.

"Oh, Cade, it's beautiful!"

"See how efficient I was? This one only erupts about every five hours, and I timed this show just for you."

Marci looked toward Cade, her eyes filled with adoration. Standing before an erupting geyser, with prism rainbows all around her, she thought she was the luckiest woman in the world. This man whom she had known for such a short time was unlike any other man she had ever known, and in that instant she knew she loved him. Whatever their differences, she was determined she would teach him to love her as much as she loved him.

FIFTEEN

When Cade and Marci went inside the hotel, they found F. Jay and Frances sitting in the great lobby with its exposed log-and-stone architecture. The immense fireplace, burning logs the size of trees, was taking the chill off the evening air. The lights in the lobby were dim, so that the faces of all who were gathered there waiting for the dining room to open were bathed orange in the light of the flickering flames.

"There you are," F. Jay said when he saw the two enter the room. "Larry's stew is long past gone for me. I'm starved."

"Don't wait for me," Cade said. "I don't have a room reserved, so I'd better see if I have a bed or if I'll be sleeping out under the stars tonight."

"You don't really mean that, do you?" Frances asked. "If there's no room left, Marci and I can double up and you can have her room. You wouldn't mind, would you, Marci?"

"Of course not," Marci said, joining Cade as he approached the registrar for the hotel.

"You're in luck, Lieutenant," the clerk said. "I'm afraid it's not our best room, but it's our last one. For how many nights?"

"Just one."

"For a soldier, it'll be one dollar. Here's your key—room 230. It's at the very end of the hall in a little cubby behind the linen closet, but at least you've got a window. Sorry, sir."

"No problem. It's a bed with a clean sheet and that's all I need. Marci, I'll take my necessary bag up, and then I'll join you in the dining room in just a few minutes."

When Cade entered the dining room, many of the diners, including Frances and Marci, were standing at the windows looking over the landscape that was illuminated with a few strategically placed gaslights.

"The bears?" Cade asked as he pulled out a chair and sat down.

"Yes, with all the wonders this place has to offer, what gets the tourists' attention first? Bears at a garbage dump," F. Jay said, shaking his head. "I just don't understand it."

"That was exciting," Frances said, coming to the table and taking her seat. "With all those bears out there, one very foolish person decided he wanted a close-up, but old bruin didn't want to pose. He turned on that young man and sent him skedaddling for the closest tree."

Marci took her seat next to Cade, not adding to

Frances's description of the scene outside the window. She did not wish to remind anyone of the incident she and Cade had experienced. That is, no one except Cade.

She purposefully moved her foot to the side until she found Cade's foot under the table. Then she pressed it, telling him exactly where her thoughts were. She smiled, cutting her gaze toward him, and with a nod imperceptible to anyone else, he acknowledged what she was doing. Instantly, his tongue came out of his mouth to wet his lips.

The action proved to be as erotic to Marci as if he had taken her into his arms and crushed her to his chest. And it continued. When the food arrived, Cade—in what seemed to be an accommodation to the waitress—moved his chair closer to Marci's, putting their legs in contact during the meal.

Marci could not concentrate on the conversation, her senses were so befuddled.

"You're awfully quiet tonight, Marci. Are you feeling all right?" F. Jay asked.

"It's been a long day," Marci said, covering for her turbulent emotions. "I guess I'm tired."

"I'm sure you are, and even though we're only forty miles from Mammoth, we're at a higher altitude. That makes a difference to people who aren't used to it, wouldn't you say, Cade?"

"That could be what has happened," Cade said, applying more pressure to Marci's leg as he spoke.

"Perhaps you could see Marci to her room," Frances said. "I'd like to visit with some of the tourists, if you'll stay with me, F. Jay. I've received some interesting commissions just by overhearing a choice tidbit here and there."

"Is that how you got the assignment to go down in a coal mine and risk an explosion when you lit the magnesium powder?" F. Jay asked.

"Nobody had ever taken a picture underground before—at least not one that anybody could tell what you were photographing."

"I think it's time we both retired," Cade said. "I'm afraid this conversation has moved to shoptalk, and it's well beyond a simple soldier."

He rose and helped Marci to her feet.

"I'll see you in the morning. Will we be going back to Mammoth tomorrow, or will we be going on to Old Faithful?" Marci asked F. Jay.

"I think we'll go back. I've left Lily and the boys a lot this summer, and she's complaining a bit."

"Well, then, I'll see you in the morning."

When Cade and Marci got to the top of the stairs, he walked with her until they reached her door.

"Here it is, 208." She withdrew her key from her pocket and handed it to Cade to unlock the door.

When the door was opened, he stepped to the side, allowing Marci to enter.

"Would you like to come in?"

Cade's eyes bore into hers, telegraphing what he wanted as opposed to what his words said. "I think not," he said as he lowered his gaze to her lips.

Marci could not respond, nor could she move from the doorway.

They stood inches apart, yet neither reached for

the other. Cade looked both ways up and down the hallway, then stepped into her room, closing the door behind him.

"Oh, Marci, I've wanted to do this all night." Cade pulled her into his arms, his kiss smothering her lips as he demanded a response.

She freely gave, returning the kiss with an insatiable desire, her arms encircling his neck. His glances and touches had inflamed her during the meal, and now he was here with her, with no restraints on either of them. No one would knock on the door to interrupt them, no bugle would sound to call him to orders, no bear would amble into their space.

This night she would prove that she loved him. She knew she would go wherever he led her, and she was ready. She dropped her arms and stepped away. Keeping her eyes fixed on his, she reached for the top button of her blouse, and as he watched, she unbuttoned it, then moved to the next and the next, allowing the tops of her breasts to be exposed.

He knew what she was doing, and he was powerless before her. Taking her hands in his, he squeezed them tightly, stopping her progress down the front of her chest.

"Don't you want me?" Marci asked as a lump formed in the back of her throat.

Cade pulled her hand down to the front of his pants, where she felt a hard bulge straining against the cloth. "Does this tell you whether or not I want you?"

Marci had no words. She had no experience to judge what he had asked her.

Cade took a deep breath. "I've got to go to my

room before it's too late." He took a step backward toward the door.

"Don't go, Cade. Stay with me."

He closed his eyes for a long moment, debating the choice he was forcing himself to make. He knew he loved Marci, and at this moment he wanted her more than he had ever wanted anything else in his life.

So why didn't he stay?

Before he could talk himself into it, he turned and left the room.

Marci stared at the closed door for a long moment. What had just happened? She had tried to tell Cade in every way she could that she wanted him, yet he had turned away from her. It stung and reminded her of other rejections.

Walking to the window seat that, were it daytime, would afford her a view of the geyser basin, she lifted the window and sat down. The strong smell of the boiling waters came drifting into the room.

Maybe providence had introduced her to Frances Johnston. As far as Marci's observations went, Frances had no thoughts of ever becoming romantically involved with a man, yet she led a fulfilling life that was as adventuresome as Frances wanted it to be. No doubt she was sitting around the fireplace right now listening to some tourist tell her about some exotic place to visit, or some cause of the downtrodden that needed a champion. If Frances was intrigued, she would be off on another adventure, her camera in tow to record for posterity some slice of time.

Marci could do that, too, if she just willed it. Mind over matter.

That's what her father would tell her. For the first time since leaving Washington, she was homesick. She wished she could talk to her mother and tell her about Cade. Tell her how much she loved him.

Marci squeezed her eyes shut.

Mind over matter! She was going to be a professional photographer and follow in Frances's footsteps.

But she couldn't get Cade off her mind. She loved him and wanted to be his wife. As she saw her problem now, she thought her only obstacle was to convince him that he wanted her as much as she wanted him.

Marci had never been a wallflower. She had been the best athlete at Wells College. When the Sargent apparatus had been brought in, who had mastered it first? Who had gone to the Académie Julian and won a prize for her work as a single-semester artist? Who had learned how to maneuver the wheel better than any other woman in Washington? Who had come to Yellowstone to take photographs that were worthy of praise from two of the best-known photographers in the country?

When she had raised her confidence enough, she decided she would march down to Cade's room and ask him outright if he would marry her. Grabbing her key and putting it in her pocket, she entered the hall, which was now lit by only a handful of flickering gas lamps.

All at once her plan had its first flaw. What was Cade's room number? She had heard the clerk tell him, but she couldn't remember the number. But he had said it was a cubby tucked in behind the linen closet. Surely there would be a sign marking that door.

Marci was making her way down the hall examining each door in the dim light when a gentleman stepped out of one of the doors.

"Oh, miss. You shouldn't be wandering around the hallway so late at night."

"Où se trouve la salle nécessaire?" Marci said, hoping the man would think she was French and hadn't understood his warning.

"C'est au bout du couloir." He pointed down the hall in the opposite direction.

"Merci." Marci now had to head in the direction he had indicated.

But as it turned out, the "necessary room" was adjacent to the linen closet. She saw a short hallway beside the linen closet. That had to be the way to Cade's room. She pulled herself up to her full height and, straightening her skirt, stepped to the door. She checked to make certain she had her key so she could get back into her room. When she felt the key, she also felt the small vial of perfume Frances had found in the tent at Larry's Lunch Station. Taking it out of her pocket, she opened it and found the scent pleasing.

"For luck," she whispered as she dabbed a drop behind each of her ears. Then she knocked lightly on the door, her heart racing rapidly.

As she stood in the hallway, the only sound Marci heard was her own ragged breathing. Did he hear her knock? Should she knock again?

Should she turn and leave? Was Cade even in this room?

As all these thoughts were racing through her mind, the door began to open slowly. A dim lamp glow was in the background, and she could see Cade standing before her clad only in a pair of drawers. The light silhouetted his muscular body.

Marci took in a deep breath as a shiver coursed through her body, taking away every ounce of bravado she had worked so hard to muster. Her knees began to quiver and she felt light-headed.

Cade stepped aside without saying a word, and with his hand he invited her into the room, which was barely a third the size of hers.

"I shouldn't have come," Marci said, looking around the room.

"Why not?"

"This is the most forward thing I've ever done."

Cade raised his eyebrows as a smile crossed his face. "How does it compare to throwing a red shirt at a bear?"

"I didn't do that," Marci said, raising her voice.

"Shhh." Cade put his finger on her lips. "We don't want anyone finding us in our hidey-hole."

"Your room is out of the way."

"It's perfect." He took her face in his hands, cradling her jaw. With his thumb he began stroking her bottom lip. "Are you afraid?"

Marci shook her head. "Not when I'm with you."

He took her hand and led her to the bed. Standing before her, he began to unbutton her blouse. When he reached the top of her breasts, he stopped. Marci pushed his hands away and quickly finished the task, dropping her blouse to the floor. She unfastened her waistband and her skirt joined the blouse. She stood before Cade with only her underclothes between her and being naked. In the back of her mind she thought of the models in Paris—how she had thought that any woman who would disrobe was brazen, but she didn't feel brazen at all.

Cade sat on the edge of the bed, pulling her onto his lap. He loosened her camisole, freeing her breasts before him. When he had removed the garment, he took first one and then the other breast in his hand, causing a low moan of pleasure to escape from her lips as he slowly massaged each. When he saw the nipple standing erect, he brushed his thumb against it, the rough texture causing her to tremble.

As she had done at Indian Creek, Marci thrust her breast toward him, urging him to take it in his mouth, but this time he did not.

"There's no hurry." He pulled her to him, falling back on the bed. "We have all night."

He stretched his arms out on the bed, inviting her to do to him whatever she chose.

She leaned over, supporting herself on her arms while she brushed her breasts against the hair on his chest. With her hand she began to fondle her own breast and with firm pressure work it toward his mouth.

Cade chuckled softly. "You like that, don't you?"

He took her breast and gently nipped it with his teeth, then pulled her to him and kissed her. Dragging his mouth to her ear, he began nibbling on it, then trailed kisses down her neck. All at once he stopped and sniffed.

She raised her head, then realized it was the perfume she had put behind her ears that he was smelling.

"Come back," he said as he pulled her head toward him. He found her ear again and began to flick his tongue in and out of it as his breath sent a shiver through her body.

Marci pulled away from the torture and rose up on her forearms, looking down at Cade with an expression that was begging for something, though she could not put it into words.

"Marci, this is the time."

"Yes," she said in a raw, husky voice. She rose from the bed and pulled off the last bit of her lingerie so that she was now totally naked. The soft light of the gas lamp gave her skin a greenish cast, lending her nude body a sensual, feline appearance. She raised her arms toward him, and suddenly a nipple was highlighted, glowing and tight, like a tiny rosebud.

Reaching down, she put her hands on the top band of his drawers, then pulled them down and off, exposing him in all his aroused glory.

Wait until he is aroused and his little worm jumps to the size of a flagpole. Then you will see big.

She smiled as she recalled Babette's comment at the art school. At the time, she had no real concept what the girl had meant. She had seen Leopold totally nude, but at no time did he look like Cade. She reached down and wrapped her hand and fingers around his shaft and was almost startled by the feel of it—the texture, the heat, even a sense of movement, throbbing as if it had a life of its own.

Cade's own hands were busy as he started exploring her body, in some cases duplicating what he had done when they were lying out on the grass by Indian Creek. Repositioning himself on the bed, he made room for her to lie down beside him, and when she did, he turned on one side. As he kissed her with a deep, tongue-tangling kiss, he let his hand slide down her body, searing a path across her stomach. His lips followed his hand from her breasts and the engorged nipples, across her ribs, then to her stomach, where his tongue probed into her navel.

Marci was panting heavily, feeling a building tension, and a pressing need such as she had never before felt. His fingers slipped into the dampness at her very core. Then he slowly began stroking that little piece of flesh buried within her, causing a whirling sensation to build.

His fingers continued the stroking—the maddening, demanding stroking that caused the sensations to heighten, and she moaned as she lifted her hips toward him.

"Now, Cade," she implored. "Whatever it is, do it now!"

Cade was feeling the same ache, the same want as she, and when he moved over her, he grasped her bottom and lifted her to him. He began rhythmically rubbing his penis against her core, following the same path as his fingers had done just moments before. Her moistness bathed his shaft, and he knew the moment she was ready as he felt her muscles tense in anticipation. When she spread her legs, he saw in her eyes the naked hunger that mirrored his own. His erection was pulsing as he put the tip of his manhood in position to enter the opening that was slick with passion. Slowly, he pushed against her, feeling her tight muscles throb around him as he plunged forward. When he was fully into her, he pulled back and began a rhythm that was the call of nature itself. As the bed rocked to their motion, the springs squeaked and the headboard banged against the wall. Cade tried to alter the rhythm somewhat to stop the sound, but Marci grabbed a fistful of his flesh.

"Please, Cade, don't stop," she said through clenched teeth.

Marci's entire body was tingling with the most exquisite sensations she had ever experienced. She rose to meet each thrust, and together they found the perfect rhythm that bound their bodies together. Wave upon wave of ecstasy began to sweep through her, and she knew something was about to happen, she knew that what she had been seeking was just there, with the next thrust.

Then, yielding to the burning need, she surrendered herself and felt herself explode into a thousand bursts of light, as if her very body had been struck by lightning. She gasped in the sweetness of it, felt herself beginning to coast down, then suddenly, she was cresting again, lifted even higher this time than the first.

And now, feeling the convulsive leap of her body in one shattering, final echo, she was aware that Cade was experiencing his own release as she felt him thrust himself into her, faster, harder, until he was as deep as he could go. Her body made one last leap against him in the final, shattering echoes of her orgasm even as Cade was spending himself inside her.

His breathing was ragged as he collapsed on top of her, his member still deep inside her. Laying his head against her, he placed a tiny kiss on her neck.

"What kind of perfume was that?" He kissed her again.

"I don't know," she said languorously, "but I want to buy a gallon."

SIXTEEN

It was just past 5:00 a.m. and the morning sun was creeping above the eastern horizon. Marci pulled Cade's wool tunic around her naked body as she stood at the window, looking out toward the Fountain Geyser. She had heard the roaring eruption once during the night, but now the geyser was silent. She watched as two elk munched on the sparse clumps of vegetation growing near the steaming fumarole, taking advantage of the first light of dawn, free for the moment of any invading tourists.

Marci turned back to see Cade, still asleep on the bed behind her. In her mind, she compared the two elk stealing a quiet moment to Cade and her finding some privacy in this little room hidden behind the linen closet. She knew their relationship would forever be altered from this day forward. She was no longer an innocent who could tease and throw out double entendres meant to draw him to her. If this had been a contest, she had won.

But what was the prize?

She knew the answer. It was love.

Last night was an experience she would never forget. She wanted Cade to know how much she loved him. Unable to say the words, she had tried to show him by coming to his room. But did Cade see that as an expression of love? Or did he consider it a part of his "duty" to see to the needs of someone in his charge?

She turned toward the bed with the thought of waking him. She wanted him to take her again— no, not *take*—rather to make love to her again. She needed to be reassured that he shared the feelings that she was experiencing.

But what if she approached him and he turned her away?

Continuing to study him as he slept, she knew that she would fix this picture in her mind, both as a lover and as an artist.

He was lying on his side, his hands curled under his face, which was sprouting the morning shadow of a beard. His hair was mussed and his eyes were closed. The wrinkled sheet covered his upper body, but his legs and buttocks were exposed. The muscles of his cheeks were defined and firm, while his legs were long and lean.

Then she thought of the powerful thrusts from this body that had caused her exquisite feelings. Even now she felt a moistness building in her core. As she pulled Cade's shirt tightly against her, the roughness of the wool seemed to increase the sensations.

Stepping closer, she took off his tunic, intending to return to the bed and reawaken his interest. But just as she was about to crawl in, Cade turned his back to her.

Had he done this in his sleep? Or had he consciously turned away from her?

It didn't matter. The moment was lost.

Reason returned and she knew she had to go back to her room. When she glanced out the window, the elk were gone and a lone man was walking toward the geyser. Her time in her own wonderland was over.

Quietly, she put on her clothes, then stepped out of the room.

As she was walking down the hall, she was startled to see F. Jay. What was he doing in the hall? Then she saw his shaving kit and realized he was heading for the necessary room.

"Marci?" F. Jay said. "Aren't you the early bird. And here Fan and I've been teasing you for always being late."

Marci smiled at him. "Maybe I wanted to see what it was like to be the first one up."

"Well, you did it. See you at breakfast."

When they reached Fort Yellowstone, Cade turned Rowdy over to Sergeant McKay, then went to see Captain Anderson to file a report on the trip to the Lower Geyser Basin.

"Cade, you're just the man I want to see. I received a telegram from Colonel Burt this morning," Anderson said.

"And what did he have to say?"

"Our suggestion has been approved. Moss thinks your idea of a shakedown run from Missoula to Yellowstone is a good one, and Colonel Burt suggested you might want to be a part of the trip. Do you think you're up to a bicycle trip that might be as much as four hundred miles long?"

"If Moss can do it, I can do it!"

Colonel Anderson laughed. "That's what I told Colonel Burt. No man of the Twenty-Fifth Infantry can compete with one from the Sixth Cavalry. I'll let him know you're coming."

Cade's step was bouyant as he started back toward the BOQ, but then he thought about Marci. This adventure would take him away from Yellowstone for at least three weeks. Three weeks out of the one month they were sure they had left to be together. Would she think he was deserting her?

No, she loved adventure as much as he did, and she would understand why he was doing this.

"You're going to ride a bicycle from Fort Missoula, Montana, all the way to Fort Yellowstone?" Marci asked with a look of astonishment.

Cade smiled. "Yes, Colonel Burt has asked me to join Daig and his men, and Captain Anderson is all for it. If it works, riding a bicycle would be a boon for patrolling the park."

"I think it's a great idea!" Marci beamed proudly.

"I knew you'd understand." Cade hugged her to him and kissed her excitedly.

Marci looked at him with a quizzical expression. "Do you think the secretary of war's order covers this experiment?"

Now it was Cade's turn to be confused. "What are you saying, Marci?"

"I can ride a wheel every bit as well as you can. I want to go, too."

"What?" Cade blurted out. "Absolutely not. Do you have any idea what you'd be getting into? This isn't like riding back in Washington, or even like riding here in the park. There aren't any roads, and besides, you'd be riding with a corps of men."

"I wouldn't do it by myself. Fan would go, too, and you'd be there to take care of us."

"No, Marci." Cade shook his head. "Even I can't take care of you on a trip like this. It will be grueling. We'll be out at least ten days in all kinds of weather, and we'll be crossing over mountains."

"Is it something you've ever done?"

"No, but I know I can."

"And I know I can do it, too." Marci ended the conversation and walked away from Cade.

July 31, 1896

Cade purposefully avoided Marci for the next couple of days, but he didn't want to leave without saying good-bye to her, so he stopped by F. Jay's house before he left for Cinnabar, where he would catch the train west.

"Marci told us about your grand adventure," F. Jay said when he saw him. "That's an ambitious undertaking."

"I expect it will be. But I'm looking forward to the challenge, and if the results turn out to be favorable, it will be well worth the endeavor."

Just then Frances and Marci joined Cade and F. Jay on the porch.

"There he is—the man who thinks he's made of iron," Frances said.

Cade smiled a deprecating smile. "I don't think it's going to be that hard."

"Well, that's good to know," Frances said. "F. Jay, I think we'd better step into the shop and let Marci have a word with Cade. All I can say is, good luck."

"Thanks," Cade said as Frances and F. Jay stepped from the porch.

"I've missed you," Marci said.

"I've been busy getting everything taken care of so I can be away for a while."

Marci didn't reply.

"I'm sorry I was sharp with you, but I had to make you understand how irresponsible it was for you to even consider that you could come along on this trip."

Still Marci did not speak.

"Oh, Marci, I can't leave you like this. Tell me you understand."

"I do, I really do. Be careful, and, Cade . . . watch out for bears."

Cade laughed. "If I see one, you know what I'll be thinking about." He took her in his arms and kissed her without thought of anyone's seeing them. This was his Marci.

When Cade had gone, Frances came out onto the porch. "Did you tell him?"

"No."

"Do you think that was wise?"

"He'll find out soon enough," Marci said.

Missoula, Montana, August 2, 1896

Lieutenant James Moss met Cade at the Northern Pacific depot.

"Daig," Cade called when he saw his friend.

"Welcome to Missoula, Cade. Come for a chess lesson, have you?" Moss and Cade shook hands.

"I shouldn't have moved my knight to queen's rook four," Cade said, shaking his head.

Moss smiled. "And Napoléon shouldn't have gone to Waterloo. Come on, I've got a rig to take us out to the post. The colonel and his wife have invited us to dinner tonight."

The next morning, following the night spent with Colonel Burt, Moss introduced Cade to the men who made up his Bicycle Corps.

"This is Sergeant Dalbert Green, and this is Corporal John Williams," Moss said. "They are the noncommissioned officers who will make the trip with us."

The two NCOs saluted. Cade returned their salute, then offered his hand.

"Men, Lieutenant McDowell will be accompanying us to McDonald Lake. And if that doesn't change his mind, then our next outing will be to Fort Yellowstone," Moss said.

"I hope you got strong legs, Lieutenant," Sergeant Green said. "You're goin' to need them."

"Well, if I give out on the way, maybe you can just give me a ride on your bicycle."

At first Green wasn't sure Cade was teasing, then when he saw the smile, he laughed out loud.

"Yes, sir, if you get tired, you just let ole Dalbert tote you on his bike," Williams said.

Moss explained the logistics to Cade, emphasizing the tremendous amount of planning that had gone into this undertaking.

Each bicyclist would carry a ten-pound blanket roll, including a shelter half and poles that when combined with another half would make a tent. Clothing was a set of underwear, two pairs of socks, and a handkerchief; with a toothbrush and powder. All of this was on a luggage carrier on the front of the bike. Each man would also carry his own rations of bacon, bread, canned beef, baked beans, coffee, and sugar in hard leather cases attached to the bicycle frame. Every other man carried a towel and a bar of soap, and each squad leader would carry a comb, a brush, and a box of matches. Two bicycles were fitted with special containers that could double as frying pans. And Private Findley, the bicycle mechanic, had a large metal box attached to his bike that would carry tools and some spare parts.

"It's lucky we've got Findley," Moss said. "Before he joined the army, he worked at the Imperial Bicycle Works in Chicago, and he swears he can fix anything."

"What will all this weigh?" Cade asked as he began choosing his own supplies.

"About seventy-five pounds," Moss said. "Plus whatever weapon each soldier is assigned. You and I will each carry a pistol."

"You've really thought this out," Cade said.

"I hope so. I've been working on this project ever since General Miles gave us permission to go. Longer than that, actually."

"Do you really plan to ride all the way to St. Louis?"

"I do," Moss said. "But it won't be until next spring. I want to make certain my men are ready."

August 6, 1896

Puddles of water were scattered about the post grounds, and where there wasn't grass, there was mud. Nevertheless, by five thirty that morning, Lieutenant Moss, Cade, and the eight black soldiers who made up this first run for the Bicycle Corps, were standing alongside their bicycles in a column-front formation.

"Prepare to mount your wheels!" Moss called, and all the soldiers threw one leg over the bike.

"Left by twos, move out!"

With the regimental band playing, and with Lieutenants Moss and McDowell in the lead, the Twenty-Fifth Infantry Bicycle Corps began riding. Colonel Burt and most of the officers and their families, as well as all the soldiers, were turned out to watch them depart the post.

Fifteen minutes after leaving the post they rode through the town of Missoula, where scores of civilians were standing alongside the road, even at this early hour, watching as the soldiers rode by.

"Where're you soldiers goin' on them wheels?" someone yelled.

"The Lord only knows. We're followin' the lieutenant," one of the soldiers replied.

Later that same day, Marci Winters and Frances Johnston stepped down from the train at the Northern Pacific depot in Missoula, Montana. They waited by the baggage car until two bicycles were off-loaded. Both women were dressed in traveling suits, and when they climbed onto the bicycles and rode away, they received more than one glance of curiosity from the others who were waiting at the train station.

They rode to Fort Missoula, and when they reached the post gate, they were stopped.

"Ma'am, could you state your business here?" the gate guard asked.

"We are here to meet with Colonel Burt," Marci said.

"What is the nature of your business?"

"I'm afraid that's between us and the colonel."

The young private stroked his chin as he considered the request. He was obviously not prepared to handle this.

A sergeant, seeing the exchange, came over to the gate. "What is it, Jackson?"

"Sarge, these here ladies want to talk to the colonel."

"All right," the sergeant said, "I can take care of it."

Marci and Frances dismounted their bicycles and walked them across the quadrangle, following the sergeant. "Just inside there," the sergeant said. "Tell the first sergeant what you need."

"Thank you, Sergeant," Marci said, flashing him a grin. He nodded in response, then went on his way.

When Marci and Frances stepped in through the door of the headquarters building, a black man, seated behind a desk, looked up in surprise. Marci had been around the army long enough now that she recognized by the stripes and diamond on his sleeve that he was a first sergeant.

The first sergeant stood quickly. "Can I help you, ladies?"

"We would like to speak with Colonel Burt," Marci said.

"Yes, ma'am, if you would wait here for a moment, I'll tell the colonel you're here."

Marci looked around the room as she waited. She had an eye for detail and was pleased that she could pick out specific ones, such as the unit guidon of the Twenty-Fifth Infantry, the map designating the regiment's area of responsibility, a picture of President Cleveland, a picture of Secretary of War Lamont, and a picture of General Nelson Miles.

The first sergeant came back. "Ladies, the colonel will see you."

The two stepped into Colonel Burt's office, and because he was already standing, he came forward to greet them. "Ladies, this is an unexpected surprise. To what do I owe the honor of your visit?"

"We understand that soon some of your soldiers will be making a bicycle ride from here to Fort Yellowstone," Marci said.

"Yes, that's right."

"We are professional photographers, and we'd like to ride along with your men."

Colonel Burt shook his head. "Oh, ladies, I don't think so. There won't be any wagons following the men. This is an experiment to test the bicycles."

"Yes, we understand that," Marci said. "And we feel we are competent enough bicyclists to accompany them. We think that a photographic journal would be outstanding publicity for the army."

Colonel Burt smiled. "Ladies, even if I agreed with you, and the truth is, if you are willing to undertake the adventure, I see no reason why you shouldn't, I don't think I have the authority to grant you permission. In fact, I'm sure I don't. To do something like this, you would need the approval of someone much higher up than a mere regimental commander."

"Can the secretary of war authorize it?" Marci asked.

"Well, yes, of course, but I hardly think you are going to be able to get the secretary of . . ." Colonel Burt paused in midsentence when he saw Marci handing him a sheet of paper. "What is this?"

"It is our authority from my friend Secretary Lamont," Marci said.

> *July 29, 1896*
>
> > *Office of the Secretary*
> > *Department of War*
> > *Washington, D.C.*
>
> > *Miss Frances Johnston*
> > *Miss Marcia Winters*
> > *c/o F. Jay Haynes*
> > *Yellowstone National Park*
>
> *Reference: Photographic record of Bicycle*
> *Corps trip*

Dear Misses Johnston and Winters:

Secretary Lamont has reviewed your request that you be allowed to accompany the Bicycle Corps of the 25th Infantry Regiment on a training ride from Fort Missoula, Montana, to Fort Yellowstone, Wyoming.

The Secretary feels that a photographic record of the Bicycle Corps trip would be a wonderful means of promoting the venture and preserving for posterity a record of the project.

Your request is approved.

For the Secretary of War

Jason Campbell

Col US Army

Adjutant

Colonel Burt read the letter, then looked up with a curious expression on his face. "Ladies, I . . . you will forgive me, but I have to have validation on this. First Sergeant?" he called loudly.

The first sergeant stuck his head back in through the door. "Yes, sir?"

Colonel Burt wrote a quick note and handed it to the first sergeant. "Would you get this out by telegraph as soon as possible?"

"Yes, sir."

"I should have a response by tomorrow," Colonel Burt said. "Where may I find you?"

"We're staying at the Brunswick. Will you get word to us as soon as you receive validation from the secretary of war?" Marci asked.

"Yes, ma'am. I will personally inform you."

The next day, at midmorning, a clerk from the hotel knocked on the door of Marci and Frances's room, and Frances responded.

"I beg your pardon, ladies, but Colonel Burt is in the lobby."

"Thank you," Frances said. "Please tell the colonel we'll be right down."

A few minutes later Marci and Frances descended the stairs and saw Colonel Burt standing in the lobby talking to a rather smallish man wearing a brown suit and a bowler. When the colonel saw the two women, he smiled.

"I take it you have heard from Mr. Lamont?" Marci asked.

"Yes, I received a rather lengthy telegram from him. Shall I read it?"

"Is it one that we are going to want to hear?" Marci asked.

"Oh, I think so." Colonel Burt nodded. He cleared his throat and began to read:

> *I am personally acquainted with both Miss Marcia Winters and Miss Frances Johnston. I cannot recommend them highly enough. It was with pleasure that I approved their request to accompany your soldiers on their bicycle expedition, and I now reiterate that approval. I believe that a photographic record of the expedition will be very good publicity, not only for the*

*25th Infantry Regiment, but for the entire
United States Army.*

*It is my request that you, Colonel Burt,
take personal responsibility in equipping
the young ladies with everything they might
need. I further instruct you make certain
all who are involved in the expedition be
apprised of the personal interest of the
Secretary of War in the participation of
Miss Winters and Miss Johnston.*

After Colonel Burt finished reading the telegram,
he handed it to Marci. "Keep this, along with your
letter of authorization. I'll add an additional letter
of my own."

"Thank you, Colonel."

Colonel Burt chuckled. "I'm going to enjoy seeing
the expression on Lieutenant Moss's face when he
finds out he has two ladies added to his roster."

"It isn't Lieutenant Moss we're worried about,"
Frances said.

"Oh?" Colonel Burt replied, curious.

"It's Lieutenant McDowell."

"Fan," Marci said, that one word expressing her
displeasure with the subject being brought up.

"I see," Colonel Burt said. Frances had said nothing further to clarify her comment, but Colonel Burt
was perceptive enough that she didn't need to say
anything more. "I don't think either of you will have
to worry about either Lieutenant Moss or Lieutenant McDowell. They are officers, they will follow
orders, and they will follow them willingly."

"Thank you," Marci replied.

Colonel Burt turned toward the man standing near him. "By the way, I would like you to meet Edward Boos. His father is the publisher of our local paper, the *Missoulian News*, and he has convinced Lieutenant Moss that he should be allowed to accompany the corps when they make their trip to St. Louis."

"I think that is a rather ambitious undertaking," Marci said as she extended her hand to the man.

"No more than what the two of you are going to do," Boos said. "When the colonel told me of your intent to ride to Yellowstone, I suggested that you might want to spend a few days training before you start out."

"That's very thoughtful, but both Miss Johnston and I have ridden a lot, and we consider ourselves quite prepared for the trip."

"I'm not suggesting otherwise, but riding in the mountains is quite different from riding on flat ground. I've been going out to the hills every day, trying to build up my endurance, and should you wish to go with me, I'd be glad to have you join me."

"That would probably be wise," Frances said. "When do you think Lieutenant Moss will leave for Fort Yellowstone?"

"The plans are for them to leave on the fifteenth," Colonel Burt said.

"Marci, I think our time would be well spent to go with Mr. Boos. We will be in training, yes, but more important, we will not be highly visible."

Marci smiled as she recognized the intent of Frances's suggestion. "Mr. Boos, where shall we meet you?"

"Right here. Tomorrow morning."

"I think you will find this to be a worthwhile excursion. Come to the post and we'll outfit you with the supplies you'll need for the trip to the park," the colonel said.

"Thank you, we'll do that," Frances said.

As promised, Boos met Marci and Frances at the hotel the next morning, then accompanied them to the fort where they drew the equipment they would need for the trip.

"Oh my," Frances said. "I had no idea there would be so much . . . stuff! The bicycle weighs a ton now."

Boos laughed. "It doesn't weigh that much, though I'm sure it is heavier than anything either of you are used to. I think it might be wise to take a short trip today, only enough to get you used to handling the loaded bicycle."

With their bicycles heavily laden, the two women accompanied Boos for what he called a break-in ride. They rode out a distance of no more than a mile or two, then back into town.

"So, what do you think, ladies? After straining your muscles to move your wheels with such weight, do you still want to accompany the soldiers to Yellowstone?"

"Yes, absolutely," Marci said.

It rained hard that evening, with great, jagged streaks of lightning renting the night sky, followed by thunder booming loudly, then picking up resonance from the hills and rolling back with a loud rumble. Marci stood at the window of the hotel room, watching the rain slashing hard against the panes. Another boom of thunder caused the panes to rattle.

"The colonel thinks the Bicycle Corp could be back as early as tomorrow," Frances said. "But if it's still raining like this, they may not make it."

"If I know the army, then they'll be back tomorrow."

Frances chuckled. "If you *know* the army? Now, just how well do you actually know the army?"

"I know Cade. And he is the army. And believe me, if he is supposed to be back tomorrow, he'll be back tomorrow."

"What's Cade going to say when he finds out you're following through with this harebrained idea?"

"I don't know." Marci turned away from the window. "I really don't know," she repeated pensively.

"Marci, are you sure you want to do this? I mean, I sense that things are going pretty well between the two of you, and this could upset the applecart for you."

Marci recalled the night at the Fountain Hotel, and she felt herself flushing. She was glad that it was too dark for Frances to see her cheeks. "Yes. Things have been going well."

"Aren't you afraid this could cause a problem?"

"It is a risk, I'll admit. But now it's sort of an all-or-nothing proposition."

"I hope it goes well for you, Marci. I really do."

Marci got in bed, then lay there listening to the rain as she thought about what she was doing. Cade had been adamantly against it when she'd suggested that she come with him on this bicycle trip.

But she was here now. This trip would either bring them much closer together, or it would drive them irreparably apart. It was, as she'd told Frances, an all-or-nothing proposition.

When Marci awakened the next morning, she turned on the bedside lamp and glanced at the clock. It was five minutes until five. Getting out of bed, she moved quickly to the window. Looking up, she could see a vast array of stars, which told her that not only had the rain stopped, but it had cleared up and was not likely to rain again today.

"Fan. The rain's stopped. If they are coming at all, I'm sure it will be soon, and I don't want to miss seeing them."

"All right." Frances sat up, then swung her legs over the edge of the bed. "I'm tired already. Remind me again—whose idea was this?"

"It didn't take much to sell you on doing it, too."

They waited at the window, and before long the bicyclists rode by. Marci saw Cade in the front, riding beside another officer. He said something to the officer and smiled, and even from her place above him, she could feel the impact of that smile.

When Edward came for Fan and Marci that morning, he announced that he wanted to ride at least five miles out for this, their first real day of training. When they returned, Marci could barely crawl into bed, so sore was she. Every muscle in her body ached and it made it hard for her to go to sleep. She was so stiff the next morning that she lay there questioning herself, wondering why she had ever had such an idea. She had ridden a lot, and she thought she would be better able to handle this, but just as Cade had said, riding on mountains was different from riding in Washington.

The next day, they rode ten miles out and back, then they increased their ride by five miles every day.

To Marci's surprise, even though they went farther each day, she wasn't as sore, and by the third day, as her muscles began to strengthen, she began to feel that she might make it after all.

"All right, ladies," Boos said when he came by for them on August 11. "This will be the last phase of your training. We're going to make a forty-six-mile trip this time, and we're going to follow the railroad all the way to the town of Duncan. We have to be back on the fourteenth, because I've been told the corps leaves for Yellowstone on the morning of the fifteenth, and you don't want to miss the colonel's soiree the night before."

"We definitely don't want to miss that," Frances said as she gave Marci a playful shove.

This trip was long and tiring, but they were blessed with good weather and they reached Duncan the first night. Edward suggested they try out their camping gear, so rather than going on into the town, Edward showed them how to put the shelter halves together and make a tent.

The next morning, they rode into Duncan, where they attracted some attention from the citizens of the town.

"Ladies, what do you say we find a place to have a good breakfast?" Boos suggested.

"I think that's the best idea you've had since we left Missoula," Frances said.

They stopped in front of the Miners Café, and as they did so, a few came over to look at the bicycles.

"We don't see many of these contraptions in these parts," one of the men said as he examined the wheel closely.

"It's a bicycle," Boos said.

"I seen you comin' in on 'em, but I swear I ain't never seen the like of it before. Is it better 'n ridin' a horse?" another man asked.

"In some ways it is." Boos smiled. "You don't have to feed or water a bicycle."

"I'll be! What'll they think of next?"

The three went into the café and ordered their meal.

"I have to say, I'm not looking forward to the long ride back," Frances said.

"We don't have to ride back," Boos said. "We can take the train if you want to, but I'm not sure you should. This is just the beginning for you two if you intend to follow through with your trip to Yellowstone. And this time we had good weather. What are you going to do when the mud is ankle deep?"

"You don't have to bring that up, Edward," Frances said as she downed the last of her coffee.

"Edward's right, Fan," Marci said. "We need to test ourselves to the limit if we want to be ready."

"I didn't say I wasn't going to ride back. I just said I wasn't looking forward to it."

⚜

The three rode into Missoula late on the thirteenth, tired and exhilarated after they had made exceptionally good time.

"I wasn't sure we could do it," Marci said as she fell onto the bed in the hotel room. "I'm glad we pushed ourselves because now I know we won't be burdensome to the corps."

"You're right," Frances said. "There's a certain satisfaction that comes with knowing what your body is capable of. Thanks for getting us into this, because I'm not sure I would have chosen this as one of my adventures."

"Fan, I don't think I've told you, but I can't thank you enough for giving me this job. I know I'm a different person from the headstrong girl who left Washington."

"*Headstrong,* you say? Just how do you think you will behave when Cade McDowell says you can't go on this trip?"

"I'm not going to think about that." Marci turned out the light.

Marci and Frances were sleeping well into the morning when they were awakened by the hotel clerk, delivering a note.

> *My dear Miss Winters and Miss Johnston,*
> *My wife, Elizabeth, and I are hosting a*
> *small reception this evening for*
> *Lieutenants Moss and McDowell, and we*
> *would be honored to have you attend as*
> *well. It is my belief that this will be an*
> *excellent opportunity for you to inform*

the lieutenants of your participation in
the bicycle excursion to Yellowstone.

I must tell you that Mr. Boos has
assuaged any trepidation that I may have
had concerning your physical ability to
endure this trip. He says you are more than
prepared for the rigors that are to come.

Sincerely,
Andrew Burt
Colonel, Commanding

SEVENTEEN

August 14, 1896

Marci and Frances were prepared for the evening because in addition to the jeans, shirts, and underwear they had for the trip, they also had the traveling suits they had worn on the train.

"I expect Cade is going to be surprised to see us tonight," Frances said.

"Yes." Marci's voice sounded stifled and unnatural.

Frances looked around in surprise. "Marci, are you all right?"

"I don't know, I . . . to tell you the truth, Fan, I'm beginning to wish that we hadn't come."

"It's a little late to be having second thoughts now, isn't it? You know Cade will be at this reception tonight."

"We could just say we came to Fort Missoula to see him off; then we could take the train back to Yellowstone."

"Is that really what you want to do, Marci?"

Marci sat on the bed. "I don't know, Fan. On the

one hand, I very much want to make this trip. I think it will do some good for the army, and especially for the colored soldiers. They seldom get the recognition they deserve, and I know we'll get some wonderful pictures. On the other hand, I feel like I'm defying Cade by insisting that we go." Marci looked up at Frances with an expression of agony. "What if he gets so mad at me that he never wants to see me again?"

"You just have to make up your mind, Marci. If this relationship between you and Cade is real, then shouldn't you have some say in how you live your life? I know the biblical injunction is for 'wives to submit to their husbands,' but do you really want to give up all personal freedom?"

"No. And I don't think Cade would want that either."

"Well, there you go." Frances smiled broadly. "This will give you the opportunity to put him to the test."

"A test? I don't know that I like the sound of that, but I guess I'm ready."

Colonel Burt had sent a two-seated surrey for them, and when they stepped out to the front of the hotel, they saw a black soldier sitting erect in the front seat, wearing an immaculate uniform.

"Are you here to pick us up to take us to Colonel Burt's?" Frances asked.

"Yes, ma'am." The young soldier hopped down from the surrey to assist Marci and Frances into the vehicle.

When the surrey rolled through the gate, the

guard, seeing the ladies, stood at attention as he waved them on through.

A hand-painted banner stretched across the front of the commandant's quarters:

GOOD LUCK TO THE BICYCLE CORPS

This sign greeted the officers and their wives, as well as the bachelor officers, of the Twenty-Fifth Regiment when they arrived.

Inside the house, the enlisted soldiers, also wearing their best uniforms, moved about serving coffee or tea and distributing tidbits of food.

Colonel Burt met Marci and Frances, then introduced them to his wife.

"Come with me," Mrs. Burt said. "Andrew wants to wait until the time is just right to introduce you. He does like his drama." She smiled.

Elizabeth Burt was particularly pleased to discover that both Frances and Marci lived in the nation's capital, and she insisted that they catch her up on all the latest society gossip. She had dozens of questions, from what parties were being given to what the ladies were wearing to what music and dances were popular.

When the three heard some applause from the parlor, the colonel's wife said, "Oh, I'd better go. I imagine the applause means that Lieutenants Moss and McDowell have arrived."

As Mrs. Burt left the room, Marci bit her lower lip nervously.

Frances reached over to pat her hand. "It'll be all right, Marci. I just have a feeling. It'll be fine."

❦

Out in the parlor, Colonel Burt greeted Cade and Moss. "Well, my lads, you will be pleased to know you are two of the four guests of honor tonight."

"Four?" Moss asked. "Who else is here?"

Colonel Burt chuckled. "Don't be distressed, James. Elizabeth, will you bring in our other"—the colonel paused for a moment to look back toward Cade and Moss—"honored guests."

Elizabeth left the parlor, then returned a moment later.

When Cade saw whom she was bringing in, he gasped. "What in the hell are they doing here?" Cade asked under his breath.

"Do you know these women?" Moss whispered.

Cade took a deep breath. "I'm afraid I do."

"Ladies, gentlemen," Colonel Burt said, "I want you to meet Misses Frances Johnston and Marcia Winters. They are both photographers by profession, but that isn't all I want you to know about them. They are two very courageous women, and it is my pleasure to tell you they will be making a photographic diary of the historic bicycle trip Lieutenants Moss and McDowell and the stalwart soldiers of the Twenty-Fifth will be embarking on tomorrow as they make their way to Yellowstone National Park."

The guests started to applaud, but they were interrupted when Cade announced loudly, "No, they won't!"

The applause ended raggedly.

"Lieutenant McDowell, with me, please," the colonel, looking toward Cade, said, the harshness of his voice matching the sternness of his visage.

"What is this, Cade? What's going on?" Moss asked in confusion.

"Lieutenant Moss, you come as well."

With the eyes of everyone on them, Cade and Moss followed the colonel from the room. Cade glanced over at Marci, and the expression on her face, a cross between fear and despair, jolted him. He wished the expression had been one of smug victory because that would have fueled his anger with her.

But inexplicably, he found himself feeling terrible that he could be the cause of her obvious distress.

Oh, **Marci thought** as she watched Cade and Lieutenant Moss follow Colonel Burt from the room. *Why am I here?* Once again, because of her impetuousness, she might have put his career in jeopardy. She had been around the army for over a month now, and though there was much that she didn't understand, she knew that to openly defy a colonel's order, as Cade had just done, was not a good thing.

With tears stinging her eyes, she turned and left the reception, feeling as if she and Cade were onstage, playing out a tragedy for all to see. She hurried back into the room where she and Frances had been awaiting the introduction. Grabbing a handkerchief, she dabbed at her eyes, which were flooded with tears.

Frances followed her.

"He hates me," Marci said as she blew her nose.

"He doesn't hate you."

"Yes, he does. Did you see the expression on his face? In his eyes? And now I've gotten him in trouble with the army. Oh, Fan, how could I have done this? The army is his life and I . . . I've ruined it for him."

Frances chuckled. "I don't know that much about the army, Marci. But I'd be willing to bet that for as long as there's been an army, colonels have had to deal with lieutenants. And I doubt seriously that this will have any lasting effect."

"I wish we hadn't come. I'm miserable and now I've ruined everything."

Fan was silent for a moment, then she reached out to put her hand on her friend's shoulder. "You love him, don't you? This isn't just an infatuation, is it? You actually love him."

"Yes, I do. And now I've ruined it."

"Dry your eyes, Marci, and go back to the reception. If Cade loves you as much as you love him, this will work out. And if it doesn't, then it isn't meant to be. I'm a firm believer in that." Frances took Marci into her arms and embraced her.

"How did I ever find a friend like you?" Marci asked.

In his study Colonel Burt lit his pipe as Cade and Lieutenant Moss stood at attention. The colonel held a match to the bowl and didn't look up at the two young officers until his head was wreathed in aromatic, blue smoke. "Stand at ease," he said as he leaned back in his chair.

Both Cade and Lieutenant Moss relaxed their positions.

Colonel Burt took a couple more puffs from his pipe before he spoke again. "Now, Lieutenant McDowell. I want to know what you meant when you countermanded my order a few moments ago."

"Sir, I . . . I didn't, that is, I'm not aware that I countermanded an order. I would never do such a thing."

"But you did do such a thing, Lieutenant," Colonel Burt said sharply. "I said that Misses Johnston and Winters would be accompanying you and Daig on this bicycle trip, and you said, and I quote, 'No, they won't.' That, sir, is countermanding my order."

"I didn't mean it like that. I was not expecting to see Marci . . . that is, Miss Winters. Colonel, she has been petitioning me to allow her to make this trip from the moment she learned about it. I've been telling her that is not practical. I resent that she went around me to appeal to you."

Colonel Burt laughed out loud. "You don't know the half of it, Mr. McDowell. She went around all of us."

"Sir? I don't understand."

"Miss Winters and Miss Johnston have permission from the secretary of war to make this trip. Lamont thinks the publicity would be very good for the army. And, apparently, these two young ladies are not strangers to him."

"Yes, sir. He knows Marci quite well," Cade said, recalling the incident at the academy.

"Well, then, there's nothing either of us can do about it. The secretary of war says she's going to make the trip with you, and she is."

"Yes, sir."

"And you, Lieutenant, will have the special duty of looking out for Miss Johnston and Miss Winters. I'm putting their safety and well-being directly in your hands, but I have it on authority that these two really are quite proficient with the wheel. So perhaps it won't be too much of a challenge for you."

"Yes, sir," Cade said.

Colonel Burt smiled. "Now, gentlemen, let's return to the reception, shall we?"

August 15, 1896

As the soldiers who had been selected to make the bicycle trip to Yellowstone lined up the next morning, they were surprised to see that two women, also equipped with bicycles, were with them.

"Men," Lieutenant Moss said, "I want to introduce these two ladies to you. This is Miss Johnston, and this is Miss Winters. They are professional photographers, and they will be taking pictures of us during our expedition."

"We goin' to be famous, Lieutenant?" Private Brown asked, and the others laughed.

"Well, I suppose we will," Moss said with a broad smile.

Cade stepped back to the two women, who had drawn their bicycles up at the end. "I think you two should ride up front behind Lieutenant Moss and me. That way I'll be able to look out for you."

"Cade," Marci said quietly, "I've been thinking about this all night long. If you really don't want us to go, I mean, you're really opposed to it, then we'll take the train back to Yellowstone."

"Well, I've been thinking about it, too. And the more I've thought about it, the more I've come to accept the idea that you should be with us. Your pictures might help James promote his trip next summer, and beside that, I have it on good authority that you're actually pretty good at this wheel stuff."

"Oh, Cade, I love you." Marci beamed a smile.

"Now, none of that. This is a mission!" But he, too, broke out in a broad smile.

As they had for the bicyclists when they'd left for McDonald Lake, the entire post turned out to see the group off. Many had not heard that two women would be going and looked on in surprise, commenting about it among themselves.

The cyclists rolled through the town of Missoula fifteen minutes after they'd passed through the gates of the fort, and again many of the towns-people had turned out to watch. Like the soldiers and civilians of the post, they, too, were surprised to see two women riding with the men . . . though, in truth, because the women were dressed as men, wearing jeans and flannel shirts, their sex wasn't immediately noticeable.

Almost right from the beginning, though, the group encountered difficulty. The rain had created a thick, sticky mud, and the mud started piling up on the wheels, making it hard to ride. Marci kept up rather easily, but Frances was having a difficult time, so Marci had to keep her spirits up.

"Come on, Fan, you know you can do it," Marci urged. "You did really well on all our practice rides."

"It's the mud. We didn't have mud like this when we went to Duncan."

"Lieutenant Moss, sir," Corporal Williams called out. "Do you think we could ride up on the railroad tracks? There ain't no mud up there."

"Corporal, I don't know why your idea wouldn't work. Let's try it," Moss called back.

The group moved their bikes up onto the tracks. There was no mud there, and because the grades had to be moderate for the locomotives, they weren't struggling to climb the hills. They did have to deal with the cross ties, but there was sufficient ballast to allow riding.

They rode forty-two miles the first day, stopping at eight thirty. Cade came back to help Marci and Frances pitch their tent.

"How was it?" he asked.

"Oh," Marci said. "I thought I was up to this, but I'm hurting in places where I didn't even know I had places."

Cade chuckled. "That happened to me the first day we rode to McDonald Lake. James plans for us to get to New Chicago by noon tomorrow. If you wanted to leave there and take the train back to Livingston, we all would understand. You've spent an entire day with us, and I know between the two of you, you've taken enough pictures to put together a photo essay."

"Cade, do you want us to leave tomorrow?"

"No, I told you, you've won me over. And you've managed to take your pictures without holding us up. I want you to make the whole trip with us, if you can. But, I also want you to know that if you decide to leave the group, nobody will think any less of you."

"I think I want to stay," Marci said as she turned to Frances. "But if you want to leave tomorrow, as Cade said, nobody will think the less of you."

"I would think the less of me," Frances said. "I may hate myself tomorrow night, but if you stay, I stay."

"I'm proud of both of you," Cade said, "and you'll get stronger as you go along. You'll see."

The second and third days proved to be much easier. They found the roads surprisingly good, and they made good time, covering close to a hundred miles in the two days.

Had it not been for their total exhaustion, Marci and Frances would have very much enjoyed being with the men. They were deferential to the two of them, offering to scrape the mud from their wheels, and seeing to it that their tires were properly inflated.

But the thing Marci appreciated most was the soldiers' demeanor. None of them complained about anything, and they constantly joked and teased with one another. As an added bonus, two of the men had beautiful singing voices, and even on the steepest climb, they would start a song, making everyone forget the task that was at hand.

On the fourth day they crossed the Great Divide, reaching the summit at a little after four in the afternoon.

"Lieutenant, we goin' to coast down this side?" Private Findley asked.

"I don't think so," Moss replied. "I think this grade's too steep; we wouldn't be able to control the bikes."

"I'll try it out for us, Lieutenant," Brown said, and mounting his bicycle, he started down the hill.

"No, wait, it's too steep!" Moss called, but it was too late. Private Brown was already going so fast that his brakes were failing him, and he was in danger of leaving the path and pitching over the edge.

Brown started screaming in terror.

"Brown! Jump off the bicycle!" Cade shouted. "Jump to your left, away from the edge. Do it now if you don't want to die!"

Marci, with her heart in her throat, saw the private lean over, causing his bike to fall. It skidded for several more feet down the rocky path, then edged out onto the lip. This lip of the cliff angled down at about forty-five degrees, and Brown and his bicycle skidded on it until he stopped his slide by catching on a rock. The front wheel of the bike protruded out over the edge, hanging precariously over a sheer drop-off.

Leaving his own bicycle on the path, Cade sprinted down the mountain until he reached the soldier. Brown was scraped and bleeding and balanced precariously on the rock that was the only thing preventing him from falling to his certain death.

"Give me your hand," Cade said calmly as he reached down toward the man.

"I can't let go, Lieutenant." Brown's voice was choked with fear. "If I let go, I'm goin' to fall over for sure."

"Give me your hand. I'm not going to let you fall. If you're holding on to me and you fall, that means I'll fall, too. And I'm not going to let that happen."

Brown hesitated for a moment, then let go with

one hand and reached up. Cade grabbed him around his wrist.

"Hold on to my wrist," Cade said, and Brown did so. Then, bracing himself on the path, Cade pulled Brown back from the precipice, far enough onto the path that the young private felt safe enough to stand up.

"How we goin' to get my bike back, Lieutenant? I ain't goin' back to get it."

"I can get it," Marci said.

"Private Brown, you go on up the path and tell Corporal Williams to take care of your cuts."

"Yes, sir." Brown started back up the path.

Then Cade turned his attention to Marci. "What are you doing down here? You saw what could have happened to Private Brown."

"I can get the bicycle."

"And just how could you do that?"

"I am probably the lightest one here. If I lie down on my stomach, and you hold on to my ankles, I can reach the bicycle."

"No. Even if it would work, I'm not going to put you at risk like that."

"Cade," Marci said quietly, "I did a lot of gymnastics when I was in college. I know I can do this."

"What is it she can do?" Moss asked, now coming down the trail to join them.

Marci explained what she wanted to do.

"Why not let her try, Cade?" Moss said. "We for sure can't leave the bike behind. If we do, that'll leave Brown afoot and he can't walk out of here."

"Better to leave the bicycle behind than to lose the woman I love."

Marci looked sharply at Cade.

"Oh," Moss said, his brows shooting up upon hearing Cade's declaration.

Marci smiled. "If you love me, Cade, I know you aren't going to let me fall. Now, either you hold on to my ankles or I'll have James do it."

By now the others had all come down the trail, bringing with them the bicycles of Cade, Moss, and Marci.

"All right, Miss Winters," Cade said. "Let's do it."

Cade sat down and braced his feet on a couple of rocks.

"Lieutenant, if you don't mind, I'll sit down behind you and put my arms around your waist," Sergeant Green said.

"Thank you, Sergeant. I'll appreciate that."

Cade got into position first, then Sergeant Green got behind him and wrapped his arms around Cade's waist.

"All right, I got you, sir."

"All right, Marci. It's all up to you, but promise me if you see you can't do this, you'll stop."

Marci got down onto her hands and knees, then crawled over Cade's spread legs.

"Grab my ankles," she said.

Cade did so, and Marci giggled when she visualized the picture they were making.

"Stop it, Marci, this is serious," Cade said. "Either do it or don't do it."

"All right." She got on her stomach and stretched out as far as she could. She managed to grab the back wheel, sticking her fingers in through the spokes. "I got it." She tried to budge the bicycle, which was wedged onto the rock. "Uhn! It's too heavy."

"I should have thought of that, Cade; the thing weighs seventy-five pounds," Moss said. "It was a good try."

"Lieutenant, I got a rope in my tool kit," Findley said. "If she could get the rope wrapped around the wheel, some of us could pull it back up."

"Yes," Marci said. "Bring me the rope, I can do that."

A moment later a rope was passed down to Marci, but as she started to wrap it around the back wheel, the bicycle dislodged and started to slide.

"It's going over!" Marci shouted.

"Let it go! Don't take any more chances!" Cade yelled.

"No, I've . . . I've got it stopped. I can get the rope through the wheel, I know I can."

With ten men and one woman watching and holding their breath, Marci was able to loop the rope through the wheel.

"Pull me back up. I'll hold on to the rope."

Cade pulled her back up until Findley was able to take the rope from her. Moss helped her stand, and a moment later—amid much backslapping and cheering—the bicycle was recovered. All the men proclaimed Marci the heroine, and they made up a little song about her:

> *Ole Private Brown*
> *He fall down,*
> *He lose his bike 'cause he so shaken,*
> *But Miss Marci, she save his bacon.*

Had Marci ever had any doubts, she knew she was now fully accepted among this group of men. Her only regret was, as she was learning, "the mission" took precedence over everything else. She wished that she and Cade could have found some private moment together because she was almost certain in the height of the excitement he had said she was the woman he loved.

They reached Fort Harrison, which was about the halfway point of the trip. Here, Moss had made arrangements to be reprovisioned with food and bicycle parts. A separate barracks had been set aside for the men, and James and Cade were told they could stay in the BOQ. Marci and Frances were invited to stay as guests of the commandant.

The men were fed in the mess hall, and they were the object of much attention, not only because they were Buffalo Soldiers, but also because of the trip they were undertaking. Dozens of questions were asked of them, not the least of which were about the two women who were traveling with them.

Everyone was pleased when Lieutenant Moss announced they would spend a day so that Private Brown might have some time to recuperate from his wounds. Marci and Frances spent the day taking pictures, promising to send prints to the commandant when they got back to Yellowstone. Colonel Ruger issued an invitation to all the officers, as well as their ladies, to dine at the officers' mess that night. The officers of Fort Harrison seemed as interested in the bicycle trip as did the enlisted men of the base, posing questions to both Moss and Cade.

Like the enlisted men, the officers, too, were fascinated that women were traveling with the group.

"Both Miss Winters and Miss Johnston are personal friends of the secretary of war, and they are with us at his behest," Moss said proudly. "That means we have the secretary's enthusiastic support for what we're doing."

"Miss Winters," Colonel Ruger said, "do you live in Washington?"

"Yes, sir. My father works in the Treasury Department."

"Would your father be DeWitt Winters?"

Everyone glanced toward Marci and she gasped, as she felt her cheeks flaming. Was Colonel Ruger aware of the scandal that had forced her to leave Washington? Was he about to say something? She looked over at Cade and saw that, like the others, he was looking at her. How would he react when he heard the gossip?

She realized that the question was still hanging in the air and had to be answered. "Yes," she said meekly, so quietly that she could barely be heard.

"I thought as much," the colonel said with a broad smile. "I met your father last year when I was soliciting more money for the post. He is a very fine man, and you must be very proud of him."

"I am." Marci's answer was almost a relieved sigh.

For the next several minutes, the wives who had lived in Washington during some period of their husband's service talked about the city, and the wonderful social functions that took place there.

"Out here we may as well be on the moon, so

bereft are we of anything even remotely social," a captain's wife said.

"Why, that's not true, dear," the captain said. "We have the Officers' Open Mess, and the post band."

"And Helena has a theater," one of the other ladies added.

As the conversation continued, Julie, the young wife of Lieutenant Purcell, found a moment to say quietly to Marci, "Miss Winters, may I ask you a question?"

"Yes, of course."

"With all those men around, what do you do when . . . I mean if . . . uh, you need a little privacy?"

Marci smiled. "You forget, there are two of us. When one of us needs a little privacy, the other will simply stand watch for her."

Julie smiled. "Oh, yes, I can understand that."

"Now, Julie, may I ask you a question?"

"You want to ask me a question?" Julie was flattered that someone as glamorous as Miss Winters would be interested in anything she had to say.

"Yes." Marci glanced around the table, and when she saw Cade conversing with Colonel Ruger, she leaned closer to Julie and asked quietly, "What is it like being married to an army officer?"

A broad smile spread across Julie's face. "Oh, it's wonderful! I love watching the men drill with Ben in charge, I love the pomp and ceremony, I love being with the other officers' wives. There is nothing else, anywhere in the world, that can compare with the closeness we have. I grew up without a sister, and now I have a dozen sisters."

"But doesn't his strict adherence to duty all the time get in the way of things? I mean, which comes first in your husband's mind—you or the army?"

"Who do you love most, your mother or your father?" Julie asked.

Marci smiled, recognizing the truth of the other woman's quip. "Thank you. That's a very good answer."

EIGHTEEN

On the trail, August 21, 1896

Daig, look over there." Cade pointed to a covey of prairie chickens. "Don't you think that would make a good supper?"

"Absolutely." Moss held up his hand to halt the squad.

"Squad, halt!" Sergeant Green ordered.

"Men," Moss said, "do you see those chickens? Lock and load your weapons."

With Sergeant Green in charge, the men, now with loaded weapons, started toward the fowl. Just before they were in position, though, Findley sneezed, and the covey took flight.

"Aim, fire!" Sergeant Green called desperately, and eight weapons roared as one.

"Cade, you want to hear what I'm putting in my report?" Moss asked later that night.

"Sure."

Moss cleared his throat, then began to read, loudly enough that all the soldiers could hear him:

"'While bounding along at a ten-mile rate, we

ran upon a covey of chickens near the road. Halting and dismounting, we formed as skirmishers and advanced on the chickens until the command was given: "Squad halt; aim, fire!" The command was executed with precision.'"

Smiling, Moss looked up, then read the last line:

"'But we had government bacon for supper, nevertheless.'"

"Lieutenant, now, you ain't really goin' to say that, are you?" Corporal Williams asked. "It warn't our fault. It was Findley's fault. When that boy sneezes, it sounds like thunder!"

Everyone enjoyed a good laugh.

The remaining four days were almost anticlimactic, and on the afternoon of August 25, ten days after leaving Fort Missoula, the bicyclists rode into the company area at Fort Yellowstone. They were greeted by the officers and men who weren't elsewhere in the park. Captain Anderson, having been forewarned by telegraph when they rode through Cinnabar, turned out the band, and they played music to welcome the soldiers. For their part, the soldiers made a show of riding by as fast as they could, making intricate maneuvers that were quite impressive, though that occurred only after the two officers and Frances and Marci had dropped out.

F. Jay and his family were there with the others to meet the arriving bicyclists, and they especially welcomed Frances and Marci back.

Smiling, Cade came over to join them.

"Tell me, Cade, how did our girls do?" F. Jay asked.

"They did well. No, let me change that. They did exceptionally well."

"I thought you were opposed to having them along."

"I was in the beginning. But I have to say they proved me wrong."

F. Jay laughed. "I like a man who can admit his mistakes. But the whole purpose of this was to get pictures. I hope you were successful."

"Oh, we took a lot of pictures," Frances replied. "I want to get in the darkroom right away."

"I can't believe you, Fan," Marci said. "You can hardly wait to develop your pictures, and I can hardly wait for a bath."

"A bath," Cade said. "That sounds good to me. If you don't mind, I'm going to say good night."

Cade wanted desperately to take Marci in his arms right now, he was so hungry for her, but just as on the trip, this was neither the time nor the place. Instead, they exchanged smiles that were so private and personal they were as intimate as a kiss. Cade nodded, then turned to head across the parade ground.

When he reached his room, he looked at Marci's picture just as he had done a hundred times before. He thought about the trip, recalling when she had put her trust in him to keep her from falling. At the time, he had said she was the woman he loved. In the aftermath of the excitement, the opportunity to tell her that he'd meant every word he'd said had not presented itself. He'd have to rectify that as soon as possible.

There was no reason why she couldn't be beside

him right now—well, not in the BOQ, but in the married officers' quarters. If he asked her to marry him, he knew she would say yes, and if they were married, he would never have to leave her again.

As Marci, Frances, F. Jay, and his family started back across the parade ground toward his house, Marci heard someone calling her name. It was a woman's voice, and it was familiar.

"Marci? Marci Winters, is that you?"

Turning, she saw a young woman coming quickly toward her, and recognizing her, Marci smiled and started back, closing the distance between the two of them. "Letitia Scott!"

Letitia smiled and shook her head. "No, it's Letitia Bramwell now."

"Oh, that's right. I knew you and Charles were about to get married. But what are you doing here? Are you on a vacation?"

"Oh, no, my dear. *Lieutenant* Bramwell is in charge of a military surveying team. We're posted here until the survey of the park boundaries is completed."

"Oh, how wonderful! Are you living in the married officers' quarters?"

"No, there aren't any available for visiting officers, so we're at the hotel."

"It's so good to see you." Marci started to reach for Letitia, then pulled back and smiled self-consciously. "Uh, no, I'd better not do that. I'm not fit to touch anyone until after I've cleaned up a bit."

"Did you really ride a bicycle for four hundred miles?"

"I did indeed."

"You always were a little crazy, but I had no idea you would do something like that. You'll have to tell me all about it."

"I will, I promise. For now I have only two things on my mind. Taking a bath, and getting some rest." Marci could have added, *And Cade McDowell,* but she thought better of it.

The next morning Cade and Lieutenant Moss went to see Captain Anderson to give him an after-action report of their trip. When they stepped into the headquarters building, they saw talking with Captain Anderson a rather tall officer, whom they both recognized.

"Gentlemen, this is Lieutenant Charles Bramwell," Captain Anderson said, "but I'm told no introductions are necessary."

"Indeed they are not, sir," Lieutenant Bramwell said. "Daig was in my class at the academy."

"Daig?"

Moss chuckled. "I swear to you, sir, I don't have the slightest idea how I picked up that nickname."

"And Cade was one class behind us," Bramwell added. He shook hands with the two.

"Hello, Charles. I seem to remember a little business between the two of us when I was a plebe," Cade said, but the smile on his face showed that, whatever it was, there was no remaining animosity.

"Come on, you remember yourself that half the fun of becoming a third classman is that you can order plebes around."

"Cade, you're aware of the problem we have with

the park borders," Captain Anderson said. "Lieutenant Bramwell is here with a detail of surveyors. Finally, we're going to have permanent boundary markers so there can be no question whether or not poachers are on government land."

"Good, that will make our patrols a lot easier, especially in the winter," Cade said.

"Lieutenant Moss, I understand your trip down was an unmitigated success," Captain Anderson said.

"Yes, sir," Moss said. "We had one potential incident, but . . . I hate to admit this, one of the ladies resolved it for us."

"Well, then, I'll look forward to reading about it in your report. Now that you're here, you will be touring the park, I suppose?"

"Yes, sir, but I think the men need a little time off today, so we'll continue on tomorrow."

"Cade, while you're out, make sure you take them to all the soldier stations, and if we're really going to consider adapting bicycles for patrols, find some places to go in the backwoods to see just how they handle. And you take the day off, as well," Captain Anderson said.

"Yes, sir, thank you, sir."

When Cade and Moss left the headquarters building, Moss said he needed to make certain his men were comfortable, and to tell them they would be off for the day, so he went off on his own.

Cade knew exactly what he was going to do on his day off, so he walked over to Haynes's house and knocked on the door.

"I wondered when you were going to come see

us," Haynes said. "We've been getting an after-action report, but I know Marci and Fan are leaving off some of the details."

"I'll bet they're still sleeping."

"You know better than that. Fan's been in the darkroom since before sunrise because she's so anxious to see her work. I think Marci's in there, too. Would you like me to get her?"

"Yes, I'd like that."

F. Jay stepped into the darkroom, and a moment later Marci came out, smiling. "Well, I think we both look better today than we did yesterday, don't you?"

"You might say that. Listen, Marci, I was wondering if you'd like to take a little walk with me. I haven't seen Rowdy yet, and I know he's thinking I've deserted him, so do you want to come with me?"

"Sure, I would love to."

"F. Jay?" Cade called. "I'm going to borrow Marci for a few minutes."

"Go ahead, Cade, you took her for ten days. What's a few more minutes?"

Chuckling, Cade led Marci out of the house and across the parade ground to the company area. When they reached the stable, Cade held out his hand to stop her for a moment, then he looked inside.

"Sergeant McKay isn't here. Come on in, we'll say hello to Rowdy. And to Cinnamon, too, if you'd like." Cade led her on into the stable.

"It always amazes me how clean this place smells. I know the soldiers keep it fresh, but that must be very hard work."

"Believe me, it is," Cade said. "I know, because I did it from the time I was nine years old until I left for the academy."

"That must have been hard for you," Marci said sympathetically. She put her hand on his arm.

"I have to say Mr. Dickey treated me fairly. He always told me all the hard work would make a man out of me, and I guess it did."

Marci took Cade's arm in both hands and leaned her head against it. "I guess it did." She smiled softly.

They walked down a wide, center area, with stalls on either side. The horses, curious about the entrance of the two, had all moved to the front of the stalls and stuck their heads out, following Marci and Cade with big, brown eyes.

"There's Cinnamon." Cade pointed.

Marci walked over to him. "Hello, Cinnamon, you old sweetheart you." Marci leaned her face against Cinnamon's head, and Cade chuckled. "What is it? Why are you laughing?"

"Cinnamon is a warhorse, and here, in front of all his friends, he's being hugged by a woman. All the other horses are going to be making fun of him now. How is he ever going to live that down?"

"Oh!" Marci pulled her face away quickly.

This time Cade laughed out loud. "I'm teasing. The others aren't going to make fun of him. They are going to envy him."

Approaching the stall at the end of the stable, Cade said, "Hello, Rowdy."

Rowdy began nodding his head up and down in obvious joy at seeing Cade.

"Did you think I'd deserted you, old boy?" Cade

began patting Rowdy on his face as Marci stood alongside. "Do you remember this lady, Rowdy?"

Smiling, Marci reached up to pat the horse as well.

"Rowdy, old boy, I brought her in here because I want you to be my witness."

"Witness?" Marci asked, confused by Cade's comment.

"You see, Rowdy, I'm going to ask her to marry me now, and I wanted you to be the first to hear it."

"What did you say?" Marci gasped, barely able to get the words out.

Cade turned to Marci, took her hand, and lifted it to his lips. "Marci, I love you. I think I've loved you from the first moment I ever saw you. Will you marry me?"

She broke into a wide, dazzling smile. "Oh, yes, Cade! Yes, I will marry you!"

Cade drew her into his arms and kissed her, not a deep kiss, but one that was full, satisfying, and gave the promise of love that would forever be shared.

"He asked me to marry him!" Marci said when she returned to F. Jay's house.

"Are we supposed to be surprised by that?" Frances asked. "The only thing I'm surprised about is that it took him this long. From the way he looked at you when he met us at Cinnabar that first day, I thought you two would be married by the time we reached the park."

F. Jay and the others laughed.

"When is this happy event to be?" F. Jay asked.

"I want my parents to be here, so I'll write tonight, to tell them the happy news."

"The wedding will be here at Yellowstone, won't it?" Lily asked.

"Oh, yes. Where could we find a better place?"

"I wish I could stay for it," Frances said.

"Oh, Frances! Are you saying you won't be here?" Marci's expression showed her intense disappointment.

"I can't, Marci, as much as I would love to. But I have some photo sessions set up with all of the outgoing cabinet members and their wives. We've had these scheduled for a long time, and I can't put them off. I do have a business to run, you know." Frances reached out to put her fingers on her friend's cheek. "But don't you worry, F. Jay will take pictures of the wedding, and I've heard that he's a pretty good photographer."

"I get by," F. Jay said, and the others laughed.

"Where are you going to get married?" Nance asked, after Cade told the other officers of his plans.

"Here, in the park."

"Where? You may have noticed, we don't have a chapel."

"I don't know, we haven't gone that far with it."

"Well, if you want us to attend, that might be good information for us to know," Nance teased.

That night, Cade decided to write a letter to the only person in the world that he would want to be a guest at his wedding. But before he began to write, he took out Libbie's reply to the telegram he had sent her on the Fourth of July. He had known she would have good advice, and she hadn't disappointed him.

> *Dear Cade,*
>
> *My darling boy, your telegram sent me into the seventh heaven of bliss. How much you remind me of your father, and even my own dear Autie. As to what you may have to recommend you to your young lady, may I say that my husband knew for some time what his future would be—years of monotonous service on the frontier—and I knew as well. We decided early in our marriage that we would take whatever life had to offer and, sweetened with our love, take enjoyment from each other.*
>
> *We managed to preserve romance throughout our entire married life and vicissitudes (so soon, and so tragically ended) and though we had our trials, Autie, as I know you to have also, had the blessed faculty of looking on the sunny side of things.*
>
> *Cade, you love this young woman, and that should be all that matters. Do you know how lucky she will feel to know that she has that love? You ask for advice, and this is the advice I give you. Do what your heart tells you.*
>
> *Your own,*
> *Aunt Libbie*

Cade folded the letter and put it away. How fortunate he was to have the love of a woman such as Libbie Custer, and to love her in return. He knew that she would always be an anchor in his life as he turned to her for support, advice, encouragement, or, as she had been by his side at the death of his mother, sympathy and understanding.

He picked up his pen and dipped it in the inkwell as he began to compose his thoughts.

> *Dear Aunt Libbie,*
>
> *In your last letter you wrote, "Do what your heart tells you." Emboldened by that advice, I have asked Miss Winters to marry me, and she said yes! We are planning it near the end of September to allow time for her parents to come from Washington, and, Aunt Libbie, it would mean everything to me if you would come as well. Of course, if you cannot make the long trip to Yellowstone, I will understand. But please know that your attendance would be, for me, blessed, as you are the closest family member I have.*
>
> *With much affection,*
> *Cade*

When Marci awakened the next morning, the smell of frying bacon was permeating the house, and for some reason she felt nauseous. She sat on the edge of her bed for a few moments, then splashed her face with cool water, and that seemed to help. She hoped she had not caught some malady on the trip down from Fort Missoula because she and Frances had been asked to accompany the Bicycle Corps through the park.

On this, the first day, the corps went no farther than Mammoth Hot Springs. Frances posed them on Minerva Terrace, the soldiers with their bikes at different levels of the terrace. It made a dramatic picture, one that Marci knew would be used for publicity for a long time to come.

For the next several days the Bicycle Corps, accompanied by Cade, Marci, and Frances, continued to ride through the park. Because the roads were well graded and well kept, the riding was much easier than it had been on the ride down from Fort Missoula.

The only interruption was from the tourists. The novelty of a corps of black soldiers, two officers, and two women riding through the national park caused much excitement. Marci and Frances were amused by how many amateur photographers snapped their pictures as they rode along.

On August 31, the soldiers of the Sixth Cavalry held a barbecue for Moss and the Buffalo Soldiers because they would be returning to Fort Missoula the next day. Though the units had been segregated during their stay at Fort Yellowstone—the Buffalo Soldiers were given their own barracks and ate in their own mess hall—the two groups had had a lot of contact, and some friendships were forged.

"Lieutenant Moss, we have enjoyed having you and your men as our guests," Captain Anderson said. "And the invitation is open for you to come again. And I wonder if you might say a few words?"

Moss stood, then looked around, and seeing all

the soldiers sitting together, black man with white man, he nodded and smiled.

"Ladies, Captain Anderson, officers, and men, you have made us most welcome during our stay here, and from myself, and on behalf of my men, we thank you."

"Here, here!" Sergeant McKay called, and all the men clapped.

"As you know," Moss said, "there were two young ladies, Miss Marcia Winters and Miss Frances Johnston, who made the trip with us in order to preserve this historic event by way of their photographs. They were courageous, energetic, and an inspiration to us all. I have been told that Miss Johnston will be returning to Washington tomorrow, and I want to thank her for what she has done and wish her a pleasant trip back. Good-bye, Miss Johnston, good-bye, Miss Winters, and good-bye to the Sixth Cavalry."

After the speeches, Brown and Williams sang a couple of songs, including the one they had made up for Marci, then four soldiers from the Sixth Cavalry made their own musical offering, singing "I'll Take You Home Again, Kathleen" in perfect four-part harmony.

When the barbecue was over, Cade walked Marci to the Haynes house, where he kissed her good night, a kiss that was as gentle as the brush of a butterfly's wing.

NINETEEN

Two days after Frances and the Buffalo Soldiers had left, Marci was in front of the Mammoth Hot Springs Hotel, taking pictures for F. Jay. She finished one set, then was placing her tripod in another position when she heard someone call, "Marci!"

Recognizing the voice, Marci felt a dryness in her throat, a tingling sensation in her skin, and a weakness in her legs. It was Stanton Caldwell!

"Marci," Stanton said, coming quickly toward her. "Isn't this wonderful? I got off the coach not more than five minutes ago, and you are one of the first people I see. This has to be fate!"

Stanton grabbed her, pulled her to him, and, before she could resist, kissed her.

"Stanton, what . . . what are you doing here?"

"Why, isn't it obvious? I've come to get you away from this exile. I told you when the time was right, I would come for you and we would wed." Still holding her by the arms, he stepped back and smiled broadly. "Well, darling, the time is right!" Stanton pulled her to him for another kiss.

"Stanton, stop!"

Stanton laughed. "I know what you're thinking. Here's staid, old, conventional, nondemonstrative Stanton, kissing right out in the open. But, darling, I can't help it. I'm just so happy to see you!"

Jeff Nance was coming out of the hotel, having just checked the guest roster against some fresh names the soldiers had found scratched into some of the park fossils. He saw Marci setting up a tripod and started toward her to offer her his best wishes. He stopped when he reached the bottom step, though, because he saw a man—who wasn't Cade McDowell—grab her and kiss her.

Nance's first reaction was to go to Marci's aid, thinking perhaps she was being accosted by a perfect stranger. But as he watched the interaction between them, he realized that, whoever the man was, he wasn't a stranger.

Cade was in front of the quartermaster building, supervising a Gatling-gun drill, when he saw Nance coming toward him. "Good morning, Lieutenant. Did you come to see how a Gatling-gun drill is supposed to be run?" Cade asked with a broad smile.

"Sergeant Dawes, could you take charge of the drill?" Lieutenant Nance asked. "I need to talk to Lieutenant McDowell."

"Yes, sir."

"What is it, Jeff?" Cade asked as the two walked

away from the men who were gathered around the three guns.

"I don't know how to tell you this, Cade, but, I just saw Marci and—"

"Jeff! She hasn't been hurt?"

"No, my friend. But you're about to be."

Cade walked quickly across the parade ground, often breaking into a run. He saw them when he was about fifty yards away, standing there, facing each other. The man was holding both of Marci's hands, and as soon as Cade saw him, he recognized him.

This was the same man he had seen with Marci at the zoo in Washington. Cade was nearly to them before Marci noticed him. He saw her gasp and drop her hands.

"Cade! This isn't what you think!" Her voice was high-pitched and shaky.

"Don't worry about it, darling, I'll take care of it," the man with her said, holding his hand out toward her. With a huge smile on his face he came toward Cade. "Hello, I'm Stanton Caldwell, come to get his bride, and I'm happy to meet Marci's friends." He held his hand out, but Cade kept his hands down by his sides, clenching and unclenching his fists. His mouth was drawn in a tight line.

The smile didn't leave Stanton's face, but he withdrew his hand. "Oh my, I think I see what's going on here. Well, as I'm sure you have learned, Marci is a passionate young woman who, how shall I say it . . . lives life to the fullest? Whatever has happened between you two, I hold no animosity toward

you. But I think you should know that Marci and I
have been engaged to be married for three years."
Stanton's chuckle was self-deprecating. "I know you
may be wondering why I've waited so long. But you
must understand, old boy, that I've been busy in
Governor McKinley's bid for the presidential nomination, and now that he is the candidate, I've had
the opportunity to think about the life Marci and I
will have together. You know, we may get married
right here in Yellowstone Park. I can't imagine a
more beautiful place, can you? What am I saying?
Of course you know how beautiful it is, you work
here."

"Stanton Caldwell, we are not going to be married," Marci said, coming over to join them. "I have
a say in this."

The practiced smile did not leave Stanton's face
as he turned toward her. He reached into his pocket
and pulled out a box, opening it to reveal an engagement ring. "My dear, you gave me your solemn oath
that we would be married. Did you, or did you not,
accept my promise ring?"

"I did, but—"

"And did you, or did you not, beg me to marry
you?"

"I did but—"

"If you back out on me now, you must know that,
unless there is a legally justifiable reason, an unwill-
ingness to perform one's promise to marry creates
a breach of contract. And with all your other scandals, I'm sure you don't want to be drug through
that, too.

"Besides, look at the comparison here. I have

been told I will most likely be President McKinley's postmaster general, perhaps the most influential job in the cabinet. This man is a"—Stanton looked at Cade—"forgive me, I don't recognize army ranks, but I think it is reasonable to assume that you aren't a general."

"He is a lieutenant," Marci said resolutely.

"Yes, a lieutenant. Tell me, Lieutenant, will you be able to take Marci to concerts, or to White House functions? She very much enjoys that sort of thing, you know. Why, we attended the wedding of the daughter of the vice president of the United States, and I must say"—Stanton looked at Marci possessively—"it was quite a memorable occasion.

"Will you be able to provide her with a big house with full-time help? Or will she forever be forced to live in some one-room hovel at a dirty and distant army post?"

Cade turned and began to walk away.

"Cade, no!"

"Let him go, darling." Stanton reached out toward her. "Let's just the two of us pass this off as an unimportant interlude. I know that you were bored and probably found this young officer to be a dashing figure with whom you could entertain yourself. I want you to know that I'm not holding that against you."

"Stanton Caldwell, what makes you think we are engaged?" Marci's words were short and clipped.

"Why, darling, we've been engaged ever since I gave you the promise ring that you are wearing on your . . ." He looked at her finger and saw that the ring was gone. "Well, no matter." He held out the engagement ring. "This is the ring you'll be wearing now. It's a diamond, which is a proper engagement ring."

"We are not engaged, and I will not wear that ring."

"Why, Marci, you are acting as if this is a surprise. I told you in the note that I sent you in St. Louis that I would contact you when the time is right. Well, as I said, the time is right."

Marci grabbed the tripod and the camera and walked off.

When Cade returned to the company area, he went into the headquarters building, where he saw Lieutenants Nance, Scott, Forsythe, and Bramwell. Captain Anderson was there as well, and the expressions on the faces of all the officers told Cade that they knew exactly what was going on. Cade didn't want their sympathy; he would much prefer that nobody knew of his shame and humiliation.

"I'm really sorry, Cade," Forsythe said.

"Yeah, we heard what happened," Scott added.

"I didn't know who you were engaged to, Cade, but Jeff told me," Bramwell said. "I know of this woman, and you are better off without her. Believe me, you are much better off," he added pointedly.

"What do you mean?"

"Well, for one thing, she was kicked out of Wells College. Nobody really knows what happened there, but I do know that they are very strict with their students and won't put up with any foolishness. Then she spent the winter in Paris, living among the bohemians. And everyone knows what loose morals those people keep."

"That's nothing but innuendo," Cade said, defending Marci. He knew why she was kicked out of Wells, and he knew that he was the cause of it, but he didn't mention that. He also knew that she had spent time in Paris.

"Yes, my friend, but here is something that isn't innuendo. Perhaps you don't know why she came to Yellowstone. She came here because her father insisted that she come. You see, she was a party to one of the most outrageous scandals to ever hit Washington. She was caught in a very, let us just say, *compromising* position with a man in a bedroom in the suite occupied by the vice president of the United States.

"And the reason I know that isn't innuendo, Cade, is because my wife is Mrs. Stevenson's niece. So trust me when I tell you you are better off, much better off, leaving this woman behind you."

Cade didn't answer Bramwell, but he looked directly at Captain Anderson. "Sir, I wonder if I might have a word with you?"

"Yes, of course. Gentlemen," the captain said to the other officers, "if you would excuse us?"

The officers left, with Jeff putting his hand on Cade's shoulder as he passed him by.

"Damn," Cade said after they left. "The only thing worse than getting dumped on is having it happen in front of every Tom, Dick, and Harry in the whole Sixth Cavalry."

Captain Anderson nodded. "What can I do for you, Cade?"

"I need to get away for a while. I'd like a temporary-duty assignment somewhere."

"How about going back to Fort Missoula? You could do a little more work with the Bicycle Corps, then write out a recommendation that we could send to both the Department of the Interior and the War Department. It would get you away, but it would also serve a real service to the post."

"Yes, sir, I would like that. Daig could help me get the report together."

"How long will you need?"

"I think a month should be more than enough time."

"All right. I'll have the clerk type up your orders, and I'll send a telegram to Colonel Burt telling him you're coming back."

"Thank you, sir."

Cade turned to leave, but Captain Anderson called out, "Cade?"

Cade stopped, then turned back.

"You aren't the only one who's ever had his heart broken. I know you feel like the whole world has dropped on you now, but you'll get over this."

"Yes, sir."

Marci stepped out of the sun and into the cool shadows of the stable. Sergeant McKay, surprised by her appearance, came to speak to her.

"Hello, Sergeant McKay."

"Miss Winters." McKay was puzzled as to why she was here. "Are you looking for Lieutenant McDowell?"

"Yes. No," Marci amended. Tears began flowing down her cheeks. "I mean, I don't know. I was wondering if I could go down to speak to Rowdy."

"Yes, ma'am, I reckon you can." Sergeant McKay looked away in embarrassment over her crying.

"Thank you, Sergeant."

Sergeant McKay led Marci down to the far end of the stable. "Are you sure you're all right, ma'am?"

"Yes, thank you."

Sergeant McKay looked at her for a long moment, then he turned and Marci watched him walk back to the other end of the stable where he resumed his repairing of bridles.

Marci turned to Rowdy, and when the horse hung his head over the stall gate, she pressed her face against his, feeling his hair against her tears.

"Oh, Rowdy, what have I done? Why didn't I write Stanton a letter as soon as I got here, telling him I never wanted to see him again?"

The horse seemed to sense Marci's pain, almost as if he were pressing his head harder against her face to soothe her.

In his room at the BOQ, Cade packed his bag with what he would need for a month's stay at Fort Missoula. When he was finished, he looked at the photos, and at the line of poetry that was written on the one of him and Marci.

As in love they fondly twine.

In a fit of anger, he lashed out at the picture, sliding it across the desk, shattering the glass. He opened the drawer, sweeping the glass and the pictures into it. He would destroy them when he got back.

Cade knew that a tourist coach would be leaving for Cinnabar within an hour and he could catch a ride, so he picked up his bag and walked down-stairs. Lieutenants Nance, Forsythe, and Scott were sitting in the day room and they stood as he entered.

"Are you leaving us for good?" Forsythe asked.

"No, I'm going up to Fort Missoula to do some more with the Bicycle Corps and then write another report. I'll be back in a month."

"You think you'll be able to beat Daig in chess while you're there?" Nance asked.

Cade knew that Nance had asked him that to lighten the mood a bit, and Cade rewarded him with a slight smile. "I'll have him begging for mercy."

"Take care of yourself while you're up there. We don't want you to like it so much you decide to stay," Forsythe said, and though Cade was junior to all of them, as one they saluted him. He returned the salute, then picked up his bag and went outside.

He started toward the hotel, but changed his mind and headed for the stable instead. He stepped inside, then set his bag down.

"You goin' somewhere, Lieutenant?" Sergeant McKay asked.

"Yes, I'm going back up to Missoula for a while. I thought I'd say good-bye to Rowdy."

"Yes, sir. Well, I'll give you two a few minutes of privacy. I'll be over at the quartermaster's if you need me for anything."

Cade watched McKay hurry off and thought it a little strange that the sergeant felt a need to give Cade and Rowdy a few minutes of privacy.

He walked down the aisle to the stall at the end.

"Rowdy, I'm going to be leaving you again. I'm sorry."

"Please don't leave, Cade."

Startled, Cade turned and saw Marci standing in the corner shadows.

"What are you doing here?"

"I wanted to see you."

"You have no right to be here."

"Cade, it isn't what you think. Stanton and I are not engaged."

"I saw you in his arms."

"I had no idea he was planning to come here. I couldn't help it when he showed up, and I couldn't keep him from grabbing me."

"I'm not talking about in front of the hotel, Marci. I saw you in his arms at the zoo, back in Washington."

"I . . . Cade, that isn't fair. That was a long time ago, this is now."

"Yes, this is now, and here he is again."

"I love you, Cade. Don't you believe that? Stanton means nothing to me."

"Is Stanton the man you were caught with in the vice president's bedroom?"

Marci raised her hand to her throat as her eyes welled with tears. "Who . . . who told you that?" she asked in a shaky voice.

"Then, it's true, isn't it?"

"Yes, but, Cade, it isn't like you think."

"Marci, maybe where you come from such carryings-on are normal. But it's like Caldwell said." Cade made a sweeping motion with his hand, taking in not only the stable, but by inference the army itself. "I am not high society. We should never have gotten involved. You don't fit in my world, and I sure as hell don't fit in yours."

"But, my parents are coming for our wedding. What will I tell them?"

"Tell them you're going home with them."

Cade picked up his bag and left.

Half an hour later, Cade was on one of the Tally Ho stagecoaches, en route to Cinnabar. He was crazy ever to think that he would have a chance with someone like Marci Winters. They couldn't be more different if they had come from opposite sides of the world.

The coach was crowded with tourists, and they were jabbering back and forth excitedly about various points of interest in the park.

"Well, let's ask the soldier boy here," one overweight, bald man said. "Tell us, soldier boy, which geyser is the highest? Old Faithful or Great Fountain?"

Cade stared at the man for several seconds, but said nothing. The talkative man grew nervous under the intense stare, then looked away.

Cade turned to look through the window, and nobody bothered him during the rest of the trip to Cinnabar.

When Marci left the stable, she went to F. Jay's house.

"Hi," F. Jay said brightly. "I'm finished in the darkroom if you want to use it."

"No," Marci said, her word coming out as a

choked sob. She went upstairs quickly, then went into her room, closed the door, and lay facedown on her bed.

Lily went upstairs behind her, then stood in the hallway just outside Marci's room. Lily put her ear to the door for a moment, then she went back downstairs.

"What did you say to her?" she asked accusingly.

"Why, I didn't say anything to her," F. Jay replied defensively. "All I did was ask her if she wanted the darkroom. What's she doing?"

"She's crying."

"Crying? What's that all about?"

"I don't know," Lily said. "But if I had to guess, I would say that it had something to do with Cade McDowell."

Marci didn't come back down for the rest of that day. She didn't join the family for dinner that night, nor did she eat breakfast the next morning.

"All right," F. Jay said, "I'm going to get to the bottom of this."

"F. Jay, don't you go upsetting her with a lot of questions. I won't have it," Lily said.

"I'm not going to ask her anything. I'm going to get it right from the horse's mouth. I'm going to talk to McDowell."

"Cade isn't there," F. Jay said when he returned half an hour later. Lily held her finger across her lips, and F. Jay furrowed his brows in question.

"She's in the darkroom," Lily said.

"Is she still crying?"

"No, she seems fairly composed now."

At that moment there was a knock on the front door, and F. Jay went to answer it. He saw a well-dressed man with blond hair, blue eyes, and a perfectly trimmed mustache. He was holding a hat in his hand, and he made a slight bow.

"Good afternoon, sir. My name is Stanton Caldwell. Perhaps Marcia has spoken of me."

F. Jay turned to look back toward Lily, who had, by now, also come to the door.

"What can we do for you, Mr. Caldwell?" Lily asked.

"I'm told that Marcia Winters is staying here, and I've come to call on her."

"Is Marci expecting you?" F. Jay asked.

"No, in fact I'm sure she isn't. We are very old . . . friends, and I'm afraid that when I arrived, unannounced, it might have caused some unforeseen difficulty for her. I would like to see her—that is, if she is willing to see me. I think I can set things straight between us."

"Well, something needs to be cleared up, that's for sure," F. Jay said. "She's been in a state for two days now."

"Please, would you tell her that I would like to see her?"

"You don't have to, Lily, I'm here," Marci said as she entered the parlor. "What do you want, Stanton?"

Stanton flashed a brilliant smile. "I would like for you to have dinner with me tonight, at the hotel restaurant. Obviously, our meeting didn't go well, and I think we have some things to discuss. Under the circumstances, I think you owe me that."

Marci was quiet for a moment, then she nodded. "All right."

"Good, I'll be in the dining room at seven o'clock."

"Who is that man?" F. Jay asked after Stanton left.

"He's someone I've known for a long time. He's from Washington."

"Is he the reason why Cade has left Fort Yellowstone?" F. Jay asked.

"You know about that?"

F. Jay nodded.

"Yes. I would say this man is the reason."

"Then, I think you're foolish for going anywhere near him."

"It might not help with Cade, but I'll be through with this man, once and for all."

When Marci walked into the hotel dining room at seven o'clock that evening, she saw Stanton seated at one of the tables. He stood, and she knew he must have been watching for her. He was smiling broadly as she approached, and out of courtesy, he pulled out a chair.

"I've taken the liberty of placing an order for us. Roasted venison, garden peas, and mashed potatoes. I hope that's acceptable?"

"It's fine," Marci said with little enthusiasm.

"First, Marci, I owe you an apology. I should have let you know I was coming because I think my unexpected arrival has been quite a surprise to you. I even suspect that it was an unappreciated surprise."

"You suspect? Stanton, after that rude and horrible note you sent me when I stopped in St. Louis, how did you expect me to react? You dismissed me out of hand. Do you have any idea how that made me feel?"

Stanton reached across the table to take Marci's hands in his. "Darling, you don't understand. You have no idea what kind of pressure I was under. It was a national convention to nominate a candidate for president of the United States, and I was right in the middle of it. I'm sorry if you considered the letter dismissive, but I did tell you in that same letter that I would contact you." He lifted her hand and kissed it. "And here I am."

"Yes. Here you are."

"Marci, I want you to come back to Washington with me, where we can be married."

"Stanton, you can't just drop in out of the blue and expect me to marry you."

"Why not? We're engaged, aren't we? In my mind we've been engaged for almost three years. Certainly from the time I gave you the promise ring I considered us engaged." Stanton frowned. "Am I to understand that your promises mean nothing?"

Marci didn't answer.

"Darling, I've saved the best part for last. I am absolutely positive that Governor McKinley will be the next president of the United States. And when he is, he'll have two people to thank. Mark Hanna, and me. I know I will be the postmaster general, and no position has more patronage jobs to hand out than that one. I plan to use that job as a springboard for running for office, Marci, and I want you—no, I *need* you by my side when I do."

"Stanton, please."

The smile left Stanton's face. "Did you, or did you not, plead with me to marry you?"

Marci looked down. "Yes," she said quietly.

"All right, if you wanted me as your husband not one time, but two times, I believe, why won't you marry me now when I need you? Marci, don't you see? We're meant for one another. We think alike. All you have to do is say yes. You know you'd like to go back to Washington and be in a position of power. There's such an exciting future waiting for us. Don't throw it all away over some . . . some affair you may have had with a . . . man who can't ever give you anything. Whatever you've done, it won't make any difference. No one need ever know except the two of us. We've both done things that are, shall we say, inappropriate. Now, let's pretend that none of this ever happened between us, shall we?"

The meal was delivered, and as Marci toyed with her food, Stanton babbled on with Washington gossip, dropping names that at one time meant something to Marci. She spoke little, but Stanton didn't seem to notice, so busy was he in selling himself.

"Stanton," Marci said when finally there was an opening in his monologue. "You don't want to marry me."

"Don't be silly! Of course I want to marry you. You'd be a tremendous asset to my career."

"How much of an asset can I be if I come to you with a bastard child?"

"What?"

"I'm pregnant, Stanton. I'm pregnant, and Cade McDowell is the father."

Stanton stared at her for a long moment. Finally he picked up a napkin, dabbed at his lips, then laid it across his plate. Without one more word he stood and walked away, leaving her alone at the table.

When she returned to F. Jay's house, both F. Jay and Lily were in the parlor, obviously waiting for her.

"Did you get rid of him?" F. Jay asked.

"Yes. I think I did."

TWENTY

When the coach arrived in front of the Mammoth Hot Springs Hotel, a woman stepped down, then turned to offer a hand to an older man.

The older man chuckled. "Libbie Custer, when I am so old and decrepit that I have to have a lady help me down from a coach, I'll quit leaving home."

"Why, Mr. Hannaday, what makes you think I was offering to help you down? You are quite a handsome man; it could be I just wanted you to hold my hand."

Cade Hannaday laughed. "You always were the biggest flirt in Monroe, and you've not outgrown it. Let's get settled in, then find my grandson. This day has been a long time coming—too long."

"I can't wait to see his face when he meets you. I don't know why Margaret never told him about her childhood. And you lived so close."

Hannaday looked down in embarrassment. "I've been a fool, Libbie. For twenty-five years. That's way too long. Such a fool." The old man shook his head.

"This is supposed to be a happy time." Libbie ushered him up the stairs.

After the hotel clerk read over the registration, he looked up in awe. "Elizabeth Custer? Ma'am, are you *the* Elizabeth Custer?"

Libbie laughed. "Since I'm the only Elizabeth Custer I know, I suppose I am. Tell me, young man, is there a telephone connection between the hotel and the army post?"

"Yes, ma'am."

"I should like to place a call."

The clerk pointed to a box telephone on the wall near the desk. "If you'll pick up that telephone, I'll connect you."

"Thank you." Libbie walked over to the phone and picked it up.

"Sixth Cavalry, Corporal Delaney speaking, sir."

"Corporal Delaney, this is Mrs. Custer. I would like to speak with your commanding officer, please."

"Yes, ma'am."

A moment later another voice answered, "Mrs. Custer, this is Captain Anderson."

"Hello, Captain. You don't know me, but—"

"Mrs. Custer, everyone in the United States Army, if not the entire country, knows you. I'm honored to take your call."

"Thank you. I'm over at the Mammoth Hot Springs Hotel. I wonder if you would be so kind as to tell my nephew that I'm here."

"Ma'am, I wasn't aware that we had your relative in our midst."

"Well, you do, and I've come to attend Lieutenant McDowell's wedding. I've also brought a guest, but don't tell him that yet, I want it to be a surprise."

"Mrs. Custer?" Captain Anderson's voice sounded a little strained.

"Yes?"

"Uh, you are at the Mammoth Hotel?"

"I am."

"If I may have your permission, I would like to see you in person."

"Of course, Captain. I'll wait in the lobby." Libbie hung the phone up and looked at it, confused. "That's strange, he said he'd like to see me. Not Cade—the captain."

"That is strange," Hannaday said.

Less than ten minutes later, Libbie saw an army officer enter the hotel. She had never met him, but because she recognized this officer's rank as captain, she knew it was him. She stood and he started toward her.

"Mrs. Custer," Captain Anderson said. "It is an honor to meet you."

"Thank you, Captain. But I must say, I'm little concerned about Cade. You seemed so circumspect when we spoke on the phone."

"That's why I wanted to speak to you in person. Cade isn't here."

"Oh? Where is he?"

"He's on temporary duty to Fort Missoula, and he'll be gone for a month."

"Captain, how could you? Didn't you know he's—"

Captain Anderson held up his hand. "Ma'am, he's there by his own request."

Libbie's eyebrows raised. "By his own request? But why? I don't understand. He invited me to come for his wedding."

"It's off. And Cade wanted to . . ."

"Run away?"

Captain Anderson looked at the old man who had spoken.

"Please excuse me for not introducing you," Libbie said. "This is Cade Hannaday, Cade's grandfather."

"Mr. Hannaday," Captain Anderson said, extending his hand.

"What caused my grandson to run away?"

"I think there was a disagreement between him and the young lady he was to marry."

"That would be Miss Winters?" Libbie asked.

"Yes."

"Is she still in the park?"

"Yes, ma'am. I believe she is."

"Captain, I wonder if you would do me a favor. If she would agree to it, I would like to ask her to meet with Mr. Hannaday and me. Perhaps for breakfast, say tomorrow morning here in the hotel? Could you arrange that for me?"

"I'll do better than that. I will personally see that she is here."

"Thank you."

Libbie and Hannaday were sitting at a table in the hotel restaurant the next morning when Libbie saw Captain Anderson come in. With him was a young woman.

"Oh my," Libbie said quietly. "I don't blame Cade for being taken by her. She's quite beautiful."

Captain Anderson picked his way through the dining room until he reached Libbie's table. Libbie and Hannaday stood.

"Here she is, Mrs. Custer. I'll leave the three of you to discuss whatever has to be discussed."

"Thank you. That is most kind of you," Libbie said. "Please, child, sit down. I've heard much about you," she said to Marci with a welcoming smile.

Somewhat hesitantly, and obviously anxious about the meeting, Marci sat down.

"Now, tell me, Marci, before we get started. Do you love Cade? Because if you don't, just say so; we'll have a nice breakfast together and this gentleman and I will take the next train back East."

"Oh, yes, I love him. I love him more than words can express," Marci said sincerely.

Libbie smiled and reached across to pat Marci on the hand. "Then, I promise you, Cade's grandfather and I will get this worked out."

"You're Cade's grandfather? I didn't know he had a grandfather."

"Neither does he. At least not yet," Hannaday said.

"Now, tell me what happened, so I know what kind of task I have in front of me," Libbie said.

For the next several minutes, Marci told Libbie everything, how she had met Cade at West Point, how she had waited for him under the sally port, and how that action had been misconstrued and had gotten her expelled from college. She told Libbie that there had been another man, and at one time she thought she was in love with him. She even told them about what happened . . . or rather, didn't happen, in the vice president's bedroom, so that she had to leave Washington under a cloud.

Libbie chuckled. "The vice president? Well, my dear, when you do something scandalous, you don't mess around, do you?"

"But nothing really happened."

"My dear, it isn't what actually happened that counts, it is the perception of what happened that counts."

Marci smiled. "That's exactly what my father says. He works in the government, so my behavior was particularly hard on him."

"Would your father be DeWitt Winters?" Hannaday asked.

"Yes, do you know him?"

"I've never met him, but I've seen his name enough times. He's in the Treasury Department, isn't he?"

"He is."

Marci continued with her story, telling how when she stopped in St. Louis to see Stanton at the convention, he had dismissed her, and in her mind whatever kind of friendship they had had was over. "Stanton was working with Mark Hanna, you see, in securing the nomination for Governor McKinley."

"If Mr. Caldwell was working with Mark Hanna, that's enough, by itself, to indict him. I know the banking business, and Hanna is the lowest of the low as far as I'm concerned," Hannaday interrupted.

"I've never met the man, but because of his work, Stanton said he didn't have time for me, and I put him out of mind, right then. I destroyed his letter, got rid of his ring, and I thought that was all behind me until, three days ago, when he showed up here. Cade saw me with him, and he misunderstood."

Libbie fished in her bag for a handkerchief, and she handed it to Marci, who took it and dabbed at her tear-filled eyes.

"Stanton is gone now, I sent him away. But it's too late. It's not what is, it's perception," she said pointedly. "And now Cade doesn't want anything to do with me."

The waiter arrived, carrying a tray with their breakfasts. He put a plate down in front of each of them.

"Oh, thank you, young man, this looks delicious," Libbie said, looking at the bacon, eggs, and biscuit in front of her.

"I . . . I . . ." Marci clutched Libbie's handkerchief to her mouth. "Please, excuse me for a moment."

Getting up from the table, Marci rushed out of the dining room, stepping out onto the porch that overlooked the Terraces behind the hotel. From his position at the table, Hannaday could see her through the window, and she appeared to be retching.

"I wonder if I said something to upset her? That was a strange thing for her to do," Libbie mused.

"Perhaps not so strange."

The old man continued to watch through the doorway as Marci touched the handkerchief to her forehead. He saw her take a few deep breaths, then she came back in.

Her face was pale as she sat back down at the table. "Please excuse me, I'm terribly sorry."

"That's quite all right, dear," Libbie said.

Marci motioned for the waiter. "Could you bring me a piece of pilot bread, please?"

"Yes, ma'am. Will you want butter and jam with that as well?"

"No, thank you, just the pilot bread."

The waiter left, then returned a moment later with a plate, with only one cracker. He put his hand on Marci's plate of bacon and eggs and looked at her, and when she nodded, he took it away.

"Does Cade know you are with child?" Hannaday asked.

Marci's eyes opened wide in shock, then she lowered her head. Libbie, too, had been surprised by Hannaday's comment.

"No," Marci answered quietly. "I only learned myself, very recently. I'm so ashamed."

"Don't be." Hannaday reached across to take her hand. "Twenty-five years ago my daughter found herself in the same situation, and I turned my back on her when she needed me most. That was the biggest mistake I ever made in my life, and I've no intention of making that mistake again. I will not let my grandson, or my great-grandchild, get away from me this time."

After breakfast, Libbie and Hannaday walked Marci back to F. Jay's house. Marci introduced them.

"I'm very pleased to meet you," F. Jay said. "It's just such a shame that the happy event we were all looking forward to won't happen."

"Oh, I wouldn't be so sure of that," Libbie said with an enigmatic smile.

Fort Missoula

Libbie was standing at the window in her room in the Brunswick Hotel when she saw a surrey pull up in front. The driver, a soldier, hopped down, tied off the team, then hurried back to help a woman down. Libbie left her room and hurried downstairs, meeting Elizabeth Burt, wife of the post commander and an old friend just as she came through the front door. The two women embraced.

"Libbie, you don't know how thrilled we were to get your telegram that you were coming."

"Seeing you and Andrew will bring back many beautiful memories," Libbie said. "Lieutenant McDowell doesn't know I'm here?"

"No, you specifically stated that he not be told. But I'm dying of curiosity. Why the surprise?"

"I'm afraid if he knew I was coming, he might not want to see me. And that would be the biggest mistake of his life."

The driver helped both Libbie and Elizabeth into the surrey, then headed back to the fort, the team stepping out in a brisk trot.

On the way, the two women reminisced about the happier times when their husbands had served together. They did not mention that Colonel Burt, then a major, had been a part of the Little Bighorn campaign, having been with General Crook in the Rosebud phalanx of the expedition that took the life of General Custer.

When they reached the commandant's quarters, Colonel Burt was there to greet Libbie, and after a few pleasantries were exchanged, Libbie got to the purpose of her visit.

"Andrew, I understand that Lieutenant McDowell is here on a temporary assignment, and I have some, shall we say, urgent business to discuss with him. I want to meet in a place where I can be assured I will have absolute privacy, because what I have to say to him—well, it should have been said a long time ago."

"All right, Libbie. I can arrange for you to meet him here in my quarters. I'll tell him at once."

"Please don't tell him the meeting will be with me."

"All right. Elizabeth, shall we leave Libbie alone?"

"I don't know what this is all about, but I do hope things go well for you," Elizabeth said.

"Thank you."

Private Findley was showing Cade how to repair a bicycle sprocket when Sergeant Green came up to Cade and saluted.

"Sir, the colonel's compliments, and he asked me to request that you report to his private quarters."

"Does he mean now?"

"Yes, sir."

"Carry on, Private Findley," Cade said.

He walked across the company area to the commandant's quarters, then knocked on the front door. He was shocked when he saw who answered the door.

"Hello, Cade."

"Aunt Libbie?"

"Come in, we need to talk."

"I know what this is about. Aunt Libbie, I'm sorry I got you involved in this."

"Please. Come in."

Libbie sat on the sofa, and when Cade started to sit on a chair, she patted the sofa beside her. "No, sit here with me."

As Cade sat beside her, Libbie opened her purse, took out a photograph, and handed it to him. It showed a rather handsome man, with piercing eyes, dark hair, a swooping, dark mustache, and narrow chin whiskers.

"Do you know who this is?"

"Yes, I've seen this picture before," Cade said, confused by Libbie's question. "It's Captain Myles Keogh, and I know he served with General Custer. Evidently he and my father were friends."

"Other than his brother, Tom, Captain Keogh was Autie's favorite and most trusted officer. He, of course, died with the General."

"My mother once told me I was named for Captain Keogh. I know he was an Irishman who fought in Italy during the Papal War, where he won two medals before coming to fight in our Civil War. And of course, he served in the Seventh Cavalry."

Libbie smiled. "Your mother told you all of that, but she left out one very important fact."

"And what was that?"

"First, I must tell you that Edward McDowell was killed in Wyoming in the fight at Goose Creek . . . in 1867."

"What? But how could my father have been killed in 1867? I wasn't born until 1872."

"Because Edward McDowell isn't your father."

"Then, who is?"

"Myles Keogh."

Cade rose abruptly and walked away, running his hand through his hair as he absorbed what Libbie had just said. "So you're saying he abandoned her and me, too?"

"No, he didn't do that. Your mother was so ashamed of getting pregnant that she abandoned him. He didn't know anything about you until he contacted your mother and brought her to Fort Lincoln. She brought a four-year-old child . . . you, to the fort shortly before the Seventh left on that last, fateful mission. When Myles discovered that he was your father, he was the happiest and proudest man in the world." Libbie's eyes shone brightly. "Even the General was proud of you. When you received your commission on the Plain at West Point, that wasn't the first time." Libbie smiled. "Autie made you a lieutenant a long time ago.

"While they were on the campaign, Margaret and I made big plans for a wedding when the regiment returned. Your mother and I sewed her wedding dress to help occupy the time." The smile left Libbie's face, to be replaced by a look of extreme sadness. "But of course, 268 men of the Seventh never returned, including my Autie, and her Myles."

"Why didn't she ever tell me?"

"I don't know. She was a very private woman. I think she made a big mistake not to tell you, just as she made a mistake in not telling Myles he had a son. Your grandfather made a mistake in banishing your mother and refusing to acknowledge you. Cade, don't be the third generation to make a mistake."

"What do you mean?"

"I've met Marci. She loves you dearly, Cade. She loves you, and she wants to marry you. She didn't know that man was coming to Yellowstone. And he's gone. She got rid of him."

"Aunt Libbie, you don't understand. It isn't just

Stanton Caldwell, it's what he represents. He represents wealth and power, the same kind of wealth and power Marci is used to. She's from a very influential family."

"Do you love her?"

"Yes, I do. I love her very much. That's one of the reasons I'm willing to let her go. I'm a soldier, I have nothing to offer her."

"Cade, did you not read my letter? You asked for my advice, and I gave it to you. You should take what life has to offer, sweetened by the love you and Marci have for each other. Don't dwell on your differences.

"By the standards of the day and the community, my father, too, was an influential man. He was a judge and was deemed to be quite wealthy. Autie came from a most modest family, but I never considered that. All he had to offer me was love, and I never needed anything more. I don't know of anyone who had a happier or closer marriage than we did. If you truly love her, that will be all Marci wants or needs. Please, come back with me."

Fort Yellowstone

When DeWitt and Rosemary Winters arrived at the park, they were met by both Marci and Cade Hannaday. Mr. Hannaday was a banker in Monroe, Michigan, whose bank was large enough and successful enough that DeWitt Winters knew him by reputation, if not personally.

Marci had to tell her parents that Stanton Caldwell had showed up unexpectedly, causing a misunderstanding so great that Cade had left Fort Yellowstone.

"Stanton Caldwell?" DeWitt asked angrily.

"Yes."

"Honey, I told you a long time ago—"

"Please, DeWitt, not now," Rosemary said. "Can't you see how distressed Marci is? There's no need to make it worse."

DeWitt's expression softened. "Your mother's right, of course. I don't have any business finding fault with you. Where is Caldwell now?"

"Marci sent him packing," Hannaday said with a little chuckle. "And don't worry about Cade. He'll be here. His aunt Libbie has gone to bring him back."

"Do you think she'll be able to convince him?" Rosemary asked anxiously.

"Mrs. Winters, I believe Libbie Custer can do just about anything she sets her mind to."

"Libbie Custer is the young man's aunt?"

"For all practical purposes she is," Hannaday said without bothering to elaborate.

Cade and Libbie returned from Missoula on the late train, reaching Cinnabar just before dark. Because it was too late for the public coaches to run, Sergeant Dawes was waiting for them in the post ambulance.

"Oh my," Libbie said as she and Cade climbed into the ambulance. "Autie and I have made many a journey in one of these. When we were tenting on the plains, this was the vehicle of choice for the officers and their wives."

As the ambulance made its way from Cinnabar to the park, Cade watched the sun, now an orange disk, settling just over the Gallatin Range. He picked out Dome Mountain, and he became melancholy when he recalled what had happened there.

Would memories be all he had of the woman he loved? Aunt Libbie had convinced him to come back, but what if she had misread Marci's true feelings?

He couldn't lose her now. He would do whatever it took to keep her love.

"Here we are, sir," Sergeant Dawes said as he drew up in front on the Mammoth Hotel. "Shall I wait here, so I can take you back to the BOQ, Lieutenant?"

"No, thank you, Sergeant. I can get back from here. And thanks for coming after us."

"Yes, sir. Nothing is too good for Mrs. Custer." Dawes snapped the reins over the team.

"Cade, I know you are worried, but there's no need." Libbie gave him a motherly hug.

"I don't know what I would do without you." Cade returned the hug. "And, Aunt Libbie, thank you for bringing me to my senses."

Libbie rewarded him with a big smile. "You're wasting time, my son. Go to her."

Marci had spent several anxious hours after Libbie had left for Missoula. Even the telegram Marci had received from her, though encouraging, wasn't definitive enough to ease all her concerns: RETURNING WITH CADE.

That was all it said. It didn't say whether he was coming back for Marci or just coming back.

She moved to the window of her room and looked out into the darkness. "Taps" had not yet sounded, so the windows of the bachelor officers' quarters just across the parade ground were glowing with light—except for one window. His window.

Then there was a light tap on her door.

"Marci?" It was Cade's voice.

Taking a deep breath, she crossed the room to open the door, her heart in her throat. Was this to be a reunion? Or a final good-bye?

"I love you, Marci." The expression on his face was agonized and anxious. "I was a fool to run away, do you—"

Whatever Cade was going to ask was smothered by Marci's kiss as she threw her arms around his neck and took his lips with her own.

One week later

The wedding was held at the Mammoth Hot Springs Hotel. The lobby was decorated with red, white, and blue bunting, with pictures of Marci and Cade displayed alongside. Some were from the long bicycle trip, and others from various scenic spots throughout the park. One picture was hung in the center of all the others—Cade's baby picture, which Libbie had brought from his mother's house in Marshall. The US flag, as well as the unit guidon for the Sixth Cavalry, were also there.

The ceremony was performed in the dining room, where the tables had been removed, and the chairs arranged for the guests. The ferns that decorated the hotel were augmented by a shipment of fresh flowers that had been brought in from the East.

"I now pronounce you man and wife," the post chaplain said. Then, with a big smile he added, "Ladies and gentlemen, I present you Lieutenant and Mrs. Myles Cade McDowell."

Those who had attended the wedding—civilian employees of the park, and several soldiers from the troop, including the first sergeant and Sergeants McKay and Dawes—applauded.

Libbie, who had acted as Marci's matron of honor, fought to control her tears, and Captain Anderson, who served as Cade's best man, handed her his handkerchief as they watched Marci and Cade leave the dining room. Cade was resplendently dressed in his mess dress uniform, with gold-fringe shoulder epaulets, and a gold sash running diagonally across the double-breasted tunic, while Marci was wearing the wedding dress that Libbie and Cade's mother had sewn so many years ago in anticipation of Margaret's marriage to Myles Keogh.

When the newlyweds stepped out onto the porch, there, lining each side of the walkway, stood six officers, three on either side. All the officers but James Moss were from the Sixth Cavalry.

"Officers, present sabers!" Lieutenant Nance said, and as they crossed sabers, an instant arch was formed. Cade and Marci passed under the sabers on their way to the buggy that sat hitched and waiting for them.

As Marci looked back at the little band of well-wishers, she smiled. At one time she had imagined her wedding would equal that of Julia Stevenson, with all the most powerful and influential people in Washington in attendance.

This small military wedding was nothing like that. But she knew at this moment, as she sat close to her husband, with best wishes and congratulations called by friends and family, that this was exactly the wedding she wanted, and never in her life had she been happier.

Fountain Hotel

Marci was standing at the window, totally nude, her body bathed in the silver splash of moonlight. Cade was equally nude, lying on a bed that was mussed from their recent lovemaking.

"Why didn't you tell me you were going to have our baby?" Cade's words were neither harsh nor challenging.

"I wanted you to marry me because you love me, not because you thought you had no choice."

"I didn't have a choice," Cade said easily.

"What?"

Cade laughed quietly. "I love you so much, I would have gone crazy if I couldn't have you."

Marci came back to sit on the side of the bed beside him.

"You don't mind that I turned down my grandfather's offer to go back to Michigan and take over his bank, do you?"

"Not only do I not mind, I'm glad you turned him down."

"Oh?"

"We're army," Marci said.

"We're army?"

"Cade, have you ever heard the term *ménage à trois*?"

"I can't say that I have."

"It's a French term; it means a 'household of three.' We are in a *ménage à trois,* you, me, and the United States Army. I won't compete with the army; I will live with it, and because you love it, I will love it as well."

"I love you, Marci." Cade reached for her. "Let me show you how much."

"No." She smiled as she reached for him. "Let me show you."

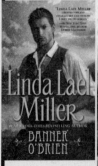

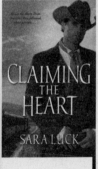